Silent TIES

Silent TIES

DAWN DAY-QUINN

KARR VALLEY PUBLISHING

Silent Ties
Copyright © 2018 Dawn Day-Quinn.

ISBN: 978-1-7321709-0-2 (Paperback)
          978-1-7321709-1-9 eBook

Library of Congress Control Number: 2018905176

Cover Art © 2018 by Dawn Day-Quinn
Cover and interior design by Book Marketing Graphics.
www.BookMarketingGraphics.com

Karr Valley Publishing
4885-A McKnight Road Suite 193
Pittsburgh, PA 15237
www.karrvalleypublishing.com

DEDICATION

To special women in my life who inspired me.

To the women who taught me to love the written word: my sisters Darlene Bainbridge and Wendy Todd who listened to me read Dick and Jane repeatedly; Mrs. Williams, the librarian at Washington Elementary, who always had a special book waiting for me; Alice McHenry, my mentor and partner at the David A. Howe Public Library, who showed me how kindness and crazy joy can change a child's life.

To the women who taught me to be kind, confident, strong, and most important, loving: Joanne Day, my mother, guide, teacher, and friend who molded me; Mary Ellen Quinn, my mother-in-law, spiritual partner, confidante, and friend who I miss so much; Harriett Day, my wonderful grandmother who we all admire for her fun-loving approach to life; Marge Neltner and Brenda Furiga, amazing women of strength and my dear friends.

I honor each of you with sincere gratitude and my deepest love.

ACKNOWLEDGEMENTS

I must thank a special group of individuals who were so gracious with their time and provided valuable feedback. Your questions, comments, and honesty helped me to see Missy's story through the reader's eyes, and led me through nine major revisions.

First to Alice Edwards, Linda Lorah, and Fran Jackson who were challenged with the first very long version; I appreciate your kindness in tackling such a daunting task. Your input, suggestions, and criticism were exactly what I needed to weed out story lines, bring more focus to Missy and Addie, and reduce the word count!

Next, I wish to thank Evelyn Pierce. Your knowledge about writing and life in the South during the 1950s and 60s guided me through the next phase. I learned so much from you, and truly appreciate your kindness and time. Thank you.

My final readers were a husband and wife team, Greg and Angie Ellison. To Greg, thank you so much for providing analysis from the male point of view. Your input was critical. Angie, you were my mood booster. Your positive excitement provided the incentive I needed. I want to extend my sincere gratitude to both of you.

I offer a special thank you to Hope Toler Dougherty. Your advice and constant encouragement inspired me to push on.

To Linda Fulkerson, when others walked away and left me stranded you rescued me. Thank you for my wonderful website, book cover, formatting, and help. You were a blessing.

To Linda Young, principal of Eagle Eye Editors, LLC, thank you for your guidance through the final phase of development. Your knowledge and encouragement were a perfect combination. I truly appreciate your dedication to this project. God guided me to you for a reason.

Finally, I must acknowledge the most important individuals: my husband Paul and my children Craig, Rich, Cristian, and Cade. Thank you for believing in me from the moment I told you I was writing a novel. You gave me the confidence to persevere, never showed doubt in my ability, and encouraged me through the many years. I am grateful for your support. I love you all!

TABLE OF CONTENTS

Chapter ONE

1945

Oone of my earliest memories was the funeral of Granddaddy Tucker. I was four and it would be the first of seven deaths that impacted my childhood. It was not sudden or a surprise. Everyone seemed relieved the painful suffering was over. I shared the front row of our newly painted Methodist church with Grandma Em, Aunt Sara, her husband Roy, their two boys, Leroy and Samuel, Momma, Daddy, and my older brothers, Ted and Cal. The church was filled with flowers and people, so you knew someone important had died. But, as it turned out, honoring him was not the most memorable event that day.

The old organ started to play. For a few minutes, the only sound was the beautiful music. Then a low murmur began from the back of the church. I turned to see our neighbor Miss Ada, her son James, his family, and my best friend Addie.

They walked slowly down the aisle to the front pew across from us. Daddy didn't turn to acknowledge them but stared straight ahead. It was like he was in a trance. Grandma Em and Aunt Sara were beside themselves, their faces turning multiple shades of red. Grandma Em called to Daddy, "J.P., do somethin'. Stop 'em." But he continued to direct his eyes forward.

A few moments later, Reverend Howell moved toward the pulpit. Everyone quieted. As he began the service, I looked at the people surrounding me. Grandma Em's face seethed with anger. There were no tears from her, Aunt Sara, or Daddy. No one was crying, except Miss Ada. I don't recall much else, but that moment stayed with me. It changed my life. That was the last day we spent with Grandma Em or Aunt Sara for many years to come, and when a sadness settled over Daddy.

I grew up in a small town in rural Alabama. Daddy was a farmer, working alongside Granddaddy Tucker. We had about 600 acres, with a large farmhouse where my grandparents lived. We were a mile down the road in a small sharecropper's cottage painted white with a bright green door. Momma made it beautiful. She was talented in that way and determined to make her country house as nice as any on Main Street. She was Melanie Gordon Tucker, a town girl, the only child of Albert and Rebecca Gordon. She was pretty, with long auburn hair that every woman envied. She was careful about maintaining her figure and many of her town girl ways. Beautiful flower gardens accented the pristinely maintained structure.

When Granddaddy died he left everything to Daddy, including the big house, the truck, and Grandma Em's car. It made perfect sense. Daddy worked the farm with his father and my brothers. Nothing would change, or so I thought.

A few days after the funeral, Daddy went to the big house to see his mother. I begged to go, but he went alone. Momma's expression told me something was wrong. She sent us to bed before he returned. I heard his truck and the sound of the screen door. Peeking into the hall, I found Ted and Cal sitting at the top of the stairs. I tiptoed out to join them. Daddy collapsed onto a chair at the kitchen table and quietly cried. Momma held him from behind. He never said a word and she didn't ask. We watched our parents in the quiet of their little house, grieving together.

The next Sunday, we went to church like normal. The Tucker family had its own pew, but Grandma Em and Aunt Sara sat at the edge, refusing to move. Daddy steered us back down the aisle a couple of rows to our new permanent seats. When it was time to go to the big house for dinner, he told us to get in the car for a new family tradition. From that day on, we drove to the Hotel in town for our Sunday meal.

From our back door, you could see another little house shaped like ours, minus the rear porch. In its place was a simple stoop. The structure wasn't nicely painted, just raw wood weathered by age. Another difference was a large vegetable garden. It occupied the place that held Momma's flower garden behind our home. Every fall, Momma split her bulbs, and sent me across the field with the extras for that dilapidated cottage.

Miss Ada lived there with her son James, his wife Emily, their three sons, Tucker James, John James, Jefferson James, and the most important person in my small world, Addie. She was named for her grandmother so I assumed someday she'd be called Miss Ada too.

Addie and I were the same age, save one month. She was taller than me, real pretty, with a thin nose, and beautiful full lips like her mother. Her hair always had several braids coming together to form a tight bun on each side of her head. I don't recall the first time we played. Addie was always part of my life.

I treasured the innocence of those early years with Addie and her family. We played for hours with cornhusks dolls Miss Ada made, or hid in the tall grass to watch the clouds moving overhead until we were dizzy. We were always laughing and happy.

In the summer, we helped Miss Ada with her garden. I looked forward to harvest time. We picked 'God's gifts' then set to work canning them. Miss Ada approached it like a fine artist. I loved to watch her in the kitchen. After we finished, she always sent me home with a new supply of my favorite Bread and Butter pickles.

That summer, I often ran across the field to spend my days with Addie, but it was different. Miss Ada didn't tend her garden. She spent hours on the front porch lost in her thoughts. We ran in and out, slamming the screen, but she didn't look our way. One day we were playing hide and seek. I was especially quiet creeping onto the porch to hide behind her chair. She stared ahead, seemingly unaware of my presence. Tears were rolling down her face. It was etched with a permanent sadness.

That afternoon I realized Miss Ada must be dying like Granddaddy Tucker. She must have caught the cancer. Of course, that meant Daddy was dying too. They both shared the same look that was on Granddaddy's face during his final months. It's difficult to describe, but it's like you've lost something with no hope of recovery and without it life stops.

That night I sobbed into my pillow until I fell asleep. I was afraid of losing so many people that made up my world. The next morning, I awoke with a sinking feeling in my stomach. Glancing in the mirror, I saw that same devastating look reflected back. In my young mind, it was the face of cancer. How would I tell Momma? Surely, she'd get the look and have the cancer too. I had to protect her. I'd tell Daddy because I was convinced he was already dying.

He was in the field working. I snuck down the stairs, past Momma in the kitchen, quietly leaving by the front door. Running toward the big house, I listened for the chugging of his tractor. I heard the familiar sound coming through the woods. He was in the back field. I ran through the trees with prickers piercing my bare feet and thorns grabbing at my nightgown. At the other side of the woods I entered the open field sobbing and gasping for air. Daddy saw me. The engine stopped. He came running to scoop me up.

"Is it Momma? Is she hurt? Stop cryin' and tell me. Is she hurt?" he ordered. I couldn't catch my breath. I shook my head no.

"Is it Grandma Em? Miss Ada?" he pleaded again. With each question, I shook my head no. Finally realizing he was dealing with an irrational child, he gathered me in his arms, holding me gently. I relished the tenderness of those big hands and the soothing power of his voice. Being in his strong arms made you feel like everything was alright. Exposing his bald head, he removed his hat to nuzzle close. I looked up into his face. He had strong features, handsome, with the kindest eyes and a wonderful smile. He made you feel warm and loved with his reassuring presence that was recognized by all.

He didn't rush me, giving me time to breathe. I finally told him the horrible news, "Daddy, I have the cancer like you, and Miss Ada, and Granddaddy Tucker." Showing him my face, I continued, "See? I have the look. We can't tell Momma, 'cause she'll get it too. I don't want her to die."

In the months since Granddaddy's funeral, it was the first time he laughed. It sounded wonderful. Soon I was giggling with him. Though I didn't understand why, I felt assured everything would be fine. Our house was filled with laughter that evening as he told the story over and over. For a few hours, the sad look disappeared from his face, and once again we were happy.

Chapter TWO
1946

The spring season brought so much rain the farmers couldn't plant. If it wasn't raining, the powerful wind blew the seed away. Once the fields began to dry, the men got to work. They started with the back fields, later moving on to the low lands by the creek. Daddy ran the tractor while Ted and Cal used the horses.

Ted was built strong like Daddy, with big shoulders tapered to a small waist, and born to be a farmer. He had Daddy's face and matching blond hair which was sure to disappear by the time he turned thirty. Cal was small and slight with red hair inherited from Momma's family. He preferred good books over the hard labor of the farm. He helped, but his heart wasn't in it.

Daddy kept the boys out of school to take advantage of the good weather. He also hired two temporary men from town. They were nearly finished, but the radio warned bad storms were moving our way through Louisiana and Mississippi. The rain could set him back again.

Momma and I were on the back porch watching the dark clouds looming in the distance. Our men arrived covered with dirt from head to toe. Climbing the steps like their boots were full of cement Daddy said, "I was afraid we wouldn't finish. The boys are dead tired. I'd be surprised if they could lift a fork."

Momma nodded as she looked across the field. "James is still working. If they don't hurry the rain could stop them from finishing."

Daddy looked toward Addie's. James was on his tractor moving slowly through the dirt. Tucker James was working their horse and plow. The other boys and Miss Emily were doing what they could with shovels. Daddy looked at the dark sky moving toward us. He knew they wouldn't make it alone. No one spoke. He led the boys back down the steps. Momma ran into the house. Grabbing shovels out of the back of the truck, Ted and Cal had a new burst of energy. She reappeared with a plate of sandwiches and three jugs of ice tea. The boys grabbed a sandwich to eat as they walked across the field and tucked the jugs under their arms. Daddy took his from Momma. Planting a kiss on her cheek, he left for the big house.

Momma ran back inside. As I watched from the porch, I heard our tractor coming down the road. It pulled into the far end of the field. I expected James or Miss Emily to wave, but everyone kept their heads down, intent on working as fast as they could.

Momma returned dressed in denims and boots saying, "C'mon Missy, you can watch with Miss Ada and Addie." She grabbed a shovel from the car barn before we set out.

She walked quickly across the field as I ran to keep up. There was one other time she dressed like that. Daddy and Ted were both sick with a fever. She argued with Daddy as he tried to insist on feeding the pigs. It was too big a job for Cal alone, and Granddaddy Tucker was too weak. Momma went out that night to help Cal, dressed in the same work clothes. Daddy always insisted fieldwork was a man's job, not for her, and usually she seemed to agree. As we marched ahead, she said, "Sometimes you have to forget you're a lady." Helping James was one of those occasions.

Miss Ada, Addie, and I stood at the edge of the field watching the two men on tractors and everyone else moving down the rows throwing seed then shovels of dirt over trenches. They'd work about fifteen or twenty feet, going back over the fresh piles to pack the dirt with their feet, protecting the seeds from the wind.

After a short time, Miss Ada grabbed our hands and said, "Ladies, let's go a stompin'."

The three of us headed out. Addie ran to Miss Emily, while I helped Momma. It took four or five steps to match what Momma could pack with one. I tried to stomp faster, allowing her to keep shoveling. My legs were hurting, but I wouldn't stop as long as she kept working. The sky was getting dark, but the air was still. God circled his protective arms around that field.

Everyone was focused on finishing. We felt the first drop of rain, but no one looked up. It was the lightest sprinkle that went on forever. Each person completed an area, moving on to help another. I don't know how long we worked, but we made it. James simply nodded at Daddy, Miss Ada gave Momma a hug, and Miss Emily squeezed her hand as she walked by. It struck me funny that no one spoke a word, not even as we left.

We drove home on Daddy's tractor. I sat in his lap helping him steer, Momma sat on one wheel hub, and Cal on the other. Ted stood on the hitch holding onto the back of the seat. We rode in silence. Shortly after we got settled, a terrible storm hit that shook the house. God had given us just enough time.

The next afternoon, Addie came across the field carrying a pie. It was not the first time she was sent on one of those missions. Anytime one family helped the other, there was an exchange of some baked good. Our families always said thank you with food, not words.

After helping with the planting, I paid more attention to my surroundings, especially how people worked the land. I noticed many people working the fields with horses. We had two big workhorses, and James had one to use with the smaller plow, but both men could do much more with their tractors. One Sunday, on our way to the Hotel, I asked Daddy why other farmers didn't buy a tractor.

He answered solemnly, "Farmin' is a tough life. It's a poor man's job. Most don't make much money. Tractors are expensive to buy and use. They can't afford 'em."

"Why do we have one? Aren't we poor?" I asked. I wasn't exposed to neighbors often, but never felt we were different.

He sat quiet for few moments, then replied, "Grandma Em's family own a feed, seed, and equipment company. They sold my granddaddy his first tractor. My daddy got the one I have now, and the new harvester 'fore he died."

His voice trailed off. I could hear the sadness. He was finally settled with the new Sunday tradition and didn't seem to miss being at Grandma Em's. I wished I hadn't made him think about the old days.

To redirect his thoughts, I asked, "How'd James get his tractor? Is he rich?"

Keeping his eyes on the road, he didn't respond for a long time. Finally, he said, "He got one, that's all." His tone said the conversation was over. We had a quiet dinner, each lost in our own thoughts. I was remembering Sunday dinner at Grandma Em's. I wondered if she missed us.

Later that summer Addie was at my house playing school. We were only five and wouldn't be going for another year. We didn't have kindergarten. School began with first grade. Miss Emily was teaching Addie her alphabet. Momma hadn't started with me yet. She said, "School will come soon enough. This is the time for you to be a child." But I wanted to learn everything Addie knew. We played school often. Addie was always the teacher, and I was her student.

One day looking for paper and pencils in the desk, we found a picture with Granddaddy Tucker and a much younger Daddy sitting atop a tractor. It wasn't Daddy's with rubber tires, but had big metal wheels.

We looked at the picture for a few seconds before she said, "Why's your family sittin' on my Papa's tractor?"

She was right; it was their tractor. Thinking back to the conversation in the car I wondered why Daddy didn't tell me James got his tractor from us. Why was that a secret? Setting my curiosity aside I simply said, "He must have bought it from Granddaddy."

Chapter THREE

1947

In June, Addie and I turned six. Momma started teaching me the alphabet, but Addie could already read. I envied her. I talked constantly with Addie about going to school together. She listened, but never joined in my daydreams. She knew all along our friendship would change with our lives moving in different directions.

Mid-August, Momma was fitting me for a dress. I shared my excitement about walking to school with Addie and sitting side by side. Momma stopped pinning the hem and listened as I rambled on. I don't know how long I talked, but when I looked down, she was visibly sad. She gathered herself for one of the most difficult tasks she'd face as a mother. She ended the innocence of my childhood that day and introduced me to the world as it really was. Her next words felt like a knife tearing at my heart. "You and Addie can't go to school together. Your school is for whites."

She tried to explain, saying something about a colored school in town, but my head was spinning, and I stopped listening. Addie and I had spent our days together for as long as I could remember. A colored girl came into our house with no problem. I likewise went to Addie's and was fine. Why did it have to change? Maybe if we told the teacher she was nice, my dreams could come true. The excitement was suddenly gone. I didn't want to go to school. I wanted life to stay as it was.

Living on the farm kept me isolated, but my parent's actions removed me from reality. Their acceptance of James and Miss Emily as our neighbors taught me a way contrary to life outside our fields. The next year would clarify how different the two worlds really were.

The sadness remained with me. The first day of school, I wanted to walk with Addie, but she and her brothers left much earlier for the six-and-a-half-mile hike. If the colored children wanted an education, their only choice was the school in town.

My brothers and I attended a country school a mile from home. There were a few of these one room buildings dotted around the country roads for the white families. Great Grandpa Tucker gave a small piece of land for our school years back. Being close to the farm was beneficial for our family, but Ted and Cal wished it was more convenient to other boys. On cold days, if a fire was necessary, it was their job to get there early. Because we owned the land, the honor was ours.

As we approached the school, I grabbed Ted's hand. Momma didn't socialize with the other farmers' wives. The only friend I'd ever known was Addie. Entering the school yard, the two faces I recognized were Sara's boys, Leroy and Samuel.

When Aunt Sara married Uncle Roy, Granddaddy Tucker gave them a piece of land two miles from the school on the high road at the back edge of the farm. As far as Daddy was concerned, it was three miles too close. I didn't know him well, but my parents talked of Uncle Roy as a mean and despicable man. In the early years Aunt Sara and Uncle Roy went to Grandma Em's for Sunday brunch, always leaving before we arrived. Everyone said it was best that way.

That morning my eyes were opened to the evils everyone else understood. Father and son shared the name, looks, and evidently personality as well. Leroy was a large boy, in height and girth, using his size to intimidate. The mean countenance on his face stopped anyone from judging him handsome.

We arrived to find Leroy picking on the younger children. He stole a small boy's bag lunch, sampling each piece of food, before throwing it in the dirt. The boy's sister and two older girls were trying to protect him, but their efforts were futile. Ted and Cal steered me to the other side of the school yard. I learned my first lesson: stay clear of Leroy.

Cal leaned down to whisper in my ear, "Don't tell anyone 'bout Addie, ya hear. Or that'll be you."

Ted overheard, slapping him on the back of his head as he said, "Don't scare her like that."

Cal replied, "Momma and Daddy didn't tell her nothin'. Someone has to."

Ted didn't respond. He simply looked at me and nodded. I watched Leroy with a new sense of fear. Just being Addie's friend could make me a target of his meanness. I didn't fully understand why, but it wasn't the time to ask.

Samuel, on the other hand, was a quiet boy, tall and slender, with the good-looking features of Aunt Sara and dark brown hair to match. He stayed off by himself most of the time reading. In the classroom, we were grouped by age, except for Samuel. He should have been in fourth, but sat with the sixth and seventh grades. It made Leroy angry. The teacher placed them far apart, but it didn't stop the abuse.

The first day I sat next to a little girl my age named Abigail. She had the most beautiful blond hair. It hung to the middle of her back in a long braid. It was smooth and straight, like I always wanted. My hair was black and kinky curly. It hurt for Momma to comb, so it was cut real short. Momma always said someday I'd be thankful for the curls, but I doubted it. Abigail was thin like Addie. I envied both of them. I still appeared to have baby fat rounding out my arms, legs, and waist. My bone structure was big like Daddy's, so I would never be considered dainty.

Abigail lived on a small farm a mile from school in the other direction. She had seven siblings, four older and three younger. Her oldest brother was 15, but dropped out after the sixth grade to help on the farm. Next were Nettie and Anna Lee. Being girls, and needing to find a husband, they were permitted to continue in school. Ezekiel eight years old, was fourth in line. He was a small boy and frequently absent due to illness. He was bright, and ahead of the other children his age. Though his body was weak, his brain was strong.

Abigail's family was kind, but poor. Most days she came to school with only a slice of jelly bread and an apple, rarely cookies or special treats. Without jugs to keep milk cool, they drank water from the well. Some days I asked Momma for an extra hunk of cheese or something to share with Abigail. We weren't rich, but I knew how fortunate we were.

Abigail had three dresses, one was new, but the other two were handed down. The children were always clean and polite. It was a good example that money doesn't make the person.

She made school bearable. She helped me when I didn't understand, celebrated my successes, and was my constant companion.

My days were occupied with my second best friend, while my evenings were spent with my first best friend. After school I ran upstairs to change before visiting with Momma in the kitchen. I watched the clock, waiting for Addie's expected return. Each day I went to the porch, standing with my feet on the bottom rail, looking for her at the fork in the road. To the right, it took you to Addie's, to the left traveled past our house to Grandma Em's, then ten more miles to the next town.

When I saw Addie, I took off for her front porch. She started running as well, arriving about the same time. Waiting for us was a cool drink on hot days, warm milk or tea on cold ones. Though I wanted her at school with me, it was fun to have different things to talk about. We'd stay at Addie's or run to my house to play, or sometimes lay in the tall grass talking until supper. Occasionally, I ate with them or she joined my family for our evening meal. I was thankful we were still friends.

I never told Addie about Abigail. I didn't want her to feel anyone could take her place. She likely made new friends as well, but never told me about them. When we were together, it was only the two of us.

I also didn't tell Abigail about Addie. I liked to think it was for the same reason, but I knew there was more. Cal's warning, and the comments I heard from my classmates, cautioned me that others might not approve of our friendship. The words used at school by many of the students showed their sentiments, but they were terms we never used. The only way Momma or Daddy taught us to speak of Addie or the others was to call them 'colored.' I apologize if the term may not be politically correct as I write this more than fifty years later; however, in keeping with my childhood, it seems appropriate. As I tell this story there were many times that more vulgar and derogatory words were used to describe the coloreds, but I cannot bring myself to write them, even though it would make the sentiments of prejudice and bigotry more real.

Chapter FOUR

1948

F irst grade was nearing the end. It was a year of sadness as Addie and I began to live in separate worlds, but also a year of joy with a new friendship that would endure the rest of my life. I learned much, but most important was about the difference between Addie and me, and that not all people are kind.

We began Easter Sunday in the third pew listening to Reverend Howell preach about the meaning of the season. Grandma Em, Aunt Sara, Uncle Roy, and the boys sat in the front pew reserved for our family. Did they hear his words about love and forgiveness?

The loss of our family was more pronounced on Sundays, but Reverend Howell's words made me question how Grandma Em could turn her back on us. He cited a verse from the book of John that during the next week, and in the future, came to mind many times: "This is my commandment, that you love one another as I have loved you." Jesus loved everyone with an unconditional love. Reverend Howell compared it to a parent's love for their children. What did Daddy do to make Grandma Em stop loving him?

We celebrated the holiday with my mother's parents. My grandfather owned a three-story building on Main Street. A store was on the first floor in the front, with a small living/dining area and kitchen at the back. The second floor had two bedrooms and a bath for my grandparents, and a separate apartment for rental. The third floor was divided into two apartments occupied by the same families for most of my childhood. Each lived in three private rooms, sharing a common kitchen and bath in the center.

In my early years, we only saw my grandparents at their home on Easter and Christmas. They never came to the country. Grandmother Gordon didn't approve of her daughter being a farmer's wife. She often made disparaging remarks about Momma's life, frequently insulting Daddy. By her standards, our life was bordering on heathen.

My grandmother celebrated her status as a respected merchant and leading citizen. She liked to portray an image of wealth. We called them Grandfather and Grandmother Gordon, which negated any feelings of familiarity or comfort. Her formality in dealing with people in town, and with us, was unlike anyone I knew in Alabama.

Grandmother Gordon presented beautiful dinners on these occasions with candles accenting the gold rimmed crystal glasses. I loved looking at the beautiful cream-colored china with pink roses and green leaves weaving a vine border. The dishes were edged in gold as well. That year I was in school, therefore permitted to use the fine china and crystal. I proudly enjoyed my new privilege.

During our week off I intended to spend every possible minute with Addie. The first morning I raced through breakfast as I listened for her screen door. Hearing the familiar sound, I ran onto the porch. Running to meet in the field, we clasped hands and began spinning in circles. With our eyes closed we turned around and around. Falling in a heap of giggles, our heads landed pointing toward my house. I said, "Well, Momma gets us today."

Every morning we'd meet to spin. Some days I intentionally dragged Addie the last turn to be sure our heads were facing her house. I loved spending time with Miss Ada. She was warm and loving, with kind eyes and an infectious smile. She was short and full-figured, probably petite in younger years. I liked it when she gathered me to her ample bosom for a hug. Always welcoming, she made me feel like I belonged with their family.

It was a wonderful vacation. I didn't want it to end, but Saturday came all too soon. It was our last day together because Sunday was family day for both of us. We decided nothing would separate us. Momma had Reverend Howell's wife and other ladies from church gathered in our parlor to plan the Spring Social, so she sent me to Addie's for the day.

Miss Ada was sick in bed with a terrible fever and needed medicine from town. Miss Emily said I had to go home. We begged her to let me go with them. In all the years Addie and I were friends, we never went anywhere together. After we turned on the alligator tears, she allowed me to ask permission, obviously expecting Momma to deny the request.

I ran home alone, calling for Momma. She came out onto the porch, signaling for me to hush as she hurried down the steps. She said, "Quiet, the ladies will hear you." She pulled me behind the car barn, out of sight from the house.

I explained my request. Her immediate response was, "No." However, that answer was unacceptable. I began to protest, emitting great sobs. She took hold of my arms, saying "Stop it. I can't have you making a scene."

I tried to calm myself, but the tears continued as I explained, "Miss Emily said the only stop is her father's store. Please, Momma."

Her eyes moved in the direction of the house. There were two choices: to let me go, praying no one saw me, or drag me into the house crying about how she was ruining the last day with my best friend. She chose to take her chances with option one. Though the ladies in the parlor were good Sunday Christians, this was certain to be an exception to the rule 'love thy neighbor.'

She said, "Alright, but don't go until I'm back in the house. Count to ten real slow, understand, then go." I nodded.

I peeked around the corner as Momma hurried to the house. "...five, six, seven, eight, nine, ten." I ran as fast as I could across the field to make sure Miss Emily didn't leave without me. They were in the truck waiting. Arriving out of breath, I gasped, "I can go. I can go."

Addie opened the door for me. As I joined her, we wrapped our arms around each other accompanied by squeals of delight. I'm sure Miss Emily wasn't pleased, but if Momma was willing to suffer the consequences, so was she. Miss Emily started the engine.

Her father owned the food, feed, seed, and equipment store for the colored families. My grandfather owned the grocery store for whites, and Uncle Frank, Grandma Em's brother, operated the white feed, seed, and equipment store in town. Sitting next to my best friend, I thought about how much we had in common.

In town, Miss Emily turned onto a side street, then back toward the business district just before we entered 'Colored Town.' We stopped in front of a building at the other end of Main Street from Grandfather Gordon's, half the distance from Uncle Frank's. Above the door was a sign reading, 'Food, Feed, Seed, and Equipment' in big black letters. Underneath was written 'John Jefferson, Proprietor.'

It was my first and only visit, though legally I could have entered at any time. There were no signs that said, 'Coloreds Only.' The customers stared as Mr. Jefferson came to greet us. He was a tall, slim man, with a full head of gray hair, and a beard to match. His hazel eyes twinkled as he smiled. I had met him once at Addie's. He bent over as he reached down to shake my hand. Smiling warmly, he said, "I'm happy to see ya again."

While Miss Emily visited with her father, Addie and I looked at the items available. Hanging on the wall were two quilts I recognized as Miss Ada's. I asked, "Why ya sellin' those?"

She looked at me, puzzled, saying, "To make money."

Walking through the rows, I noticed Miss Ada's bread and butter pickles, and other vegetables. I suddenly realized the quilting and canning were her contribution to the family. We moved on to the farm section with the tools, as well as feed and seed. Written on the bags were the words 'Cooper Farm Supplies, Montgomery, Alabama.' I recognized them from Uncle Frank's store. That was odd. I thought the coloreds needed a separate store because they used different things. If they bought the same items, why did we need two stores?

It wasn't long before Miss Emily was calling us to be on our way. Addie and I said goodbye to Mr. Jefferson. He surprised us with two peppermint sticks. On the steps Miss Emily gave her father a kiss on the cheek, and he gave Addie a hug. I looked down the street toward the white feed and seed. Uncle Roy came out carrying two bags of lime, one over each shoulder. As I watched him maneuver down the steps, three colored boys were running toward him passing a rock between them. They were not much older than me. They didn't see him, and he couldn't see them. One of the boys ran into him. It was like watching a slow-motion play in a football game as he swayed and stumbled forward. First one bag fell. Trying to save it, he lost his grip on the second.

The boys stopped. He called them terrible names as he ordered them to pick up the bags. Two took off running as fast as they could. The third boy stared at Uncle Roy. I watched that boy take his first step toward him. I've often wondered if he knew what he was walking into. He bent over to grab the corners of the bag resting on the steps. Uncle Roy drew back his fist hitting the boy so hard he crashed to the ground. The boy got up. He walked over to the bag of lime again. Uncle Roy hit him a second time, only harder. Once again, the boy moved toward the bags. As he bent down the third time, Uncle Roy kicked him with all his might. The boy fell, but Uncle Roy didn't wait for him to get up, kicking him repeatedly. I let out a scream, but Miss Emily quickly covered my mouth. There was fear on her face mixed with tears rolling down her cheeks. I looked around at the people, colored and white, watching. No one dared interfere.

I turned back to see Uncle Frank in the open door of his store. Finally, someone would help the boy, but he retreated inside as he slowly closed the door. Our new sheriff Roland Hosper was walking up the street toward Uncle Roy. I wanted to yell, "Run, Sheriff, run!" But nothing came out. He sauntered toward them like he was on his way to get a cup of coffee. By the time he reached them, the boy wasn't moving.

Miss Emily quickly herded us into the truck. She drove the other direction for two blocks, turned down a side street, and again on a back street to head home. She was crying. Addie and I sat beside her stone faced. Addie reached for my hand. I looked at my friend, but she continued to stare forward. We held tight on the quiet ride home.

Now I understood why Daddy disliked Uncle Roy. It also explained my cousin's behavior at school. I wondered, 'are you taught to be that cruel, are you born that way, or does it come with the name?' The two meanest people I ever met were both named Leroy.

What other names could test my theory? James was an interesting name, because many men in my life were named James. Daddy, though they called him J.P. was named after his father. Addie's father was James, and all of her brothers used James in their names. Each of them was a kind person who would never hurt anyone. Every man I could think of named James was decent and good.

Testing the theory further, I examined the name Emily. Thinking of Grandma Em, she was a good person. Though I didn't understand how she could turn her back on us, she never harmed anyone. I saw her angry only when Momma bought something for the house, at Granddaddy Tucker's funeral, and if she saw Addie playing with me. I assumed her dislike of Addie was rooted in ignorance. She simply didn't know her. In my childish reasoning, that didn't make her a bad person.

I looked over at Miss Emily. She was good, like Momma in many ways, always taking care of people. She was a loving mother, and kind to me. However, she and Momma were different in one way. Whenever Daddy came into or left the house, he always got a kiss. I never saw Miss Emily kiss James. Though she wasn't mean to him, I didn't see a mutual love like my parents.

I thought of Emily Thomas at the country school. She was fourteen, the sweetest person, and a favorite of the teacher. It was decided. Emily was a name for good people, just like James. Was it really that simple? Was degree of kindness or cruelty all in a name?

Arriving home, Miss Emily turned off the engine, but we didn't move. We were surrounded by silence for a very long time. Without looking my way, she said, "Missy, ya need to go home."

I turned toward her with my tear streaked-face and said, "The church ladies are in my parlor."

She looked at me with such sadness. After a moment she said, "Then ya best come in."

We followed her into the house. She went directly to Miss Ada's room. Addie and I waited in the hall, not wanting to be alone. After a short time, she came out. Moving on to the kitchen without a look in our direction, we quietly followed. She moved around, trying to busy herself with no specific purpose. Finally, she stopped, turning to look at us. Her eyes traveled from one to the other as we waited. She walked toward us. Cupping each of our faces with a hand, she said, "Help me with some mendin', alright?"

We nodded, grateful for any task to occupy our minds and keep us with her. Near supper time there was a knock at the back door. Emily told us to wait there. Soon she was calling me. Addie accompanied me to the kitchen. From the concerned look on Momma's face I knew Miss Emily told her about the events in town. I gave a slight bow to Miss Emily as I passed by, and squeezed Addie's hand as we parted.

The walk home was quiet. Though no one could hear, I felt open and exposed. I waited to speak until we were in the safety of our kitchen. I told Momma what I saw, crying for that little boy. She listened carefully to my words. I finished with, "Why didn't the Sheriff stop Uncle Roy? He just walked up the street like nothin' was happenin'."

She said, "That's why he's sheriff now. Some people thought Fleming was too nice to the coloreds. People like Uncle Roy worked hard to get him out and Roland Hosper in. There's not much protection for people like Addie. He's the law and there isn't anything we can do." I thought of Hosper. He was young, barely out of high school, but he was big and strong looking. He wore his sleeves rolled to accentuate the size of his arms. He would be a formidable sight for any man. She continued, "You shouldn't have gone to town with Miss Emily. Don't ever ask again. Do you understand?"

"It wasn't her fault. She didn't make it happen," I said.

She replied, "I know. I'm just saying it isn't safe for you to be seen in town with them. So don't ask. And don't ever make a scene like that in front of the church ladies. Do you hear?"

I nodded, but the forceful tone of her voice made me angry. Uncle Roy did wrong, but it seemed like Addie, Miss Emily, and that little boy were the ones being blamed.

With school in session, Addie and I returned to our schedule of a couple of hours before supper each day. One afternoon we helped Miss Emily bake bread. Because Miss Ada was feeling better, she joined us in the kitchen. She was too weak to be running around, but it was nice to have her company.

I often thought about the boy, but it never felt right to ask. Addie was talking about school, so it was my chance. "Did ya see that boy today? How is he?" She didn't look up, intent on punching her ball of dough, and folding it repeatedly. I turned to Miss Emily next, but she remained focused on her task. I looked at Miss Ada. She was watching me with sad eyes. She would tell me. Miss Ada always answered my questions.

Solemnly she said, "Missy, that little boy died. God's protectin' him now."

The room was quiet the rest of the afternoon as we baked our bread. Miss Emily sent a warm loaf home with me. I was grateful for my time with them. They understood how I was feeling. Roy was my uncle, but they knew the hatred that drove him was not in me or my family.

The following days and weeks I waited to hear that Uncle Roy was going to jail. After all, if you did bad things, you were punished. I wondered how long it would take the authorities to act. However, nothing happened. I didn't understand how he could kill a little boy with no consequence.

That year I learned many new things in school, but I learned the most important lesson on Main Street. All men are governed by laws, but which laws and how depends on the color of your skin. I never looked at my little town the same. People watched a man beat a child to death, and greeted him as always in church on Sunday. When Reverend Howell said the Bible says to love one another, did he leave out the part that said only if they look like you?

Chapter FIVE

FALL *1948*

I moved up a row at our country school with Abigail at my side. Addie began second grade at the colored school in town, but we still enjoyed our few hours together each day. I was becoming increasingly aware of my double life but never felt I was living a double standard. I simply kept my two worlds separate.

The focus at school was the upcoming election. President Truman was running against Dewey. We shared news about the candidates, both national and local, with tidbits of information we gleaned from conversations at home. Miss Walters wanted us to experience the process. A wooden box with a slit in the top sat on her desk. We would vote on Election Day! It wouldn't count for real, but it was exciting.

As we were leaving the Hotel one Sunday, a group of colored men were gathered in front of Mr. Jefferson's store. Two men I didn't recognize were on the steps speaking. I heard Momma take a breath as she reached over to touch Daddy's arm. Standing in the middle of the group was James. I was the only one in the car who didn't understand the significance of the event. In the mirror I saw fear and anger on Daddy's face. Why did James standing around with other colored men cause alarm? I started to speak, but Cal hit my arm, silencing me.

That evening Daddy went out on the back porch. I watched him through the screen. He stood a few minutes, came back to sit in his chair, only to return to the porch again. A few times he picked up the newspaper, but set it back down without reading a word. In the evenings we listened to the radio, but not that night. It was quiet in our house. Momma drove the boys to the barn to take care of the animals while Daddy stayed behind. She left me to play in the parlor. When they returned, she sent us to bed earlier than usual, but I didn't argue. Watching Daddy fret frightened me.

I was unable to sleep. I heard the porch door open and close several more times. He was watching for something, but what? Before long, I heard the sound of metal banging against glass, and the creak of a door. It was his gun cabinet at the bottom of the stairs. After his footsteps moved back to the parlor, I quietly crept toward the hall. Ted and Cal were at the top of the stairs listening to the familiar sound of Daddy's shotgun being cleaned and loaded. They signaled not to speak as I joined them. We huddled together until we heard Momma's footsteps heading toward us. Running to our rooms, we climbed into our beds. She came up to her room. I listened to the silence for a very long time, before drifting off to sleep.

The next morning Momma woke me for school. The boys had eaten, and were feeding the animals. Daddy was finishing breakfast as I entered the kitchen. He looked tired. He wasn't making frequent trips to the porch. Whatever worried him had passed. I finished my oatmeal as the boys came in. We grabbed our books, milk jugs, and food. Momma came out on the porch with Daddy. I turned frequently to see them watching us until the house was out of sight.

The short trip to school was my opportunity to find out what the boys knew. I asked, "What was Daddy waitin' for last night?"

Cal turned toward me, his face fire red. "This is nothin' for ya to know 'bout. Don't speak of it to anyone, ya hear! Not anyone!"

The tone of his voice was low and threatening. I stopped in the middle of the road, unable to move. The boys turned toward me. Ted punched Cal, warning, "You'll pay for scarin' her."

Ted walked back, taking my hand as he said, "Ya can't speak of last night. James should've known better than to be seen talkin' to those men. It makes people nervous when strangers come to town, that's all. Now come on. We gotta get to school." We continued to walk in silence.

A group of boys were gathered around Leroy. Ted and Cal exchanged a knowing look. We stayed far away. Feeling safer in a crowd, Samuel and several children joined us.

One of the girls rang the bell. We were relieved, but it was temporary. After the Pledge of Allegiance and morning-prayer, came sharing news about the upcoming election. It was my favorite activity of the day. However, Miss Walters told us to take out our spellers. There were a few murmurs from the older children, with cries of disappointment from the younger, me included. She returned to her desk without a word.

Leroy stood. "But Miss Walters, I have news 'bout the election. Don't ya want to hear?"

She braced her hands to face him. "We won't be discussing the election today."

He flashed a smile saying, "But Miss Walters, don't ya want to know which darkies won't be with us tomorrow."

I turned my head to see her reaction. Her face drained of color. Her hands trembled as she pressed them against the desk. Her arms began to shake. I studied the faces around me. Did everyone understand but me? I looked at Abigail. Her head was down with her eyes glued to the floor. She wouldn't look at me.

A movement at the back of the classroom drew my attention. Cal started to stand, but Ted reached up with a hand on each shoulder forcing him to sit. Losing his balance, Cal fell against Abigail's sister, Nettie, pushing her off the bench. At any other time, the class would have roared with laughter, but not that day. Fear permeated the room as Ted rushed to help her up.

Leroy wasn't finished. "Seems there was a couple northerners tryin' to stir things up, tellin' people they can vote. I heard their talkin' days are over. Tomorrow I'll have more news 'bout lessons learned." Satisfied, he sat down.

I looked at Ted. He gave me a soft look as if to say, 'I'm here. Don't worry.'

Miss Walters was shaken. She didn't want to give Leroy another opportunity to speak, so we worked independently at our seats. Even at recess we were quiet. It continued on through the long afternoon.

We were in our own thoughts on the walk home. I didn't need to ask Ted or Cal what Leroy meant. I understood what Daddy was watching for, and why those men in town alarmed him. I didn't hurry to change or eat my snack. Momma moved slowly as well. She wouldn't stop Addie and me from playing, but it was safer at our home.

I was afraid for me, Addie, James, Daddy, Miss Emily, and Miss Ada. I was afraid for all of us, but of whom? Was it Leroy, his father, or someone else? How could one or two instill fear in everyone? I suspected there was more, but it didn't have a name yet.

My thoughts were interrupted by a soft knock on the back door. Momma tried to look and sound extra cheerful as she greeted Addie. Did Addie see beyond the smile to the concern in Momma's eyes? I saw it.

We played like any other day, but Momma wouldn't let Addie stay for supper. She walked with us to the middle of the field, sending Addie on from there. We waited until she was safely inside. Turning toward home, I held tight to Momma's hand. My fear and sadness made it impossible to speak, but the closeness was comforting.

Usually we didn't eat until the last glimmer of daylight passed. That night Daddy was at the house before dusk. Momma had supper ready. We ate in silence. Everyone was listening for any noise. All I could hear were the crickets in the field beginning their nightly song.

After we finished, I stayed in the kitchen to help Momma. Daddy was in the parlor reading. Again, Momma drove the boys to the barn and there was quiet in our house. Daddy made several trips to the back porch to look and listen with his gun leaning in the corner. Leroy's words kept playing in my mind. "But Miss Walters, don't ya want to know which darkies won't be with us tomorrow?" I understood what Daddy was afraid of, or rather for whom. I was certain Leroy was speaking of James, and Daddy was waiting.

Momma and the boys returned. Joining us in the parlor, she picked up her sewing while I played with my dolls. I fell asleep on the floor. I woke for a moment when Ted carried me to bed. Momma helped me change before tucking me in. The peaceful sleep felt wonderful.

A loud noise woke me. It was the slamming of the porch door. I heard Momma yelling for Daddy, and the boys' hurried footsteps. Running into the hall, I followed them down the stairs. The absence of Daddy's gun in the corner made me shiver. Momma was kneeling on the porch crying. I could hear the roar of horses' hooves. Lighted torches bounced up and down as they approached the fork leading to Addie's house. It wasn't only Uncle Roy. Who were they, and what could Daddy do against so many?

Ted moved toward the steps, but Momma grabbed him as he tried to run past. Holding him back, she pulled him to the floor. I knelt, encircling Momma and Ted with my little arms. Cal stood next to Momma with tears running down his face. She reached up to take his hand. We cried and prayed as we watched those torches get closer to that little house so much like ours. I looked up to see a car stop at the fork in the road. I pointed it out. We waited for them to help Daddy and James, but it didn't move. The sudden silence that fell over the field drew our attention back to Addie's. The house blocked our view. All we could do was listen but for what?

Then we heard it, the loud bang of a shotgun. Was it Daddy or someone else? We waited. The bright glow of a fire illuminated the sky. The tall dark shadow of the house was silhouetted against the light. Momma gasped.

A few moments later images in white bounced in the glow then disappeared into the darkness. We heard the pounding of horses on the road, at first loud but growing fainter. There were no torches, just the retreating sounds. We looked toward the waiting car, but it didn't move. I saw the shadowy shapes of the horses move down the road behind it. After they were gone, the car slowly moved toward our house. It didn't pick up speed, but kept the same pace as it crept closer. Cal ran to the rail to see who it was. After the car passed, he turned to us saying, "It was the sheriff." Momma remained silent. I remembered her words. There would be no protection for Addie and her family but not for Daddy either.

We waited for Daddy to come walking across the field. The glow from behind the house died down, but still no Daddy. Soon we saw a shape running toward us. It was one of the boys. Momma's body trembled. Standing to face Tucker James, Ted broke free of her grasp. Fear shot through all of us. Where was Daddy?

Tucker James leaned against the rail. We anxiously waited as he took several deep breaths. He finally said, "Miss Melanie, everyone's alright. Papa and J.P. are watchin' for anyone who might come back, but they think they're gone. Your Mister says to get some rest. He'll be home later."

Momma slumped against Ted, her body limp. I thought she fainted, but a moment later she whispered, "Thank you. Is the house fine? Did the fire do much damage?"

"Oh, no mam, they didn't burn the house. They threw the torches at the base of that old oak. For a minute we thought it might catch, but it didn't even flicker. The torches burned 'emselves up. It was a sight ya wouldn't believe. Even that old tree was tellin' 'em no harm was comin' to our family. The good Lord told 'em loud and clear!" He smiled as he told the story. We gave praise right along with him, for the Lord's protection and that tree.

After a few more questions, he ran back across the field. Momma guided us inside. We each kissed her goodnight before heading to bed. Drained by the emotional ordeal, it didn't take long to fall asleep.

I woke in the morning to coffee brewing. I ran downstairs to be sure Daddy was safe. My parents were holding each other in front of the sink, giggling like teenagers. He saw me in the doorway. I ran across the kitchen, leaping into his arms. He swung me around, both of us roaring with laughter. Ted and Cal were at the barn doing morning chores as I sat down for a special breakfast with him.

When the boys returned, I was ready for school. We set off immediately. My parents again watched us from the porch. As we neared the school a car approached from the direction of town. I could see the light perched on top. It began to slow as it came close. Sheriff Hosper crawled past us giving a slight nod. I grabbed Ted's hand. We all stared as he passed by. Ted said, "Come on. We're late."

I thought of Momma and Daddy. I worried for them and James. Hosper was the law. What could they do against him?

At school the children were inside with the doors closed. We entered, moving quickly to our seats. I felt the stares of everyone around us. Miss Walters kept talking. The big boys at the back of the class mumbled a few things, but I didn't turn their way. I wouldn't give Leroy the satisfaction of knowing he frightened me.

Throughout the morning, I waited for him to make his announcement, but he never did. Only once did I dare to look back. He was staring at me. I could see the hatred and anger in his eyes. At recess, Miss Walters allowed everyone to eat inside on the pretext of the cool weather, but everyone knew it was to protect us from his wrath.

I worried about the end of the day. Miss Walters changed the schedule. Quiet independent work was our final activity. She

walked around the classroom checking each paper. Stopping at
Leroy's desk, she noted he was having trouble with the math and
would need to stay after school. We pretended to focus on our
work, but a quick look and smile toward her said, 'Thank you.'

We wasted no time getting home. Ted told me to hurry so they
could help Daddy, but we all wanted to be sure our parents were
fine. They ran, each holding one of my hands swinging me
between them. My feet bounced off the ground every few steps to
send me flying forward until they caught up. Feeling free for those
few moments, we laughed all the way home.

We rushed into the house. Cal said, "Where's Daddy."

Momma replied, "Working in the fields."

He said, "Have ya seen him?"

She nodded. Ted grabbed Cal's arm, "Hurry and change so we
can help."

After the boys went upstairs, I asked, "Did you see Hosper?"

She nodded, "Everything's fine. He was just checking on
things. Drove by early and hasn't been back."

I asked, "Can I play at Addie's?" I wanted to see that tree.

She smiled. "Just for bit. I'll come get you before supper."

After changing, I perched on the porch rail for the first glimpse
of my friend. Seeing me, she took off at the same time. Running
across the field I lost sight of her but was sure I'd be there first. I
rounded the corner of the house. She was standing on the steps
breathing hard. I didn't care who won. I was happy to see her.

I cried out, "Addie." She rushed off the porch. Throwing our
arms around each other, we filled the air with laughter. I glanced
from her to the tree. You could see the blackened soot on the
trunk, but not one inch of bark was burnt.

Miss Ada came out on the porch to admire that old oak with
us. After a few moments she said, "C'mon. I got baked apples with
cinnamon sugar waitin'." It felt like someone's birthday.

When we were alone, I asked Addie, "Were ya afraid?"

She said, "Not much." But I didn't believe her. She continued,
"Granmama said everything'd be fine. We huddled in the kitchen.

She prayed so loud it was hard to hear. I wanted her to hush, but didn't dare say it." She smiled, causing me to giggle.

I asked, "But what was outside? We couldn't see and no one'll tell me."

She claimed to not know, but I pressed for more. She said, "I heard your Daddy yellin' at Roy, tellin' him he should've rode another horse if he wanted to hide under that hood. Then he said somethin' 'bout hurtin' Sara. He said they'd have to kill 'em both if they're gonna kill one of 'em. I didn't hear anything else 'til I heard the horses leavin'."

"But we heard a gunshot?" I asked.

"Your daddy let 'em know they was ready," she answered.

Between us, I had enough information to satisfy my curiosity. I wasn't surprised to hear Uncle Roy was there. I was scared to think Daddy was willing to die for James, but it made me proud too. What he did was important. Celebrating them as the two bravest men, Addie and I basked in the story of our fathers.

The relief of that day was not permanent. Daddy continued to fret and remain on alert in the evenings. Hosper drove by every night. I wasn't sure if he was checking on us, or warning us. I was glad when the election was over, but there would be another one the next year.

Chapter SIX
1949

Spring and summer continued much the same with Addie a central part of my life. In the fall we entered the third grade. A memorable event happened at Christmas. It was a special time of year in my family. Momma started preparing the day after Thanksgiving. We began with a trip to the woods to collect pine boughs to make wreaths for the door and windows. After wrapping the boughs around metal rings, we attached pinecones and beautiful red ribbons.

The first Saturday of December was Christmas tree day. I woke to the sound of rain on the roof. Momma continually watched for a break in the weather. Daddy was working in the barn, but ready at a moment's notice.

Late morning the rain stopped. We drove to the barn. After loading on Daddy's tractor, Momma guided him while we searched for the red ribbon she put on a tree in the fall. I spotted it first. It was a full beautiful tree. Ted had the privilege of sawing the trunk while Daddy and Cal held the bottom boughs. As they worked, I searched for a nest buried in the branches. Momma smiled and pointed to a spot in the middle. I clapped with excitement because it meant a year of blessings was ahead.

want to expose you to Missy any longer than necessary. It's best if we open our gifts at home."

Grandmother Gordon didn't argue. As we gathered our coats Momma said, "Your gifts are over there, Merry Christmas."

Grandfather Gordon said good-night. Though saddened by the events of the evening, even he didn't challenge his wife.

I asked Daddy to drive through town to see the decorations. The shops were dark except for the colorful lights framing the buildings. As we approached the far end of town I saw a light and people coming from Mr. Jefferson's store with packages of meat and handfuls of potatoes. We looked at the scene in silence.

We rode home listening to Christmas carols on the radio. Was everyone thinking of the unpleasant evening or the line of people at Mr. Jefferson's store? For me, it was the latter. There were many questions racing through my mind. Momma stopped in town yesterday to buy everything for our Christmas dinner. Why were those people in Mr. Jefferson's store on Christmas Eve?

That night I crawled under my covers and waited. I heard Momma's footsteps outside my door. Opening it a crack she expected me to be asleep. I whispered, "Tuck me in?"

She sat on the edge of my bed. The questions couldn't wait. I told her about Mr. Jefferson and Tucker James. She listened to my story patiently. I waited for her to explain, but she turned away.

I said, "Everyone looks at me and shakes their head, but I know things. I can't tell anyone Addie's my friend, and men like Uncle Roy hurt people 'cause they're colored. I'm old enough. Why was Mr. Jefferson at Grandfather Gordon's, and why were all those people in his store tonight?"

She closed her eyes for a moment. Opening them, she looked at me and explained, "There are suppliers that charge double or triple to stores like Mr. Jefferson's for food that's rotten. One of those men bragged to my father. It made him angry, so he decided to help. He orders a little extra, and sells it to Mr. Jefferson. Between the farmers, family in Montgomery, and my father, Mr. Jefferson manages. If anyone ever found out, they'd both be in danger. Do you understand? You shouldn't have seen that." She paused for a moment, then said, "I'm trusting you. You have to protect them."

I said, "But why tonight?"

"My father needed to sell to his customers first. That was the extra left over," she said.

I was afraid for Grandfather Gordon. I understood how serious it was if people like Uncle Roy found out. I smiled at her, saying, "You can trust me." She was still afraid as she kissed me goodnight, but I would show her. I drifted off to sleep thinking of my grandfather, proud of his kindness. He was a good man.

desperately to see her, but at the same time I was afraid. I felt ashamed, embarrassed, and guilty. How would she feel seeing me on a bus while she was walking? If I didn't acknowledge her, she'd be hurt. Oh, and Abigail! What would she think if I waved at Addie, or if she waved at me? The bus ride was no longer exciting or fun. I became afraid as awareness of the situation washed over me. I shouldn't have sat next to the window. Maybe Addie was walking on the other side of the road and wouldn't see me. I prayed she was at school. While all these emotions were swirling inside, I began to feel ill.

As we approached the town limit I saw Addie and her brothers. They didn't look up, but it was too late for me. I can't blame it all on the bus ride or my anguish over Addie, because fear of the unknown overwhelmed me as well. At the school, Cal came to the front of the bus. Looking at me, he knew something was wrong. That evening he told Momma my face was green as grass.

Many big brothers might ignore their little sister, but not Cal. He stopped the line of boys behind him. Abigail moved quickly to the door, but my legs began to wobble. Putting his hands under my arms, he swung me into the aisle. He carried me down the steps into the fresh air. Sitting me on the sidewalk, he kneeled beside me. A tall man with a bald head, and enormous pot belly bent down next to us. It was a nice face, making me feel at peace. He was wearing tan pants, a white short-sleeved shirt, and a big wide tie that fell three inches shy of his waist. The next thing I remember was waking in the nurse's office.

What a way to start my first day at the town school. Later the principal stopped to check on me. "Hello, little lady. That's the first time I ever made someone faint. Your brother told me your name is Missy. I'm Mr. Beaker. Are ya feelin' better?" I nodded, finding comfort in his voice. He told the nurse to give me some orange juice. His smile was warm and reassuring. He squeezed my hand as he said goodbye.

The nurse escorted me to my classroom. The introductions were done and books distributed. Many of the children snickered.

Some of the boys laughed out loud. Abigail was in the far row next to the windows. I was afraid she'd pretend not to know me, but she motioned to the seat in front of her piled high with books. Thank God we could sit together.

My teacher, Mrs. Dennis, was beautiful, with short brown hair, a wonderful smile, and soft sweet voice. She thanked the nurse, announcing, "This is your new classmate Melissa Tucker. Melissa, you may take your seat in front of Abigail."

No one ever called me Melissa. I whispered, "Missy."

She bent down to see my face as she repeated my name, "Missy."

After I was in my seat she said, "Missy, leave your spelling book out. I was explaining the first lesson to the class." I put my other books away quickly.

The rest of the day was uneventful. In the cafeteria each class was assigned a set of tables, one for boys and one for girls. Forced to sit with us, the girls seemed nice as they asked about our country school. They seemed like us except two, Charlotte Pearl and Virginia Graves.

Back in the classroom, the afternoon passed quickly. Boarding the bus for the ride home, we sat behind the driver with Abigail by the window. Shortly after we left town I saw Addie and her brothers. I was nervous. Could she see me? Abigail was talking about our first day. She didn't notice my attention was focused outside. Addie walked with her head down as we drove by. I was relieved and sad at the same time. Maybe she didn't realize it was my bus, but part of me believed she did. She was always more aware of the rules regarding our friendship while I was naïve and unsure of how to be. My parents avoided discussing our relationship, but her parents taught her the facts.

Moving to the town school was a big change, though a few things stayed the same. Abigail remained my best white friend throughout my childhood and beyond. The other constant was Leroy. He instilled fear in everyone. No one could control him. Grades first through twelve were in the same building with the

the look on Daddy's face. On the ride and at home, I was too preoccupied with Abigail to notice the growing conflict between my parents.

That evening Abigail tried on the socks. Which would Charlotte and Virginia envy the most? Which complemented her clothes for the next day without question? We chose a pair with a thin pink ribbon woven around the lip of the sock. Folded down, there were matching pink roses with green satin leaves. I admired them, but didn't order a pair for myself so they would be special for Abigail.

The next morning Momma packed matching sandwiches and milk, but added the cake for Abigail. It was fun waiting for the bus together. In our classroom the reaction was exactly as we hoped. Abigail's socks were the talk of every girl in the room. Charlotte and Virginia showed their disdain, but held their attacks against Abigail. I became their target, but I didn't care. It was Abigail's birthday. She was honored by everyone.

After school I told Momma about our day but left out the abuse I suffered in Abigail's place. Momma tried to show interest in my stories, but her mind was elsewhere. Disappointed, I went to Addie's.

At supper I monopolized the conversation with stories about Abigail's day, the girls' reaction, and my joy at seeing Charlotte and Virginia jealous. However, everyone was focused on their food with their heads down intently eating. Momma gave me one short nod, briefly making eye contact. Daddy didn't look up at all. Something was wrong.

Once we finished, he pushed away from the table without a word to anyone and walked out. That was my first clue he was angry. The boys thanked Momma for supper, before following him down the back steps. She exhaled in frustration as she shook her head back and forth. Later I learned he was angry about Momma making cakes for money. It challenged his manhood in front of the entire town, especially her mother. Momma, on the other hand, was excited at the prospect of having an income of her own. She felt honored to be recognized as talented and special.

She wasn't a typical farmer's wife. She didn't grow or can vegetables. For years she helped Grandma Em with her garden, but since the falling out, our shelves held only Miss Ada's canned goods. Momma didn't dress down animals. Daddy prepared the meat; she only wrapped it. She didn't raise chickens or sell eggs like many of the wives. She collected apples, berries, or pecans, and did occasional sewing for people, but not as a business. Baking cakes could be her contribution to the family in lieu of canned beets or pickles. Daddy, however, felt it provided ammunition to Grandmother Gordon's attacks against him. They were at a standoff. Momma was not willing to give up something that made her happy, and also helped the family. His pride stopped him from supporting her.

She moved forward with her plans. She ordered two round pans in different sizes, and materials on credit from her father. She met with her first customer to plan the cake. She never talked about it in front of Daddy, and hid the evidence before he came in. But each evening was quiet with an undercurrent of anger. She needed a new plan to resolve the dispute.

During the week she made the flowers to edge each layer. Thursday, she made the fondant to cover the red velvet cakes. Friday morning, she was up early baking the cakes to create the four-layer tower. She was working hard, but the excitement and happiness were missing. I blamed him for stealing her joy.

After school she was finishing the decorations. A round plate with posts for six columns was in place on top of the bottom layers. It would hold an arrangement of real flowers from her garden. Another small bouquet would top two additional rounds placed on the columns.

She put everything away before Daddy came in for another silent meal. Previous evenings I filled the quiet with my constant chatter, but that night even I didn't talk. I was angry with him.

Addie joined us Saturday morning to help finish the cake. We picked flowers to soak in water for several hours. Momma taught us how to arrange them in the moistened mold that would be added to the cake later. We finished with time to play a game on the parlor floor. Soon Momma told us it was time for Addie to go. I walked her halfway across the field. Waving goodbye, I said, "See ya Monday."

I accompanied Momma to the church basement to help assemble her creation. Praise from the family and friends brought the smile back to her face. My grandparents, guests at the party, beamed with pride. If Daddy could see her joy, would he continue to deny her dream?

Momma wanted a little more time to be happy and celebrate her success. We went for ice cream sundaes before returning to the farm. She prepared cold sandwiches on a plate in the refrigerator, leaving a couple cans of soup warming on the stove. The men came in, but she didn't join us. Daddy tried to make conversation, but I gave him the same silent treatment he had directed at Momma the previous two weeks.

Climbing the stairs that night, he found their bedroom door locked. He'd gone too far. They had always been partners, working together, sharing all decisions. She supported him and encouraged his dreams. She deserved the same in return.

In the morning she was up early, ready for church. She woke me with instructions to hurry. She called Abigail's mother to arrange an early pick up for breakfast at the diner. Without a word to Daddy or the boys, we left.

Momma was seething. After breakfast we drove to church. Daddy and the boys were waiting outside. She walked by without a glance in their direction. Abigail and I followed to our regular pew. The men joined the procession. Daddy went around the outside aisle to sit by Momma, but she looked at him saying, "NO!" Then, placing her purse and our sweaters in the space beside her, she turned toward the front of the church. He was left standing with nowhere to go but back around to the center aisle. The entire church community watched. The women nodded approval. Even I smiled. He deserved it.

After church Momma, Abigail, and I exited by the side aisle. I looked back to see him hang his head. We got in the car, with the men staring after us. We drove to my grandparent's store. If Daddy's reason for objecting to the cake business was Grandmother Gordon, Momma was giving him something else to be afraid of.

We stayed for several hours, enjoying a midafternoon meal of chicken and biscuits. They told us about the party and accolades regarding Momma's cake. She sent us to her old room to find some games to keep us busy. At some point we had to return home, but she was in no hurry.

Near supper time she called us to leave. We dropped Abigail before heading home. I joined Daddy in the parlor as Momma proceeded directly to their room. He looked at me as we heard the unmistakable click as she locked their door. He closed his eyes. Tipping his head back, he let out a sigh of exasperation. He said, "I think we're on our own."

He made eggs with toast, the only thing he knew how to cook. She didn't come out of her room all evening. He would spend another night on the sofa. I gave him a kiss whispering, "Her cake was beautiful. People loved it and she was happy."

In the morning Momma was making breakfast when I came down. Announcing she was helping her parents at the store, she offered to drive us to school and home later. Cal preferred to ride the bus, but I accepted. I called Abigail to apprise her of the plan.

We would walk to the store after dismissal. Excited all day, we were anxious to pretend we were town girls. We didn't rush. Walking casually, we peered in the windows on Main Street as though we were shopping. We said hello to people on the sidewalk, giggling after they passed.

At the store, Grandfather Gordon gave us each an orange Coke. Momma was stacking bolts of fabric. It was difficult to imagine her spending the day with Grandmother Gordon, but again she was in no hurry to leave. We stayed until supper. My grandmother brought a hot casserole of Goulash out to the car. It smelled good all the way home.

We walked into the kitchen to find four square cake pans in descending size, as well as a couple of square plate forms on the table. She stared at Daddy's apology with a knowing smile. He must have driven far to find that peace offering. She put the casserole in the oven before admiring her gifts. She set the table with candles waiting for him. When he entered, they simply kissed, hugged, and sat down to eat.

That summer Daniel came every day to help on the farm. He found a rickety old bike to ride to the barn. It wasn't pretty, but provided transportation.

Early on Momma gave him a cloth bag containing a piece of ham and biscuits. She told him Daddy saved back too much meat. He smiled, gratefully accepting the food. A few times a week Daniel carried part of our evening meal, muffins, or cookies to his family. Momma would have sent it every day, but a man has his pride even at fifteen.

One day it was raining hard, but Daniel was coming to do maintenance on the equipment. I rode out with Daddy to get him. I couldn't believe my eyes. The house was still dilapidated, but the fence next to the barn was repaired, with a chicken coop made of scrap wood standing nearby. There was a garden, with two fields plowed and planted. It was a working farm! Though small, it was a start. Daddy beamed with pride, and so did I.

Daniel joined our men for breakfast before heading to the barn. I couldn't wait to tell Momma all he accomplished. I wanted her to know what an industrious young man I'd chosen. But she already knew. Once again, and very indignantly, I realized everyone knew but me.

Addie and I resumed our summer routine. The familiarity was wonderful. We enjoyed our time together as much as ever.

However, Addie began helping her mother one day a week. Miss Emily was a housekeeper for a few families in town. On Wednesdays she cleaned, did laundry, and ironed for Miss Evelyn. With Addie's help, she took on a temporary client for a couple months. The second house wasn't as large, but the owner, Miss Myrna, was more particular. Another woman normally worked the job, but she was babysitting her grandchildren up north for the summer. Miss Emily agreed to help while Addie wasn't in school.

At times I felt a pang of guilt knowing Addie had to work, but a part of me was glad. A day in the middle of the week was available for Abigail. Many Wednesdays I spent the day at Abigail's. She continued to join us for church, and back to my house on Sundays.

Thursdays Addie shared the details of her day in town. She had many stories about Miss Evelyn's kindness, but working for Miss Myrna was very different. Knowing how difficult their afternoon would be, Miss Evelyn provided something to eat before they left. Miss Myrna did not permit breaks, and often required they redo jobs two or three times to meet her satisfaction. Their work often kept them until after dark.

Each Wednesday, Addie's father or Tucker James drove to town around dusk to bring them home. Frequently they were still working. If only Miss Emily could have called when they were ready, but it wasn't allowed.

At the beginning of the summer, James stopped in front of the house to wait one evening. Miss Myrna told him not to sit there again, so they started parking out of view. One Wednesday Tucker James was sent to get them. He arrived, but Miss Emily motioned him on. He moved around the corner, turning the engine off. It was a hot August evening; he sat back with the windows down. No one knows what happened next or how. Some said he appeared to be sleeping, though Sheriff Hosper said several residents stated they couldn't be sure why he was really there. There were no witnesses or at least none that came forward.

I had spent the day at Abigail's, joining her family for supper. Momma picked me up around eight. Sitting with my parents on the front porch, we listening to the radio as the daylight disappeared. The lights were off so we didn't attract bugs. You could barely see the road because of the partial moon. We were enjoying the peacefulness of the evening when we heard a horn honking repeatedly. I looked up at headlights coming fast and weaving on the road. As it came closer we could hear hollering. Daddy shook his head. "Kids!"

As it reached the fork in the road we heard cheering. It continued speeding past our house, still honking, with several people in the back celebrating. In the dark it looked like every other old truck in Alabama. We watched the tail lights moving down the road. Suddenly it braked, spun around, and headed back toward us. We stood on the porch watching as it flew by. The wild cheers erupted again.

Approaching the fork, the headlights illuminated its path. Daddy gasped. I strained to see beyond him. Something was in the road. It was hard to tell what, but Daddy wasn't waiting. He vaulted over the rail and started running. Momma and I followed. Hitting the object, the lights of the truck jumped. It came back down with a loud thud. Daddy reached the intersection. He yelled for Momma to keep me back, but it was too late. I caught up. Even in the faint light I could see it was a body. There were shreds of clothes hanging from it, drenched in blood. There was a rope tied around the ankles with the tail leading toward our house. Daddy looked up whispering, "It's Tucker James."

We knelt around his body. Daddy's cries of anguish echoed across the fields. He gathered Tucker James in his arms as he sobbed. Daddy stood slowly, and began the long walk toward Addie's. We quietly followed.

In front of the house, he stepped behind the oak tree, cradling that gracious young man in his arms. Momma climbed the steps. She knocked on the door. I stood back to distance myself from the pain that was about to erupt. James greeted Momma as he unlatched the screen. She guided him out on the porch. Closing the door behind him, she told him about his son. He collapsed into her arms. She held him while he emitted loud wailing moans. Addie's brothers were in the window. Miss Ada peered outside before joining us. Momma simply pointed to the tree. Miss Ada moved down the steps. She looked toward Daddy. Without exchanging a single word, she slowly walked past him, toward the barn. He followed. Momma helped James to a chair. The boys came out to kneel at their father's feet. We left them clinging to each other.

I followed Momma around to the back of the house. In a few minutes she headed toward the barn with a bucket of water and rags she found in the kitchen. I waited outside. She reappeared. Taking my hand, she guided me toward home and to the car. I waited in the back seat while she got the keys. We drove to town to get Miss Emily and Addie.

They were waiting in front of Miss Myrna's. Momma's presence told them something was wrong. They sent Addie to join me. Momma took Miss Emily a few steps away to tell her about Tucker James. I expected Miss Emily to collapse, but she didn't. She walked toward the car, opened the front passenger door, and got in. Momma followed. On the ride home Addie sat beside me, silent, with her eyes focused on Miss Emily.

At Addie's, James was still in the chair with the boys gathered around him. Miss Emily got out of the car and slowly climbed the stairs. She knelt in front of him. Placing her head on his lap, she began to cry. Addie fell to the floor beside her.

Momma and I left them to their grief. Ted and Cal returned while we were gone. In the parlor, Momma relayed the horrible events of the evening. When she said, "Tucker James is dead." I folded to the floor. Speaking it out loud made it real. My body melted under the pressure.

Early the next morning Daddy and the boys went looking for James's truck. They found it in a field. There was blood on the front seat and in the bed. The other end of the rope dangled from the hitch. It was the truck we saw speeding by our house, but they never told James. He didn't need to know.

The following days were difficult. We took supper across the field the first two nights, but they told Momma to stop. There was an overabundance of food coming from everywhere.

They belonged to the colored Baptist church up the road from our house. Most of the country churches closed, but a few were still around. It had been Miss Ada's church since childhood. One of the colored farmers functioned as the pastor for Sunday service, but few families remained members. Most people traveled to the larger and newer church in town.

We attended the funeral. That old building was packed, with people standing outside under the open windows to hear the service. Our family and Miss Evelyn, along with her husband, were the only white people in attendance.

I was amazed by the music created with their voices. There was no piano or organ, and no hymnals, but they all knew the songs, and sang them with such feeling. It was powerful to witness.

Daddy and the boys worked James's farm for the week. Daniel came in the mornings to help, but wouldn't let Daddy pay him. We couldn't make things better, but needed to show we cared. It was sad when Granddaddy Tucker died; however, the death of someone young, in such a vicious way, left a deep inconsolable void. Momma cried constantly. Daddy was visibly distraught, and my brothers were overwrought with emotion. I woke every day with a feeling of dread. Depression ruled our home. However, our grief couldn't compare.

No effort was made to find who killed Tucker James. The sheriff claimed he investigated, but there was nothing to uncover. As far as he was concerned, Tucker James must have done something wrong, thus giving them the right to punish him. Tucker James was dead at the age of eighteen.

A few days after the funeral, I gathered the courage to venture across the field to visit my friend. She joined me on the porch.

Sitting side by side in the rockers I said, "I'm sorry 'bout Tucker James. We all are."

She didn't respond, simply nodding as she looked away. I tried again. "How's your Mama and Papa?" She shrugged her shoulders. I said, "Do ya want to listen to the radio or play dolls?" She shook her head no. I asked, "Want to go in the field?" She nodded.

Walking in silence to the middle of the field, we collapsed in the tall grass, hidden from view. She stared at the clouds overhead. Tears began to trickle down the side of her face. I reached for her hand to cradle it in both of mine. It would be a while before we returned to normal. She wouldn't talk about Tucker James or her family, and I respected her wishes.

Miss Emily and Addie returned to cleaning both houses the following Wednesday informing Miss Myrna she would either take them home or they would use the telephone. No other colored woman in town would work for her, so making a call was the lesser evil. They finished out the summer, but Miss Emily never worked for Miss Myrna again.

I was shocked they went back. There were many things about Addie's family that puzzled me, but also kept me in awe. Through much adversity and difficulties, they demonstrated amazing strength and pride; a strength no one would defeat and a pride no one could take from them.

Chapter TEN

FALL 1952

When summer ended, we began our second year at the town school. As the bus approached Aunt Sara's, I was expecting Samuel, but was surprised to see Leroy as well. The school board and principal tried to fail Leroy, his parents fought them. Eventually they settled under the condition Leroy would be permitted to finish by Christmas. Surprisingly, he was agreeable to the compromise, and soon we learned why. Early that fall he was caught with a girl named Jessie. Her father told Uncle Roy and Aunt Sara he'd kill their son if he came near his daughter again. It was one of the rare times Uncle Roy was faced with someone who made him feel threatened. Throughout the fall Leroy appeared to respect the order as he fulfilled the academic requirements in his same scary way. Everyone was counting the days until he finished.

The 1952 presidential election was looming. The previous three years had been uneventful, focused more on local contests. However, the national campaign between Eisenhower and Stevenson created tension throughout the South. There were reports of agitators encouraging the coloreds to register to vote. Though we had not heard of any strangers in town, Uncle Roy and his fellow thugs were making their presence known. They held meetings at the church and organized patrols in the community. Several nights a week Sheriff Hosper drove by our house real slow. If Momma and Daddy were on the porch, he'd give a spin of the light on top. We didn't mistake it as a courteous hello. It was a warning "to keep James in line," as Daddy put it.

One evening Hosper stopped at the edge of the road. Momma and I stayed on the porch while Daddy walked out to talk with him. He rejoined us shortly and said, "There's no problem, just askin' if I've seen anyone who doesn't belong."

Momma stared past him. He continued, "I talked to James. He's havin' nothin' to do with it."

She replied, "If those Northerners would go home, we'd be fine here."

During those times it was frightening to live in the South, not just for the colored folk, but for any whites who might be seen as sympathizers. Daddy spent most evenings at the house while Momma escorted the boys to the barn. Ted's visits with Nettie were sometimes cancelled, and Grandfather Gordon closed the store early if there were gatherings in town. It wasn't just our family that lived in fear. Threats were issued by Leroy and his kind at school, with orders to deliver the message to parents at home. They controlled our community through intimidation, whether it might be risk of injury, or loss of livelihood, home, or sometimes life.

My mind was consumed with these menacing threats until the election was over. Our community escaped unscathed, with everyone safe as we moved toward Thanksgiving. My focus returned to the more docile harassment inflicted by Charlotte and Virginia. We tried to ignore the comments, but if others participated, it hurt. When Abigail wore my dress from the previous year, Charlotte made sure everyone knew. I shared the problem with Momma. She devised a plan. Sunday, we collected Abigail, along with her school clothes. Momma took a couple dresses apart to make skirts. She used new fabric and ribbon to change the other items. They were unrecognizable. From that time on, Momma altered my clothes before giving them to Abigail.

In sixth grade we were eligible to join the choir. Abigail and I signed up, along with all of the girls in our class, including Charlotte and Virginia. There were two performances, one at Christmas, and another at the end of the year. The director required everyone dress the same with white tops and black skirts for girls, black pants for boys.

We arrived at school that December evening. My family went to the auditorium while I joined the girls from my class in the cafeteria. Each had a white ribbon holding back their hair. Charlotte was glowing with satisfaction. She said, "Missy, where's your ribbon?" Turning to the others, she continued. "I'm so silly. How would she even put a ribbon in that hair?"

Many of the girls laughed along with her. As they were enjoying my discomfort, Abigail walked in, also missing the prerequisite white ribbon. My embarrassment became insignificant when I saw the pain on her face. A few of the girls dropped their eyes. If only one had the courage to remove the ribbon, others might follow. But no one dared to cross Charlotte. Her vengeance was worse than her everyday meanness.

I wanted to diffuse her victory. I looked at Abigail. She was wearing one of my blouses. Momma had removed the collar to add stand up lace around the neck. Pretending I was seeing it for the first time I said, "Abigail, I love your blouse. The lace is beautiful." Some of the girls murmured in agreement. The look on Abigail's face changed from sad heartbreak, to grateful pride.

One of the older girls standing nearby witnessed the entire scene. She joined in. "Oh my, I love that blouse." Calling to her friends, she gushed over Abigail. Charlotte and Virginia were livid, but didn't dare speak. They knew their place.

Soon the director told us to line up. One of the older girls called out, "Mrs. Darr, the sixth-grade girls are new to the choir. They don't know the rules. We like everyone to look the same so people will focus on the music, but they're wearing ribbons. Shouldn't they take them off?"

She hesitated a moment. Another girl said, "It'll be distracting if we have to look down at those during the performance." The others chimed in with agreement.

Mrs. Darr had no choice. "The ribbons have to come off, girls. You can reclaim them after the performance. In the future, please don't add anything to the required dress." Abigail and I exchanged a quick look of satisfaction. We smiled at the older girls. The performance I'm sure was a huge success; however, the most important event was Charlotte's plan thwarted. It wouldn't happen often, making it a memorable moment.

Chapter ELEVEN
1953

Leroy, as promised, had finished school by Christmas. In January it was a relief to see Samuel waiting for the bus alone. There was a visible difference in him. The tension on his face was gone. It was peaceful on the bus and in school. Without Leroy, the other boys were controllable. Everyone appeared to smile more, or maybe it was my relief painting such a rosy picture.

With the cloud of fear lifted, Cal and his buddies claimed the back seats. I'm not sure what Leroy did after he graduated, and no one cared. We didn't have to see him, and weren't hearing about him.

Several boys made their intentions known for Jessie, but she wasn't allowed to date. The boys could sit with her in the cafeteria, or walk her in the hall, but were not allowed to see her outside of school. Because they dared to pursue her, we assumed Leroy was in the past.

Nettie graduated in June. During the summer months she helped her family, and would babysit for Mrs. Dennis during the school year. Most girls with a steady boyfriend got married, but with only two houses on the farm, Ted was trapped. It was sad for them both.

The summer passed calmly. Miss Emily took on two new houses. She maintained the basics most of the year, and Addie helped during the summer months with the annual cleaning like washing of walls, carpets, beddings, curtains, windows, and more. It freed another day a week for me but I kept my schedule of Wednesday and Sunday with Abigail. Friday became special time with Momma for shopping, going to the diner, or house cleaning of our own.

In the fall I moved on to the seventh grade. Charlotte and Virginia continued to criticize us no matter how diligent we were with our appearance. However, the new privilege of club membership would ease the situation slightly. We wanted to be in the Library and Newspaper clubs, while Charlotte and Virginia chose Future Nurses and Cheerleading. During club meetings the girls were kind, but they remained guarded in the classroom. No one wanted to be subjected to the abuse reserved for us.

Eventually a couple of the girls began sitting at the end of the cafeteria table, and occasionally included us in conversations. We weren't as isolated, but it didn't deter the evil pair. They were even more intent on embarrassing us. However, it was more bearable if the others didn't participate. Life improved a little.

Overall, it was an uneventful year. We celebrated Christmas with our many traditions: a beautiful tree, Divinity Fudge, and our daily surprises. Ted downplayed Momma's efforts. She was disappointed to see her first child stepping away from the family. It was the beginning of many changes to come.

Chapter TWELVE

1954

As school was coming together, an event would change life at home. One Saturday morning I was cleaning with Momma when the telephone rang. It was Daddy. Something was wrong with Grandma Em. He noticed there were no lights or movement at the big house. He found her on the floor, unable to move or talk.

Momma sent me to change out of my cleaning clothes as she called Mr. Emerson, the undertaker. I feared Grandma Em was dead until she emphasized the urgency of getting her to the hospital. Without an ambulance service in town, Mr. Emerson used his hearse to transport people. I heard her say Daddy called Doc Batt, and he was on his way. I quickly dressed in the hall as I listened to the conversation. Putting on my socks, I noticed they weren't carefully matched to please the critical eyes of Charlotte and Virginia. Even in that moment, the torment of those two girls was in the forefront of my mind. I thought to change, but realized how silly, and to heck with them. Momma came up the stairs saying, "Grab a change of clothes in case we have to stay."

I suddenly remembered Addie. Telling Momma, I raced down the stairs. Running across the field I saw Doc Batt's Oldsmobile at the fork in the road. Not wasting time to run to the front porch, I pounded on the back door. Miss Ada came, followed by Addie. I told them we were taking Grandma Em to the hospital, and I wouldn't be able to see her. Not waiting to hear their response, I returned home.

Mr. Emerson's hearse was moving fast as it drove by. I ran in telling Momma both Doc Batt and Mr. Emerson were at the big house. She was gathering food in a bag. I checked the lights, while she loaded the car. In a few minutes we were on our way. It was my first time at the big house since Granddaddy Tucker died.

We pulled in the drive, clear of Mr. Emerson's hearse. I hurried after Momma through the front hall, and started up the stairs. I stopped suddenly to look at the empty spaces on the wall. You could see the markings left by pictures that once hung there. Seeing the ghostly shapes made me catch my breath as I remembered what occupied each place. One missing picture was of Daddy as a little boy, dressed in a suit with big buttons, standing by an old-fashioned tricycle. Another was a wedding picture of my parents. The other three empty spaces had been baby pictures of Ted, Cal, and me. I stared for a long time at those missing memories, shocked that she had removed us from her life so completely.

Momma came out of Grandma Em's room to see me staring at the wall, crying, my heart truly broken. She put her arm around me. "Let's go downstairs. I need to find Sara. Daddy called several times, but no one answered. I have to try again."

We went into the kitchen. Momma tried Aunt Sara. When there was no answer, she called her neighbors. They said there was a ruckus at the house the previous day. Roy, Sara, and the boys left. No one knew where they were. Momma relayed the story about Grandma Em. She asked them to put a note on the front and back doors. By then Daddy, Ted, Cal, and Mr. Emerson were on their way down the stairs carrying Grandma Em on a large flat board. Doc Batt followed. Daddy's face showed the trace of tears. Her eyes were moving around. They stopped on me. Realizing it may be my only chance I mouthed, "I love you." Her eyes welled with tears, but there was no response. I was overwhelmed by many emotions including fear, sadness, and hurt.

The men put her in the hearse. Daddy climbed in next to her. Doc Batt wasn't going. There was nothing more he could do. Daddy told Ted and Cal to take care of the farm, while instructing Momma to follow in the car. We waved at the boys as we pulled away. At the fork in the road, Miss Ada, James, Miss Emily, and their children were waiting. James was holding his hat over his heart. The others watched with a solemn face.

I said, "Why'd they come out for her? She's not nice to them."

Momma said, "Maybe a little is for Grandma Em, but it's for your daddy."

Traveling down Main Street, past Mr. Jefferson's store, I noticed him standing out front. He bowed his head as the hearse passed. Watching the scene, I shook my head in confusion. Why did he go out of his way for us? I was sure neither Grandma Em nor Daddy was acquainted with him. Suddenly I remembered Grandfather Gordon and the night he gave food to Mr. Jefferson. I looked at Momma because this tribute was for her. There was a tear resting on her cheek. I watched it break apart to finish its journey down her face.

The drive took almost an hour. The hearse pulled up to the Emergency Room entrance. Momma came to a stop behind it. She told me to fetch someone to help. Mr. Emerson came around to open the back door. She rushed to check on Grandma Em. I heard Daddy say there was no change. I was relieved. At least she was alive. I ran inside, bringing back a nurse and a man pushing a gurney. Together with Daddy and Mr. Emerson they moved Grandma Em. Momma stayed behind to see Mr. Emerson off. Following Daddy, I entered the hospital for the first time.

They took Grandma Em to a room with Daddy, showing me to the waiting area. I was relieved when Momma came in. Daddy emerged later to say, "It was a stroke. She likely won't walk again, maybe not talk either, but it didn't damage vital organs so it's not life threatenin'. She'll have trouble at first, but they said it gets better with time. They need to do more tests, but are takin' her upstairs for now. Y'all go on up. I'll wait for her."

I rode the elevator, but couldn't enjoy the new experience. As we walked through the halls, I could see into the rooms. I heard some people talking, and others moaning or crying out for help. It smelled like urine and disinfectant at the same time, making me ill. I wanted to get out of there. Realizing I was in distress, Momma hurried us along to the privacy of Grandma Em's room.

It wasn't long before they brought her in. Seeing her, I became weak in the knees and swayed against the wall. Momma looked at me. "My goodness. What was I thinking? You haven't eaten. Why didn't you say something?"

She pulled out muffins, a school jug of milk, and a large hunk of cheese. Momma offered Daddy some food, but he wouldn't leave his mother's side, saying, "Later."

In the evening, Aunt Sara arrived. She ran to Daddy, letting him comfort her, but pulled away when Uncle Roy entered. The look on Roy's face did not escape any of us. It wasn't a quick flash of anger, but a long seething glare. Momma attempted to diffuse the situation with welcoming words as she hugged Aunt Sara. Roy couldn't be appeased. He complained about having missed eating because of the unnecessary alarm, and excused himself for the cafeteria.

After he left, Aunt Sara broke down. I sat quietly in the corner, forgotten for a while. She cried, "He's upset 'bout other things. It's such a mess. Jessie's father came to the house lookin' for Leroy. The girl's expectin'. She's been sneakin' out of school to meet up with him. We thought it was over, but he's been seein' her the whole time. Jed said he's gonna kill him. He and Roy got in a fight. Jed's gun went off. It was horrible. We told him Leroy wasn't home, but he wouldn't believe us. Roy beat Jed real bad. He drove his car and him back to town. Roy swore he wasn't dead, but I didn't know for sure. We needed to get out of there 'til Jed calmed down. I called Fran Cooper in Montgomery. We took

Leroy there yesterday. They're gonna give him a job at the feed and seed. We stayed in Montgomery last night. When we got home, I saw the note. We came right away."

My father's jaw dropped and Grandma Em began to moan, thrashing about with the parts she could move. Daddy looked at his mother, then back to Aunt Sara. He said, "Did ya tell Mother?"

Aunt Sara said, "I called her from Montgomery this mornin'. I was afraid Jed might show up at the house. I told her to call you, but she was screamin' at me to get Leroy out of there. Roy took the telephone tellin' her it was done and there was no undoin' it." Grandma Em pounded the bed with her fist.

A nurse looked in. She demanded to know what was going on. Daddy yelled, "We're fine. Get out." Closing the door, he turned to Aunt Sara, saying, "What were ya thinkin'? Why would ya take him to Montgomery? In our whole life did Mother ever take us to see family there? Do ya know what you've done?"

She looked at him, confused, saying, "Cousin Fran came to visit when we were young. She was always real nice. Don't ya remember? What else did ya want me to do? I had to protect my son!"

He continued, "Sara! What have ya done?"

She responded, "I took my son to family." Each time she said it Grandma Em moaned loudly.

Then he said, "Daddy told ya. I know he did. If your husband finds out, he'll kill us all."

She said, "Ya mean those stories? They weren't true. Daddy was a bitter angry man. Right, Mother?"

He was shaking his head in disbelief, looking from his sister then to his mother saying, "Did ya tell her that, Mother? Did ya tell her it wasn't real?"

Suddenly Momma said, "J.P., Missy's here." He turned toward me with panic returning to his face. He ordered me to the hall. Momma closed the door behind me. Grandma Em's room had a big window. I could see the back of his head, as well as Aunt Sara's face. Whatever he said frightened her. The panic on his face was now on hers. She began shaking her head no, but he kept talking. He grabbed her by the shoulders while she kept shaking her head.

Uncle Roy was coming down the hall. I couldn't see him, but I heard him yelling at someone to get out of his way. I instinctively knew whatever was going on in that room needed to be kept from him. I impulsively started knocking on the window mouthing, "Uncle Roy is comin'. Uncle Roy is comin'."

Terror filled Aunt Sara's eyes as Momma put her arm around her. I could tell Momma was saying, "J.P. will take care of everything."

By then Uncle Roy was almost at my side. He said, "What's goin' on? Why are ya out here?"

I panicked, but was able to say, "Daddy needed to talk to Aunt Sara. He told me to leave."

He pushed me out of the way to charge into the room. Seeing Sara in tears, he started threatening Daddy for upsetting his wife. Daddy turned full face to Uncle Roy and said, "Jed knows Leroy's in Montgomery. It won't be long 'fore he finds him. We need to get him out of there. Sara had to know. I'll help, but I have to get to Montgomery. Jed's beat up pretty bad and won't be goin' anywhere today, but that's where he's headed as soon as he can. We have to get Leroy somewhere safe tonight. Do ya want my help or are ya gonna stand there yellin'?"

Uncle Roy stepped back saying, "I didn't know. I made some calls, but nobody said nothin'. Who told ya?"

"Doc Batt. I was just tellin' Sara. I can take him to my father's cousin near Huntsville. Nobody knows we have family there. But I gotta leave now. We're closer to Montgomery so I shouldn't have any problem. I just have to finish things for Mother." I knew it wasn't true from the conversation I overheard earlier, but Uncle Roy believed.

Daddy reassured Sara before ushering Momma into the hall. Closing the door after them, he whispered, "Call Doc Batt. Tell him what we need. He'll go along. He's patched up enough of

Roy's victims." Turning to me, he continued, "Missy, ya keep quiet. Do ya hear me?"

I nodded. He returned to Grandma Em. Bending down, he kissed her on the cheek. He said, "I'll take care of it. It'll be alright."

Grandma Em, Momma, and Aunt Sara were crying. I didn't understand what it was about, but I knew it was dangerous for the family. Telling Momma and Sara he'd make it right, he kissed each of us goodbye.

He said, "Roy, take care of Sara. Melanie, I'll be back tomorrow."

After he left, Momma asked about Samuel. "He's at the house," she said.

Momma said, "That's not safe. I'll send Ted to get him."

Momma went in search of a telephone to call Doc Batt and the boys. Aunt Sara went to Grandma Em's side. She knelt down. Putting her mother's hand to her face, she started to weep. "I'm sorry. I'm so sorry."

Later I told Ted and Cal the story. Cal was puzzled, but Ted walked away. He knew. If Daddy felt Ted was old enough, hopefully someday he'd trust Cal and me.

Daddy moved Leroy to Huntsville. Even I didn't know about this branch of the Tucker family. They gladly helped Leroy find a job and settle in. Jessie was sent to stay with relatives in Arkansas on the pretext of helping a sick aunt.

After several days in the hospital, they moved Grandma Em to a ward for stroke patients. The stroke affected her ability to speak and paralyzed her right side. Fortunately, she was left-handed. For the next several months we had a new routine. Grandma Em never went more than a day without a visitor. Aunt Sara went on Tuesdays and Saturdays. On Thursdays, Momma left when we got on the bus, and returned before I came home.

On Sundays after church, Momma, Daddy, and I went to the hospital. Ted and Cal stayed behind to tend the farm. We packed sandwiches or biscuits to eat on the way. Returning home, we often stopped at a diner. Daddy loved the home cooking with huge portions, and I loved their ice cream sundaes.

Each week we spent several hours with Grandma Em, all of us talking to fill the dead air. She often moaned, kicking her leg and pounding her fist on the bed. None of us misunderstood her message. She was telling us to get out, but we ignored her. If she was particularly difficult, we stayed longer.

I missed Sundays with Abigail. It was apparent Grandma Em would be there for quite some time, maybe forever. I wanted to see her, but asked if one Sunday I might stay behind. Momma thought I should make the trip each week, but said Abigail could join us.

The following week, we collected her for church, then went on to the hospital. We had no idea the effect it would have. I introduced her, "Grandma Em, this is my best friend Abigail. She went to the country school and now we're at the town school together. I hope ya don't mind that I brought her. We usually spend Sundays together."

It was the first time we saw part of a smile at the left corner of her mouth. She was happy the entire visit. Daddy said we needed Abigail every Sunday to put his mother in a good mood. He started calling her Happigail. We stopped at the diner on the way home. I was glad to once again spend Sunday with my friend.

That evening I snuggled into bed, so happy after our visit. Momma came in to say goodnight. I went on about Abigail, extoling her sweet nature, celebrating how much Grandma Em liked her. Momma nodded with a sad look on her face. She could have let it go, but I was glad she wanted me to understand the truth. She said, "Abigail's a wonderful girl, but that's not why Grandma Em's happy. You introduced her as your best friend. Em thinks you're no longer friends with Addie."

It didn't occur to me, but she was right. It was about Addie. I was certain as well. A smile began forming on her lips. I feared she found humor in my ignorance; however, she clarified the reason, "If she only knew the truth. She'd still be pounding her fist and kicking her foot." We giggled uncontrollably. Grandma Em was nice because she thought Addie was no longer my friend. It was her ignorance that had us near tears.

Abigail didn't make the trip every week. But each time she came, Grandma Em was happy. Momma and I could barely contain ourselves. It was truly an enjoyable time, especially after the years of sadness when Grandma Em was missing from our lives.

Before the stroke, Grandma Em had started preparing her vegetable garden. Momma never thought to continue the process. One Saturday, Addie and I walked to the barn to give Daddy a message from Momma. As we neared the big house, I was surprised to see Miss Ada and Miss Emily working out back. It was a futile project. Grandma Em wouldn't need the vegetables; the doctor said it was unlikely she would return home, but I wanted to be part of it. Addie readily agreed. After school and on Saturdays we helped in the garden. Each time we gathered, it made me feel good. The puzzle was why they were helping? Grandma Em never showed kindness to them, not even when Tucker James died. My respect for those two women grew.

The end of our school year coincided with an important political event. Mrs. Moore, my history teacher, came in one day angrily brandishing a newspaper. She spent the morning educating us about why it was necessary to assign people to their place in society and the importance of keeping them there. She read an article about the Supreme Court decision in the case of Brown vs. the Board of Education of Topeka, Kansas. It was a landmark case that changed the South, but not willingly or without a fight.

The discussion impacted me emotionally. Prior to that day I didn't know someone was fighting to allow children like Addie and me to attend school together. In my isolation I assumed all schools were separate and everyone liked it that way. Listening to Mrs. Moore rant about another civil war opened my eyes to the differences that existed beyond my small town. Her words were surprisingly reminiscent of days at the country school with Leroy.

I thought back to how desperately I wanted to attend school with Addie and my despair over the rules that kept us apart. Mrs. Moore's news should have brought great joy and elation, but it didn't. I was terrified. From her reaction, I thought perhaps by the end of the week, or surely very soon, Addie and the other colored children would join our class. My secret would be out. What would people think or do, especially Charlotte and Virginia? Would Mrs. Moore still like me? How would they treat me if they knew I was friends with a colored girl?

I was very good at balancing my two lives. The naïve innocence of my childhood was gone. I understood the social rules of Alabama, but with that event came the realization that not only had I learned to live by those rules, I accepted them. The ride home on the bus is etched in my memory. It wasn't the event, but the feelings that remain with me. Fear and panic were present; however, it was the guilt and shame that was overpowering. I no longer wanted Addie in school with me. I wanted her to stay at the colored school. I didn't want anyone to know she was my friend, but mostly I didn't want Addie to know how I felt.

What was I going to do? As ashamed as I was of my feelings, I was also saddened at the thought of losing Addie, of not seeing her after school or taking turns at each other's home. I treasured the friendship and memories of our childhood. She was always part of my life, but if she came to my school, it would end. I would choose to let her go. In front of everyone white, I would pretend I didn't know her. My shame at this realization was great, but no greater than today as I write these words so many years later. I allowed the unconscionable rules of Alabama to become part of my value system. Even more disturbing is that some of those fears are so deeply ingrained, that they are still part of me today.

As my life was consumed by my worries about Grandma Em and desegregation, a milestone was achieved in Addie's family. John James graduated. Miss Ada was so proud, as was James and Miss Emily. He was the first person in their family to receive a diploma. I assumed he would work the farm with his father, but the family made different plans. He needed to be available during planting and harvesting, but James did not want that life for his son. John James joined Mr. Jefferson in town. One day the store would be his.

I thought about Miss Emily and her family. She, like Momma, was the only child of a store owner and married to a country farmer. I wondered if her mother disapproved as well. One afternoon I asked Addie. She explained, "Mama's mother took off just after she was born. Granpappy and her lived with family in Montgomery for a long time. When Mama was eight, he met Mina. He didn't marry her right off, but she stuck around six years waitin'. He decided it was time, and moved here to open the store. She's not like a mother to Mama. They're not close. She's just Mina."

I was surprised. I asked, "Did Mina have any children?"

Addie shook her head, "No. She wasn't blessed. That's why she don't like Mama comin' around much, 'cause Granpappy dotes on her. Mina's real jealous."

Addie was in a rare mood, willing to talk about her family. I pressed for more. "How did your Mama meet your Papa?"

Addie smiled. It was a story she liked and therefore was willing share. "Granmama seen her at the store and tells how with that fine yellow skin, smooth black hair, and face everyone admired, she knew Papa had to marry her. One day Granmama told him to put on his finest 'cause he was goin' to meet his bride. Everyone saw 'em comin'. They moved to one side or the other allowin' 'em to pass. Mama says she saw Granmama's kind eyes starin' back from his face and knew she'd marry him. Mina was glad when Mama moved out. They're never gonna be like family, but they're friendly now."

I wanted to hear more, but I could see the embarrassment on her face, almost like regret. She shook her head, more at herself than me. She rarely shared personal things, keeping the truths of her family a secret. She wouldn't tell me anymore that day. I wanted to tell her I saw Mr. Jefferson and Tucker James on Christmas Eve a few years back. I wanted her to know she could trust me, but I remained silent, never telling anyone.

Chapter THIRTEEN

SUMMER & FALL 1954

The following months I nervously awaited an announcement regarding changes at school. With Addie, I pretended I didn't know and she never mentioned it. Our reasons were very different. I was ashamed that I didn't want her to join me. Addie couldn't tell me the truth and she wouldn't lie. It was dangerous for any colored person who supported desegregation. It was better to avoid all conversation about real-world issues.

The summer schedule now required she help Miss Emily Monday, Wednesday, and Friday. They took on the homes of Mr. Beaker, my principal, and his mother. Miss Evelyn also passed Miss Emily's name on to a new young couple with three children. She cleaned there after Miss Evelyn's. She also added a Saturday job, with Addie helping. That only left Tuesday and Thursday along with Saturday evening for our time together.

Cleaning for my principal and his wife Miss Bea concerned me. I was afraid Addie would learn about Abigail. The first few weeks I anxiously waited to hear of her days away from me. She told how Miss Bea let them make sandwiches before leaving for her mother-in-law's. Addie's stories made me feel good about my principal and his wife. I believed if she joined my school, he would treat her fairly. She rarely saw Mr. Beaker. He worked through the summer, typically returning home after she left. As time passed, I began to relax a little feeling secure my deep secrets were safe.

As kind as his wife was, his mother was equally mean. She was never satisfied, always complaining or adding more work than agreed upon. They had to take a jug of water, but drank sparingly because they were not permitted to use the facilities and there was nowhere else to go.

Miss Bea knew the difficulty of working for her mother-in-law because she lived with the same abuse. She had been going each week to clean for years. If Miss Emily refused to continue, the job would revert to Miss Bea. However, if she didn't interfere, Old Ms. Beaker wouldn't let them leave. Miss Bea arrived at five during the summer and seven in the fall. Driving them through town to Mr. Jefferson's store was evidently more tolerable than doing the job herself.

One week Miss Bea went to visit her sister. Old Ms. Beaker raised such a fuss they decided to keep Miss Emily's schedule. James purposely arrived late, after six. However, they weren't allowed to leave. James sat in front of the house at first, but the old lady called Sheriff Hosper. James was told to move on. He drove to my principal's house, but he wasn't home. He stayed at Mr. Jefferson's store for short periods, returning to see if the women were waiting out front. It continued for almost three hours. It was the last time they ever cleaned unless Miss Bea could pick them up.

Addie always had a story to tell. Sometimes it was about the beautiful things she saw, or the kindness of some and the cruelty of others. The new young couple was the Babcock's. They were not particularly mean, but the mister believed there was a proper place for coloreds. One Thursday we were spending a lazy day in the field watching the clouds move overhead. We tried to identify the various shapes of each one. I called out, "That's Mississippi!"

She added, "The Babcock's come from there. They're different from people here. Mama says to speak only if spoken to, never sit on the furniture, don't touch anything less I'm cleanin' it, and keep my eyes down when addressin' 'em. I don't even know what Miss Anne looks like."

We laughed, but for Addie it wasn't funny. It was serious. She went on, "Miss Anne's nice and usually likes what we done. She always says thank you, and if the mister isn't there, she lets us use the toilet. But we gotta finish 'fore he gets home or it's bad. There's always somethin' wrong with our work and he makes us do it again and then maybe again. And he won't let us use the phone to call Papa." It was difficult to hear Addie's stories, but that was life in Alabama, and no one dared speak against it. You just accepted it.

The schedule continued through the summer. In the fall they would ask Miss Evelyn to let them clean her house later in the day so Miss Emily would be gone when he arrived home. Miss Evelyn took it upon herself to tell Miss Anne.

As Addie was taking on the responsibility of helping her family, I enjoyed my childhood. Momma required me to help in the kitchen and with cleaning on Saturday mornings, but she believed I'd grow up soon enough. I often found myself feeling guilty over my limited responsibilities and the opportunity to be young.

Addie's schedule opened another day of my week. Though it saddened me to see so much expected of her, the guilt was diminished by my time with Abigail. Each year Addie and I saw each other less as her need to help the family increased.

As the summer passed, my panic over Addie joining me at the town school lessened. By August, I realized it wouldn't happen that year. I never dealt with the situation. I continued on through school and graduated while she attended the colored school. Even though that law was passed in 1954, a colored child didn't attend a white school in the South until 1960. My little town in Alabama did not comply for several years after that.

Throughout the coming months we harvested the vegetables from Grandma Em's garden. Miss Ada, Miss Emily, Addie, and I canned them. Momma took the jars to the big house as we finished each batch. I left that job to her, intent on avoiding the empty wall by the stairs.

Grandma Em made steady improvement and was gaining strength daily. In July the doctor said she could probably return home. Though she needed a wheelchair for long distances, she was able to stand and move around the immediate area with the aid of walking devices. They discussed modifications that would allow her to function adequately with some assistance.

Different options were discussed. Grandma Em disliked Uncle Roy, thereby ruling out living with Aunt Sara. Our house was too small and our only bathroom was upstairs. Keeping her at the big house was the best solution. Fortunately, the bathroom was downstairs and the wood floors simply required removal of the area carpets. The main hall, parlor, and kitchen were easy for maneuvering. The biggest concern was how to care for her. They decided Ted would move to the big house to assist during the night. The days were divided between Momma and Aunt Sara.

We started getting the big house ready. Daddy and the boys built a ramp from the drive to the front porch, while Momma turned Granddaddy Tucker's office into a bedroom. She painted the walls and made curtains. Momma worried about Grandma Em's reaction. Though she hadn't regained the ability to speak, her opinions were made clear to everyone by the noises she mastered. A grunt told you she was clearly unhappy, a moan meant 'you're frustrating me', and her special shriek meant 'if I could talk I'd be kicking you out.' When she was happy, she almost purred like a kitten.

News spread around town that she was returning home. Several people drove out with preserves or other goods, though, food was the last thing she needed. The canning we did throughout the summer provided more than enough. Momma told

Miss Ada to keep some for her family, but she wouldn't, just as Momma didn't keep any for us.

The biggest gift both in size and shock was delivered a week before her release. One evening Mr. Jefferson and John James arrived at the house with a porch swing in their truck. Daddy went outside, but I stayed within earshot. Mr. Jefferson said, "I made it for your Momma to get her out in the good air. I understand if ya think it's not best. She don't need to know where it came from. Probably better that way."

I waited for Daddy's response. I was certain his answer would be no. Everyone was afraid of another stroke. As impossible as it was, keeping her calm was a priority. I was surprised when he said, "It's a kind thought. Take it on up to the big house. I'll follow directly."

I could hear the emotion in Daddy's voice. He came in to see me standing nearby. He said, "No one's to know where that swing came from. Understand?" I nodded.

I asked to go with him. He nodded. We arrived to help move it into position. Mr. Jefferson invited me to have the first swing. I sat down, but it didn't move. I tried to push it with my feet, but it wouldn't budge. He instructed, "Ya unhook here on the left. She can't sit if it's movin'. Lift this latch and it'll swing for ya."

Beautiful carvings of honeysuckles and hummingbirds adorned the top center of the back. The arms were rounded to make it more comfortable. Beyond each arm was a shelf providing a small table within easy reach. It was sanded smooth as glass. The natural varnish highlighted the beautiful grain swirling through each piece.

She would love it. I was sad his kindness would go unrecognized, but Daddy was right. If she knew it was from Mr. Jefferson, she'd use every bit of strength to destroy it. I couldn't understand why he went to such trouble. He didn't know her and she certainly never showed him kindness. I looked at him. There was a slight smile on his lips, but sadness in his eyes. Without a word he turned to leave, followed by John James.

In early August Grandma Em returned to the big house. Daddy and Aunt Sara drove her home while Momma made sure everything was ready. She didn't ask me to help. It still hurt to see the front hall. Later I walked to the big house. Sitting on the beautiful swing, I moved the latch to slowly glide back and forth.

Before too long, the car pulled into the drive. Grandma Em was in the back seat with Aunt Sara. Daddy removed a wheel chair from the trunk. After helping her transfer, he pushed her up the ramp. She grumbled, swatting him with her good hand. He locked the wheels in place so she could stand. She grabbed the cane from Aunt Sara. Slowly, she made her way to the swing. I put the lock in place before standing to give her a hug. She couldn't hug me back, but she cocked her head to the side to rest it against my face. It was better than a hug because the effort showed she truly meant it.

Her eyes rested on the swing. She bumped it with her cane, but it didn't move. Knowing it was secure, she turned to ease her body onto the seat. I joined her. Showing her the latch, I released it and the swing began to move.

Momma set a glass of ice tea and a lemon bar on the shelf, but Grandma Em continued to push us back and forth. I watched her hand caress the arm like she was petting a cat. Eventually, she slowed the swing to a stop. Sliding the latch in place, she reached for the tea. She was happy. You could see it at the corner of her mouth and in her eyes. Grandma Em was home and so were we.

After a time, we went inside to show her the new bedroom. The room was simple, no wallpaper or fancy things, but painted a soft shade of green. A quilt from women in town covered the bed. Her dressers were strategically placed around the room, with a wood pole mounted on the wall for hanging clothes. Momma arranged a couple of chairs in the bay window that faced the barns with a table between them, a radio, and a reading lamp. Grandma Em smiled as she nodded her approval. Momma was relieved.

Next, she turned toward the kitchen. I stepped aside to let her by. My eyes looked to the wall going up the stairs. The spots where my family once resided were still bare. I wanted Momma to hang our pictures in their places, but it was Grandma Em's decision to welcome us back. I turned to find Grandma Em watching me. I dropped my eyes, ashamed that she saw. I didn't want her to know the pain it caused. It was a good day, and I was glad to be there.

We moved on to the kitchen. Momma showed everyone the pantry teaming full with pickles, beans, peas, corn, and every other vegetable grown in Alabama. Grandma Em chuckled. There was more food in her pantry than on the shelves of Grandfather Gordon's store.

She was tiring, but instead of going to her room she returned to the swing. She motioned for me to join her. My picture was not on the wall, but I was welcome at the big house again.

The remainder of the summer Momma helped Grandma Em get ready each morning. I followed later. Sometimes she was waiting on the porch. If not, I sat on the swing until she joined me. I told her about my life while we were separated, including my first day at the country school, meeting Abigail, and it's closing. I shared my fears of moving to the town school, with details about Charlotte, Virginia, the choir, Library and Newspaper Clubs.

We enjoyed our mornings. It took time away from Addie and Abigail, but the special moments with her were important. While I was there Momma took care of things at home, returning at noon with the mid-day meal. I rang the dinner bell in the yard before entering the kitchen through the back door. It allowed me to avoid the front hall. After we ate, Grandma Em rested, which gave me time for my friends. Aunt Sara brought supper in at five, and stayed to help her get ready for bed. She continued to improve and began helping in the kitchen. She was gradually gaining the ability to care for herself.

Miss Ada came to the big house while she was resting to tend the garden. One day Grandma Em saw her from the bay window as James loaded baskets of vegetables in his truck. Momma was afraid she would accuse them of stealing, but Grandma Em didn't react.

Addie and I helped can the vegetables that evening. Her brothers carried crates of jars to the trunk of our car. The next day when the men came in for the noon meal they transferred them into the big house. Grandma Em watched the procession from her swing. Coming into the kitchen, she went to the pantry. Pointing to a jar of Miss Ada's bread and butter pickles, she motioned for me to take it to the table. I did as instructed. She hit Daddy's hand. He opened the jar. She stabbed a cluster of the cucumber and onion slices for her plate. We joined her in eating every last one. It was her way of saying she accepted their kindness. No one was more surprised or pleased than Daddy.

School days arrived too soon. Each morning Momma woke me before going to the big house, but left breakfast waiting on the table. There were many changes that year including a new seat on the other side of the bus. After collecting the children beyond the big house, we turned to travel back toward the farm. Getting closer I saw the swing moving. Grandma Em was there. I waved wildly and called out the window. She raised her left hand in return. Each morning, if the weather was acceptable, she was on the porch to see me off.

Coming home the first day I asked to be dropped at the big house. Going up the steps, I knocked. I wanted to see Grandma Em, but couldn't face going in the house. Momma came to the door. "She's resting. Come help me while you wait." I shook my head no, but she said, "Trust me. You want to come in."

I tried to avoid looking at the wall as I entered, but couldn't help it. I caught my breath so loud it startled Momma. She was beaming. The empty spaces were filled with pictures of my family. She said, "I came this morning and they were there. Sara must have done it." She put her arm around me as tears rolled down my face. We heard a noise behind us. I turned to see Grandma Em clearly smiling. She made her way out into the hall to nudge me with her elbow. I gave her a squeezing hug, happy to be accepted back into her life.

Another change was Momma's time at the big house. Grandma Em continued to improve, allowing Momma to leave her alone part of the day. Aunt Sara reduced her time, often not coming until late evening to assist at bedtime. I came each day. Tuesdays and Thursdays Momma cut my visit short on the pretext of homework and chores so I could spend time with Addie.

The daily schedule included Ted showering at the big house after work, occasionally joining us for dinner or grabbing a snack before seeing Nettie. One evening after cleaning up he returned to the kitchen to find Grandma Em at the table with eggs, toast, and a glass of milk. She motioned for him to sit. She found a purpose cooking for Ted. Momma missed having him at our table, but it made Grandma Em happy.

One day he asked if Nettie could join them for supper. Grandma Em made ham steaks with baked potatoes. She used a can of Miss Ada's beans, with slices of bread, and Nettie brought an apple pie. The meal was fine, but what excited him was her reaction to Nettie. They bonded immediately. Nettie came most days to help with supper, and spend the evening with Ted. Whatever made Grandma Em disown us was forgotten. We were glad to have our family back.

Christmas of '54 was memorable. We had our regular tradition with the Gordons, but celebrating with Grandma Em made it special. Ted and Nettie got a tree for the big house. On Christmas morning we opened presents there as a family. After we finished, Nettie joined us for brunch. We stayed until Aunt Sara arrived late afternoon. Ted spent the evening at Nettie's, and the four of us enjoyed open roast beef sandwiches and a game of cards in the peacefulness of our little house.

Chapter FOURTEEN

1955

The Christmas break passed quickly. I enjoyed my time with Grandma Em, Abigail, and Addie. Before I was ready, it was time for school. In January, Jessie returned. Though the family gave excuses for her absence, we knew the truth and many others in town likely suspected.

She was a different person, quiet and removed. She didn't get involved in clubs or activities. She came to school each day, cordial and polite, but disconnected from everyone. It was difficult to watch. She was a ghost of the sweet girl we remembered.

Leroy continued to live and work in Huntsville. He was not missed by anyone except Aunt Sara and Uncle Roy.

Distressing for me was that Daniel started spending time with Ruth McCabe. She was kind, thoughtful, quiet, and reserved like him. She was wonderful to his brothers and sister. This boy with the permanently etched look of sadness on his face was frequently caught with a small, but unmistakable smile.

Seeing them together in the cafeteria was devastating. I tried not to look, but frequently found myself staring. One particular day I saw Daniel place his hand over hers. She continued talking so natural, accustomed to his touch. It was too much to bear.

Complaining of nausea, I fled the cafeteria. I couldn't let Abigail or the others see my tears.

After school I watched for Addie from the porch. I needed my friend. She would understand. I had shared my dreams with her. Though we no longer played with the corn dolls, the memories of our make-believe families stayed with me. When I saw her, I began a slow walk to the middle of the field. I didn't want anyone else to see my pain. Giving her books to Jefferson James, she walked directly into the field. As she approached I collapsed into a sobbing heap. She sat next to me on the cold ground. I said, "Daniel's in love with someone else."

She put her arm around me as I told her about Ruth and the cafeteria. There was no consoling me, and she didn't try. My friend let me cry and grieve like I had done for her in the same spot years back.

That spring my parents were focused on Cal. He and Samuel were looking ahead to graduation and making plans for college. Though my parents encouraged Cal, Daddy made it clear he had to help financially. Low rain had affected our crops the previous couple years, with a full drought in '54. Daddy was concerned the weather patterns would not improve. Extra money could be difficult to come by.

Samuel didn't discuss his plans with Uncle Roy, but Aunt Sara was supportive. Both boys were researching colleges, writing letters, and exploring ways to pay for it. Cal was a good student, but Samuel was exceptional. The teachers worked hard to help them find opportunities. They encouraged Cal to pursue Alabama Polytechnic Institute in Auburn. Though he might not qualify for a financial award, they believed with a little help from Daddy he could work his way through. He applied and was accepted. He secured a room at a boarding house for a modest price. Because he was willing to share with two other boys, it was manageable.

Samuel received a scholarship to Columbia College in New York City. Everyone was thrilled for him and proud, especially my family. That kind, considerate boy would be free of both Leroys. Though we were happy for him, there was sadness knowing he would eventually leave for good.

Daniel was also graduating. I was sad he wouldn't be on the bus, but I would still see him. He was growing his operation but continued to need outside income to expand. We paid him a minimal wage, however, Daddy and Ted helped him with his land and let him use some of our equipment.

One Friday Aunt Sara brought Samuel to stay at the big house until Sunday. They were surprised by a visit from Leroy. She was not happy and concerned for his safety as well as Samuel's. They still feared Jessie's father, and Leroy was angry about his brother's plans for college. As Aunt Sara explained, Grandma Em snorted and said, "Mean, mean." Shaking her head back and forth, she turned away saying, "Bad." Aunt Sara made excuses to justify Leroy, but Grandma Em brushed her comments away with her good hand.

Aunt Sara couldn't take her mother's judgment. She left, but I stayed to visit. Samuel shared his plans for New York and school. As disgusted as she was about Leroy, Grandma Em beamed with pride over Samuel. It was a shame Uncle Roy and Aunt Sara couldn't see beyond their oldest son to appreciate that remarkable young man.

I spent one Saturday morning with Grandma Em while Addie worked. We made Lemon Crunch Bars. After finishing, we sat on the swing drinking tea and enjoying the quiet. She ran her hand over the smooth carvings of the arm next to her. She tapped the arm saying, "Who, who?"

I pretended not to understand, but she persisted. I shook my head saying, "I can't."

She became more adamant. I said, "Daddy will be mad at me. He made me promise. Can't we just enjoy it?" She was unrelenting. I continued, "But ya won't sit on it, and I love swingin' with ya."

She used her left hand to make a cross over her heart. I shook my head, not believing she could keep that promise. She moaned as she made the cross again. She struggled to say, "Promise."

With the heaviest heart, I let out a deep sigh. Closing my eyes, I said, "Mr. Jefferson made it for ya."

I waited for her to stomp away from that swing. When I didn't feel any movement, I opened my eyes. She was no longer looking at me, but straight ahead. Her left hand was again caressing the arm. She gave the swing a push and we glided in silence. She continued to enjoy the swing, seemingly more after that day.

As Cal was making plans for his future, so was Ted. He talked with Grandma Em about bringing Nettie to live at the big house. With her approval, he proposed. He bought a ring with a square ruby in the center and two small diamonds on each side. It was simple, but beautiful. He didn't plan anything big. He showed up at her house one night, inviting her to sit with him. I swore Abigail to secrecy, but her entire family knew before Nettie. As the couple sat on the porch, the others watched through the window. Abigail gave me a detailed description of how my brother asked her sister to marry him.

Prior to Grandma Em's stroke, Ted couldn't move into the big house, there wasn't room for them to live with us, and there was no other option. The stroke changed many things for the better. After a four-year courtship, there would finally be a wedding. Plans were made for a small ceremony and party at the big house so Grandma Em could attend.

One Saturday morning, Grandma Em motioned me toward the stairs pointing up. She said, "Box, chest," then gave me a push. I went toward the first bedroom, she yelled, "No." At the next door, again she said, "No." I went into the bedroom that was hers. She said, "Yes."

There was a blond cedar chest against the wall. I removed a large box inside. Taking it to the top of the stairs, she nodded. I carried it into the parlor. Opening the lid, I pulled back layers of aged tissue paper to uncover a veil. It was made of simple netting edged with lace. I carefully removed it from the box. It reached from my head to my knees. It was slightly yellowed, but still obviously white. Under a couple more layers of tissue, I found Grandma Em's wedding dress. I gently grasped the shoulders to draw it out. It had a fitted bodice of white satin, with a V-neck trimmed with the same lace. The sleeves were long with more lace edging the bottom. The skirt of plain satin was fitted at the waist, flaring outward all the way to the floor. The back of the dress was longer to make a short continuous train. It was simple, but elegant.

I asked if it was for Nettie. She nodded. I begged, "Can I be here when she sees it? Please?"

She nodded, pointing to the clock on the mantel saying, "Ten."

I said, "She's comin' at ten?" She confirmed.

I went to work draping the dress across the arm and seat of the sofa with the veil overlaying the dress on one side. I heard Momma's car pulling in with Nettie. I ran out to hurry them. Momma was frustrated, but obeyed. Asking Nettie to close her eyes, I guided her until she was facing the sofa. Momma saw the surprise. She let out a small gasp. I moved Nettie into position. I stepped back to watch her reaction, saying, "Open."

Her eyes fell upon the dress. She turned to Grandma Em, with a gentle whisper, "It's beautiful. I'm honored." Then turning back to the dress, she whispered, "It's like a cloud in heaven. The most beautiful dress I've ever seen."

My excitement took over. I asked, "Can she try it on?"

Momma nodded. "That's a wonderful idea. You two go on. I want to bring your mother to see. Don't come down until we get back."

As she was leaving I yelled, "Bring Abigail."

I carried the veil to Aunt Sara's room, while Nettie carried the dress. Placing it carefully across the bed, she gently began to undo the satin buttons down the back commenting, "It's so fragile. I looked at fabric in town, but didn't want to waste money on such a

SILENT TIES

frivolous thing. I mean it's a dress ya wear once. There are other things we need, but this... Oh Missy, do ya think it'll fit? I'm not gonna be upset if it doesn't. I was fine with wearin' my best dress and it'll be fine now. I'll treasure the gesture." She continued to undo the buttons.

I helped her change. After fastening the veil in place, I heard tires on the gravel. She glowed. I said, "Wait here." I looked over the railing. Everyone was waiting. Motioning to Nettie, I adjusted the dress as she moved to the top of the stairs. There were gasps of delight. Her sisters began to clap as she carefully descended to the front hall.

Momma walked around her saying, "We could take in the bodice a little here..."

Nettie interrupted, "No, the fabric's too fragile. If we make it too tight, it may shred." Grandma Em was happy to see Nettie in her dress. Even the right side of her mouth appeared to be turning up at the corner. A thought flashed through my mind. Thinking back to Granddaddy Tucker and Grandma Em, I feared the dress could be a bad omen. A shiver passed through my body.

The next month was all about the wedding. Momma and I were busy getting the big house ready. It hadn't been cleaned well in years. Daddy had been keeping up the exterior and painted everything except the porch area. I wondered if it was because he was too afraid, or if Grandma Em wouldn't let him. It didn't matter. We painted it that summer. It was sparkling new and a beautiful place for Grandma Em to sit.

It was my first wedding. Grandfather and Grandmother Gordon were included, as well as Aunt Sara and her family. Uncle Frank, Aunt Marilyn, and their two children were invited. Daddy's cousins called with regrets, but we never heard from their father.

I kept Addie informed about the plans. There was no guilt knowing Addie and her family would not be invited. Though we were neighbors, and the relationship between our families was

- 97 -

friendly, it was kept private between the properties. We would not have thought to invite them, just as they would not include us in a social affair.

The day was clear, a little on the warm side, but not too bad for July in Alabama. Momma asked Mrs. Wheeler to play music on the pump organ in Grandma Em's parlor. We opened the windows so it could be heard out front. Cal and Nettie's sister, Anna Lee, stood up with them. Nettie came out on the porch, beautiful and radiant. Her parents were waiting at the top of the steps to guide her to Ted.

It was a short ceremony with Reverend Howell, but very sweet and happy. Nettie and Ted reminded me of Momma and Daddy. Ted was quiet, peaceful, and loving. She was her own person, yet, like Momma in the important ways. Her kind nature was evident in her every look and word. My concern washed away, confident it would be a good marriage.

Uncle Frank and his wife did not attend. Several days later I asked Daddy why, but he shook his head and walked away. It was one more thing he didn't think I could understand.

Later that summer Jessie disappeared. Her father was frantic. He came out to ask Daddy for help. After the last time Jed confronted Uncle Roy, he was afraid to go there again. Sheriff Hosper refused to get involved.

Jed was trying to find Leroy. Daddy refused to tell him where he was, but offered to find out if Jessie was with him. He tried to convince her father it was more important to know she was alright. He reluctantly agreed, though being with Leroy did not mean she was safe.

That evening Daddy confirmed she was in Huntsville. I listened from the parlor. He said, "Your father's worried. He needs to know you're fine." She initially refused. He continued, "If ya don't, I'll have to tell him where ya are. That's dangerous for both of 'em, but I won't have a choice." He listened again before saying,

"That's fine. Ya don't have to tell him where, but he needs to hear from ya." Silence again as she spoke. He finished the conversation saying, "Call him once a week and I won't tell him anything. Understand? Take care."

After he hung up, Daddy turned to Momma. "Well, I guess we know why Leroy came to visit."

Taking his keys from the hook, he left for town. When he returned I heard his heavy footsteps on the porch. The screen door slammed after him. He walked to the parlor. Momma signaled for me to stay in the kitchen as she joined him. I strained to hear their conversation, but they were using hushed tones. I felt for Daddy. The burden he carried for others was too great.

Within a week, Leroy and Jessie married. Usually a wedding was good news, a time for happiness; however, most comments were, "What a shame." Aunt Sara was thrilled hoping Jessie could settle her son. Everyone knew that was an unrealistic expectation. Sweet Jessie couldn't change him. Instead, concern for her made it the most melancholy news.

Chapter FIFTEEN
FALL 1955

After Ted's wedding, we focused on preparing Cal for college. I was sad, already missing Ted and what our family had been. I was nostalgic for our times together on the stairs listening to Momma and Daddy, Sunday trips to town, or the sound of our three men as they climbed the porch steps after a day in the fields. I didn't welcome the loneliness.

Too soon, the first Sunday of September arrived. Momma, Daddy, and I drove Cal to Auburn. Though the three of us were struggling with our emotions, Cal was excited and ready for the new beginning.

I moved on to the ninth grade. There was a noticeable difference. High school produced feelings of self-importance and independence. I missed Cal, Samuel, and Daniel on the bus, but the consistency of Abigail helped with the transition.

A bright spot was time at the big house with Grandma Em and Nettie. She took over caring for everyone, the house, and the garden. She no longer worked for Mrs. Dennis. She was now a farmer's wife with a chicken coop, selling eggs and canning vegetables. She enjoyed finding ways to involve Grandma Em. It was a happy home. Many days I hated to leave, but I also looked forward to spending time with Addie.

Our relationship remained constant as life changed. Even into high school, it was like our years as children. We continued to run across the field, at times spinning each other until we fell. Instead of using it to direct us to a house for the afternoon, we often stayed in the field watching the clouds move overhead and talking.

From the beginning of town school, I told her about my trials with Charlotte and Virginia. It was nice to bemoan the aggravation they caused. When I shared the comments about my hair, Addie and I would commiserate about our mutual black mass of mess and the time we spent trying to make it do impossible things.

We talked about school, the changes in our families, and our dreams for the future. We continued to occasionally join the other family for meals. It was a piece of my childhood that according to societal rules should have ended. However, I was determined to keep the relationship alive, avoid reality, and deny I was changing.

A couple months into the fall Daniel came one evening to talk with Daddy. The school had called him in for a meeting. Without Daniel there, his brother Patrick was skipping school. He needed to get the children on the bus each morning before coming to work. It confirmed how much responsibility fell on him. He was the bread earner, the parent, and caretaker in every respect.

After he left, I asked Momma why the school didn't call their father. Momma was usually sympathetic and kind in her words, but compassion for Daniel overwhelmed her. "Because he's a drunk. That boy works hard to feed that family, and his father drinks it away. Those children are lucky they have Daniel."

Daddy walked into the room. He shot Momma a stern look. She turned on him saying, "Don't tell me to hold my tongue. That boy's working himself to death and making that farm his life. But that man could sign it all away in a drunken stupor. Someone needs to protect those children." He simply nodded.

A few nights later a call came for Daddy. I heard him say, "He's home? Is he drunk? Good. We'll be right over." Next, he called Ted telling him to be out front. He told Momma it was a good time. She wished him luck as he leaned over to kiss her goodbye.

I asked where he was going. Momma said, "The lawyer drew up papers transferring the farm to Daniel. He's taking them for Ben to sign with Ted and him as witness. Let's hope it works." We clasped our hands praying Daddy was successful for the sake of the children.

We tried to keep busy in the kitchen, but I couldn't study and Momma couldn't sit still. Every now and then one of us said something like, 'He has to sign,' or 'Daddy won't come home until he signs.'

It was over an hour before we heard Daddy's truck and his footsteps on the porch. I tried to see if they sounded heavy and down-trodden, or light and successful. I looked at Momma as we each shrugged our shoulders. He came into the kitchen and dropped the folded papers on the table. She said, "Did he sign?"

He nodded. "Yeah, he signed. I'll take Daniel to town tomorrow and make sure these get filed. That farm is his."

I wanted more details. "Was his father angry? Is Daniel alright? What if he changes his mind?"

"Ben was fine. I explained Daniel was payin' the bills and needed to show he owned the property to get loans for seed and such. He's a farmer, he knows how it works, and without Daniel, he wouldn't have a place to live." Daddy reassured me.

Momma gave him a hug, but suddenly backed up. "Oh my goodness, you've been drinking!"

He smiled as he said, "Well, we had to entice him to talk. Then we needed to seal the deal." He winked at me as he laughed. She didn't care how he accomplished it, as long as Daniel and the children were protected.

Aunt Sara made short visits to Grandma Em once or twice a week, but no longer came each evening. There were new traditions at the big house for Ted and his bride. In September Nettie invited her parents and siblings to Sunday dinner. Abigail didn't join us at the Hotel. It was lonely with our small family of three. My only other friend was Addie, but she wasn't allowed to dine there.

The first week of October, Nettie invited us to the big house. I was excited. The next day I told Abigail I was sorry, but we wouldn't be going to the Hotel. She looked at me confused saying, "Aren't ya goin' to Nettie's?"

"Nettie's?" I responded. I wasn't shocked that she knew my plans, but upset at the way she called Grandma Em's house Nettie's. It's our big house. It belongs to my family. I continued, "Well yes, I am goin' to Grandma Em's. How did ya know?"

"We're all goin'. Nettie invited everyone." I was hurt and angry. If Momma knew the whole story I'm sure she would have told me. Why didn't Nettie say it was for both families? I didn't want to share it with them. I wanted to enjoy a dinner at the big house like years before. I wasn't very pleasant the rest of the day. We planned to stay after school, but I pretended to not feel well. We took the bus home. I was anxious to tell Momma it wasn't a Sunday dinner for us like we thought.

She was taking clothes off the line when the bus dropped me off. I walked around back, my anger building with each step. I immediately told her, "We weren't invited to Sunday dinner at the big house like Abigail's family. We're invited to a barbeque with all of them."

She said, "I'm aware we've been invited to a barbeque and that Nettie's family is coming. And my parents have been invited as well. Nettie and Ted want everyone there together."

I was dumbfounded, replying, "You knew? But last night you said we were invited to Sunday dinner at the big house."

She said, "No, I did not. I said Nettie invited us for a family dinner on Sunday, meaning the whole family. And weren't you supposed to stay after school?"

I nodded, still not happy. "I thought they invited us to the big house for Sunday dinner. It's our turn." I was near tears.

She put her arm around my shoulder, saying, "I didn't know you were waiting for that. Nettie asked us several times, but I told her it wasn't necessary. They need time to themselves. It's hard to be the new wife in a farm family. Honey, we do everything together and, because of Grandma Em, we're always there. Can you imagine how it feels? She's living in someone else's home, and that person is still there. She doesn't even dare move the furniture because it isn't hers. Sunday afternoons when Grandma Em is napping is her only time alone with Ted. She shouldn't spend it cooking for us. Don't be mad at Nettie. Anyway, I like our new tradition. I thought you did too. With Cal gone, it's you two girls out for the day with us, special. Maybe some days we can go to the diner, or do something different."

I was embarrassed. Leave it to Momma to think about someone else first. Nettie was wonderful with Grandma Em. She genuinely loved her. I never realized she felt like an observer. It was supposed to be her home, but it wasn't. Still, I felt a small pang of sadness. I wanted to relive the Sundays of my childhood.

I said, "I never thought of it that way. But if they invite us again, could you say yes?" She nodded.

The next day I was extra sweet to Abigail. I didn't say I was sorry because I couldn't explain why. I was afraid she might share my selfish desires with Nettie. Instead I told her I was excited about spending Sunday together at the big house.

The week dragged by slowly. I was glad Addie was available Saturday afternoon. It made the day go faster. We listened to music on the radio, sang along with the songs, and helped Miss Ada in the kitchen. I joined them for supper. Later, we walked across the field to our halfway spot. Falling onto the cool dry earth, we watched the clouds disappear into dusk and the stars begin to peak through. It was comfortable. We shared normal teenage things, talking about school and boys, though we didn't share the same people or places. There was a feeling of everything in common for two fourteen-year-old girls.

The next day Abigail's family was at the big house when we arrived. I'd forgotten about the barbeque pit behind the garden. It had grown over, but Ted restored it. Seeing the men gathered around it, ghostly memories of picnics at the big house flashed through my mind. I wished I could remember Granddaddy Tucker, but it was more the smells and sounds that flooded my senses.

Ted was beaming as he welcomed us to his home. It suddenly dawned on me it was exactly how Daddy wanted it. We could have moved to the big house and all of this could be his. But instead he gave it to Ted. He chose to pass the future over to his son with no sign of envy.

Tables and chairs from the church were in the front yard where it was easier to maneuver Grandma Em. It was a festive atmosphere. As everyone savored Momma's cake, Ted and Nettie stood up. He began with how happy they were to have their family gathered, but stopped, overcome by his emotions. She stepped in. "We're lucky to have all of you and glad you're here to celebrate with us."

I suddenly realized why we were there. Turning to my parents, they were beaming. Together Ted and Nettie said, "We're havin' a baby." Everyone cheered and applauded. The men shook hands and the women hugged, the cake was forgotten.

I ran to Grandma Em on the swing with Ezekiel. Hugging her I said, "You're gonna be a great-grandmother. Great Grandma Em." She started to laugh as I realized how it sounded. I added, "Well you are great. Now you'll have the title officially." It was a wonderful day, better than any Sunday dinner at the big house.

As we were moving on with life, outside our isolated world other things were happening. In December of 1955 Rosa Parks refused to give her seat on a Montgomery bus to a white man. She was arrested. It set off a firestorm and began a chain of events that changed life in Alabama. After her arrest, a bus boycott was organized for Montgomery. Most believed it wouldn't last. It was commonly thought that through pressure and need, the colored community would return to the buses within a few days. No one imagined the boycott would last a year.

As a result, racial tensions all over the state were at heightened levels. In our small community, Sheriff Hosper began an agenda of constant intimidation in order to keep people in line and make sure nothing happened. It was a scary time for Addie and her family.

Christmas found Cal home for the entire break. It was nice to hear him coming and going. Momma loved having him back with the family. She still created little surprises for me every day, but waited until Cal returned for the Divinity Fudge and to get our tree. It was a joyous time with our family gathered for familiar traditions with the Gordons and at the big house.

Chapter SIXTEEN
EARLY 1956

The year would bring happiness with the gift of new life, but also much sadness. A bright spot was Nettie's pregnancy. I was excited, but Momma was often quiet with an air of concern. Over the months I frequently saw that look on her face. Once I asked, "Aren't you happy 'bout the baby?"

She pretended to smile saying, "Of course I am," but quickly turned away to hide the fear in her eyes.

I continued, "Is something wrong with the baby?"

She shook her head no, but couldn't look at me, saying, "The baby's fine." Ending the conversation, she walked away. There were other times I caught her trying to put on a happy face, but it wasn't real.

We prepared the baby's room, painting it yellow and making curtains. I made pillows for the twin-size bed, one side yellow and the other blue. Grandma Em wanted to help, but it was difficult to find a job for her. Feeling excluded put her in a bad mood, which made it miserable for everyone.

One evening Momma came into the parlor with our baptism gown. The satin fabric was still in good condition, but the lace was yellowed and fragile. She called the big house to ask if we could stop by.

Through the kitchen window we saw Ted at the sink finishing the dishes. Entering, Momma set the gown on the table as she said, "Now feel free to say no, but I wondered if you'd want to use it. It was J.P.'s and Sara's, then I used it for Ted, Cal, and Missy. I hadn't brought it out because of the lace, but maybe Em can fix it. She made it, so..."

Grandma Em was in the front room, and unable to hear the conversation. Ted gave Momma a quizzical look saying, "She can't sew anymore."

A slow smile spread across Nettie's face. "We can build a frame. By adjustin' the gown, she can use her left hand. She has time 'fore the baby comes. We should use this for another generation of Tuckers. Let's show her."

Ted shook his head, but it didn't dampen our excitement. Momma gathered the gown. Moving to the parlor, she set it on Grandma Em's lap saying, "We have a job for you. Ted and Nettie want to use this for the baby, but it needs new lace. Since it was your work in the first place, you should do it."

Grandma Em shook her head no, but Momma continued. "J.P. can build a frame. I'll bring samples of lace for you to choose from. Missy can help pin the lace, but you still have your good hand. You can make those beautiful stitches."

Nettie joined in. "And I want to help. I'd like this for our children 'cause it's a part of you. Please say yes."

Grandma Em looked at her, then back at the gown. She was shaking her head no, but said, "I'll try." We erupted in celebration as Ted rolled his eyes. He went back to the dishes while we made plans. Grandma Em was happy.

We were anxious for Daddy to build the frame, but he was too busy. The drought the previous two years had financially hurt our family. He added more fields in hope the rain would come. He couldn't use his time for a frivolous project like a sewing frame, no matter how happy it made his mother. Momma took lace samples to Grandma Em the next week. The selection process occupied her mind and eased the pressure on him.

Nettie and I began removing the old lace under Grandma Em's supervision. She looked forward to our sewing sessions. I enlisted Abigail's help Sundays after the Hotel. Grandma Em loved having her around.

Daddy and Ted eventually finished the adjustable frame, and sanded it smooth with a coat of varnish. We blocked a piece of fabric. Pushing the frame close to rest Grandma Em's arm on the bottom rail, we manipulated the height and tilt for comfort. She practiced on scraps to fine tune her skills.

Soon the old lace was removed. Nettie invited us to spend the weekend pinning and sewing. I was excited, but torn. I dreaded telling Addie I was busy Friday and Saturday. As we grew older, our time was limited. I was saddened to lose our evening together and also felt guilty knowing I'd be with Abigail. But God has a way of taking care of things. Thursday after school I arrived home, changed my clothes, and watched for Addie and Jefferson James. Seeing them at the fork, I went down the steps. She started running as I began to move across the field. She arrived at her front porch first. I rounded the corner to find her sitting in the rocker next to Miss Ada. Trying to mask her gasps for air, she said, "You're gettin' slow. Ya took so long I had time to finish this tea." Miss Ada smiled as we laughed.

I shared my news from the big house. I was obsessed with the baby and sewing project. Addie didn't get a word in that day. Part of my jabbering was nerves. I dreaded telling her I was busy Saturday evening. The guilt of spending the time with Abigail was distressing. My feelings of betrayal were making it more than it was.

Before I gathered my courage, she told me relatives were coming from Montgomery. The bus boycott was causing tension and fear throughout the South. There were frequent bombings, arrests, and attacks. It was a dangerous time. Addie wouldn't be available until they returned home.

I had mixed feelings of relief because my quandary was solved, but also sadness knowing I might not see her for a while. I stayed for supper, enjoying Miss Ada's poached chicken with hot apple preserves and butter biscuits. Later, I reluctantly said goodbye to my friend. Friday as I was leaving for the big house, I mentioned the visitors. I explained Addie wouldn't be looking for me that weekend. I didn't give the information another thought.

Abigail, Nettie, and I took turns working alongside Grandma Em. We talked, laughed, and danced to the radio. Some of the girls had televisions, including Charlotte and Virginia. They talked about the new dances, but we'd never seen them. Anyone watching us jump around the parlor would have agreed with the town girls. We did look like country hicks.

It was a wonderful weekend. Grandma Em was tired from the work and laughing, but happy. We asked Nettie for another sleepover. Smiling she said, "Oh my goodness, I don't think me or this baby can handle two weekends in a row. Not to mention Ted. That poor man has been banished from his own home. Every time he heard gigglin' girls, he ran for his life. How 'bout one night, Friday, and ya can stay 'til four on Saturday. Ted'll be workin' all day, but when he comes home for supper I want it peaceful. It'll give the baby some quiet time too. Will that do?"

We readily agreed. I'd forgotten about Ted. He spent the weekend in his old bed. He ate breakfast with Daddy, joined us at noon, but escaped to our home for supper. He did it willingly because the time was so important to Grandma Em.

Returning home, the smallness of our shrinking family seemed more pronounced, especially for Momma. Having one of her boys fill the house with his presence, snoring through the night, and pounding down the stairs made her happy. She prepared supper for the three of us while I sat in the kitchen doing my homework. We worked in the melancholy silence.

Daddy came in after dark. He was unusually quiet. I thought his mood was about the absence of Ted and Cal 'til I started to clear the table. Momma pulled me back into my chair. He had a solemn look on his face. I wondered what could be so serious. Was someone ill? Was Daniel alright?

His delay frightened me. He took a few minutes to collect himself before he began. "Momma said ya know 'bout the relatives stayin' at Addie's?" I nodded, so he continued. "Problems in Montgomery are makin' Hosper nervous. He wants to make sure none of that trouble spreads here, so he's crackin' down on the colored folk. If he finds out they got people here, there'll be trouble. Ya can't tell anyone. Not a word. Do ya understand?" I nodded. He added, "Did ya tell the girls at Ted's?"

I shook my head no, saying, "I know not to speak of Addie."

Momma's face was changing colors, turning a bright red. She pushed herself up from the table saying, "They're putting all of us at risk. How could they do this? We're nice to them."

Walking to the sink, she dropped the pan in with such force I was afraid it cracked the porcelain. He said, "Melanie!"

She turned on him replying, "Don't Melanie me. If the Klan gets wind of this, it won't be only them standing out there. It'll be you and Ted too. He has a baby on the way, and you have me and Missy. I can't stand they put us in danger. What were they thinking? If Hosper shows up they deserve what they get."

Daddy didn't move from his chair or raise his voice as he said, "They're family. Things are bad in Montgomery. People don't know if they'll get dragged out of their cars, out of their beds, or beaten to death for standin' on the corner or walkin' down the street. People are scared. Ya help family, and James has to do this. I went over 'fore I came in. He's keepin' 'em inside. Jefferson brings whatever they need out here, and I'm takin' him a side of pig. He understands not to raise suspicion."

"And what about us? What if one of them says something?" There was fear in her voice.

Now Daddy was mad. "Melanie! They won't be talkin' to anyone."

Momma turned back to the sink shaking her head. What could they say about us, that we were helping them? Why would they tell? He continued in a kinder tone. "Ya protect your friends. We need to be seen as friends."

Turning his attention to me he said, "Missy, ya understand? Don't tell anyone, not Abigail or Nettie, and not Grandma Em."

I nodded. "I never do." Outside of our little world I pretended I didn't know Addie and that I didn't care. As I was reassuring him, I felt the shame of my words.

We lived on alert. Each morning I looked across the field. It was always quiet. When I arrived home from school I asked Momma if everything was fine. It seemed like such a normal question, but we both understood the hidden meaning. I often found my parents gazing at that sharecropper's cottage. I never saw anyone except Addie's family. I hoped Mr. Jefferson was being careful as well.

There wasn't an extra vehicle at the house. If they took a bus, surely Sheriff Hosper or someone might have seen them. But with a bus boycott in Montgomery, that wasn't logical. At supper I asked Daddy. It was more than curiosity. I needed to relieve my fear. He said, "The car's in the barn. They came durin' the night. Even I didn't see 'em. As long as they stay in the house, everything should be fine."

Each evening we listened to the news on the radio. There were reports of arrests, attempts by the police to stop illegal carpools, attacks on colored cab drivers, and the response of both groups. Even then we understood how one-sided the reports were, but we weren't concerned with the facts. We were hoping to hear the unrest was over.

It was hard to believe this was happening in my state. It seemed like a world away. What made it real were the people hiding in my backyard. Arrests of several leaders caused concern. There was fear of riots if they were found guilty and reprisals against the coloreds if they were found innocent. Either way, Miss Emily's family would not return home soon.

Sheriff Hosper began making trips past our house several times a week. He drove real slow to look across the field. He was there during the day making sure James didn't have extra help, and in the evening looking for anyone walking around. However, everything looked normal enough. The curtains were typically drawn, and few lights were lit. There appeared to be nothing out of the ordinary. It provided some relief.

At the end of the second week Daddy left Saturday morning as usual, but came back before noon. I was helping Momma in the kitchen when he and Ted arrived. There was a large box labeled Zenith in the bed of the truck. Ted backed up to the front steps to move it inside.

It was a television with a wood case that came to my waist. The front had a glass window in the top, with a brown fabric square on the bottom. They set it against the back wall in the parlor. I begged Daddy to turn it on. He laughed saying, "Not yet, ya won't get a picture. We have to put an antenna on the roof." Next, they unloaded a bundle of aluminum poles and a coil of wire. It took several hours to build the antennae and strap it to the chimney. They ran the wire down the side of the house and through the wall.

Finished, Daddy came in to turn it on. I was disappointed by the gray fuzzy picture and static for sound. He and Ted worked the next half hour to adjust the antennae and test three channels until they were clear.

I asked if Abigail could sleep over. It was a rarity to have Saturday evening free, but since Addie and I couldn't see each other, it was the perfect time.

I was too excited to eat, trying to hurry my parents. Momma agreed to save the dishes for later. Daddy watched the news while we picked up Abigail. Our first television shows were the *Honeymooners*, *People Are Funny*, *Jimmy Durante*, and *Gunsmoke*. I couldn't wait to see the look on Charlotte's face Monday.

We got ready for church quickly the next morning so we could watch cartoons. We skipped dinner at the Hotel. Ted and Nettie joined us while Aunt Sara visited with Grandma Em. We crammed together in the parlor for family time.

Monday on the bus, Abigail and I were giggling with anticipation. The girls were gathered by the windows sharing funny anecdotes about the weekend programs. We joined them talking about the funniest scenes on the *Honeymooners*. Charlotte turned saying, "Did you stand outside someone's window all weekend?"

I was beaming as I said, "No, we watched it on my television."

She fumed a moment, but quickly regrouped. Changing our victory into bitter defeat, she looked at Abigail saying, "Well we certainly knew it wasn't yours." Abigail's face fell, crushed by the words. A few smiled at Charlotte's ability to turn the tables, but others were sad that once again she triumphed. I wanted to come back with something to embarrass anyone other than Abigail but I was speechless.

Over the next few days I saw the pain our television was causing my friend. In the past it was us against the town girls, but the television in my parlor isolated her in the fight. As others talked about shows during the week, she was excluded. It didn't stop me from watching. I enjoyed our television. Trying to stay involved in the conversation, I told Abigail about *I Love Lucy* or *Red Skelton*, but after a few days I gave up. If you'd never seen the programs, it was too difficult to imagine.

We stopped joining the girls. Sometimes Charlotte or Virginia called out questions about the shows. Trying to ignore them made it worse, but if I answered it called attention to Abigail's ignorance. If I said I didn't see the show it was best. I hoped the novelty of tormenting her would grow tiresome, but it didn't. Watching television on the weekends wasn't enough to get by during the week. It became more painful to watch a little. We returned to spending our time at Nettie's and eating at the Hotel.

Television made the events outside of our small-town part of our life. The national and local news showed us the world, but most important for Momma, it brought the reality of Montgomery into our living room. She stopped being angry with James and Emily. When the signal wasn't blocked, we saw and heard of the protests, beatings, arrests, and the force being used to bend the will of the people. The fear they were living became real.

One day after school Momma was baking pies. There were two cooling on the counter and two more in the oven. I asked if someone was coming. She shook her head no. Next, I asked if some were for the big house. Again, she said no. I waited, but all she said was, "Get your work done so you can help me."

I studied in the kitchen. She went about peeling potatoes, soaking them in a pan of water on the stove. She told me to grab one of the apple pies as she picked up the pumpkin and berry. Following her, we started across the field.

The house was quiet. I knocked at the back door. Miss Emily peered from behind the curtain. I heard the lock as she opened the door. She called to Addie. Soon my friend was standing by her mother. I felt the painful awareness of how much I missed her. They smiled when we presented the pies. I asked Addie how she was doing. She gave a short 'fine.'

Momma said, "Enjoy," as we parted.

It was several more weeks before I could spend time with Addie. Momma and I often walked across the field taking bake goods or pork from one of our pigs. It was Momma's gift.

As the baby's due date approached Nettie's skin had a yellow pallor. One day Momma took her to the doctor. She arranged for Abigail and me to walk to the store after school.

When we entered, my grandfather came out from behind the counter to give me a hug. I was caught off guard, but hugged him in return. He offered us candy from the jars, but told us to hide it before my grandmother returned from their apartment.

We talked with him until a customer needed his attention. Alone again, he turned to us saying, "I better get back to work. I have to get these shelves cleaned and stocked. You can sit and visit with me."

I asked, "Can we help?" He gave us each a rag, showing us how to move the stock and clean the shelf before re-stacking the merchandise. We told him about school, the newspaper, Nettie, and Grandma Em. He was very pleasant.

Grandmother Gordon entered, ending the peaceful moment. She said, "Stop bothering him. You won't do that right."

He said, "Nonsense, they're doing fine. They finished one section already. You girls keep going. Now, tell me about what you're doing on that newspaper. Are you writing any articles?"

Grandmother Gordon was not happy, but she didn't raise any more objections. She took out a big ledger and started counting items on the shelves. She didn't join in the conversation, but listened to our stories with an occasional look our way.

Momma arrived. Abigail and I rushed to hear the news. The baby was fine, but Nettie was anemic and needed rest. Momma thanked her parents. Grandfather Gordon said, "They were a great help. In fact, if they want to stop in after school other days, we could use them."

Grandmother Gordon interjected, "We don't need them disturbing things around here. Do you expect to pay them?"

He said, "Let me finish. We could barter for their services." Turning toward us he continued. "You come a couple days a week after school in exchange for things in the store. Melanie, would you mind? And it would help if you could pick them up."

He looked at his wife with a flash of anger. She refrained from objecting again. My mother responded, "It's their decision."

Abigail and I simultaneously said, "Yes."

We arranged to work a few afternoons each week. After thanking them, we ran to tell Nettie. On the ride home, we began a list of things we wanted. Momma reminded us a few hours a week wouldn't buy much, but we kept dreaming.

Wednesday after school we hurried, anxious to get to the store. My grandparents were waiting for us. She sent us to the kitchen for a quick snack. Back in the store he told us to look around and choose what we wanted to work for. He'd decide how many hours were required for each item. I noticed a familiar box at the back of the store. Inside was a television. I asked, "Can we earn this?"

Grandmother Gordon said, "My goodness, you girls aren't worth that!"

Grandfather Gordon tried to ease the impact of her words as he reminded me I had a television. I said, "It's not for me; it's for Abigail." The look on their faces was shock and puzzlement.

Abigail touched my arm saying, "Missy, it's too much. Let's look for somethin' we each want." She tried to pull me toward the girl corner of the store. Avoiding my grandmother, I turned to him. His brow knit together and lips pursed as he thought about my request.

My grandmother interrupted, "Don't be ridiculous. How silly …" she stopped herself from finishing the sentence, but the intent was clear. How silly for people like Abigail to have a television. After a pause, she continued. "My goodness. I've told your mother living on that farm gives you no sense. Pick something reasonable and stop this foolishness."

Much of the time I didn't like my grandmother. Her insult toward Abigail brought those feelings close to hatred. It was like looking at Charlotte or Virginia in fifty years. My disdain for her must have been evident. I turned to see the dismay on my grandfather's face. I didn't care. She deserved it.

He broke the silence of my hate. "Now wait a minute. Maybe we can work it out." She started to object again, but he held his hand up to silence her.

He continued, "A customer bought a television, but had an accident. The speaker and wood on one side is damaged. His wife and boy brought it in to get a new one in exchange. Of course, they had to pay some, but I hoped someone else would take this one for a discount. It still works and has sound. It just doesn't look pretty. With your Papa's talent, he could probably fix it up. Would you girls be willing to work for that one?"

Grandmother Gordon tried to object, but we both screamed 'yes.' He said, "We have a deal. Let's shake on it." As we were shaking hands he said, "There's one problem. I need to get it out of my storeroom. It's taking up space. We have to come up with an honor arrangement. I'll figure how much time it'll take, and you girls have to promise to work those hours." We nodded.

Knowing Abigail's truck wasn't working he asked, "Missy, see if your daddy will take that television to her place." Turning to Abigail, he said, "Do you think your parents could take it now?" She told him absolutely. I promised to talk to Daddy.

The next hour flew by. We unpacked boxes of canned goods, carefully stacking them on the shelves. Momma arrived soon. My grandparents lit up. Their reaction showed me the real reason my grandfather offered us a job. It was to see his daughter regularly.

Before she could say hello I told Momma about the deal. At first she objected, but Grandfather Gordon cut her off saying, "No, now listen. This helps me out. I can't sell it, so this way I get something out of it. It'll take six months, but if they're willing so am I. Does that sound fair?"

She looked puzzled at first. Seeing our excitement, she finally consented. Grandfather Gordon told her about a bent antenna we could take as well, certain Daddy and Abigail's father could figure out how to attach it to the roof.

On the way home, we told Momma about the 'customer,' Mr. Wilkins. Harry had told the story at school. His father came home drunk and as Harry said, "Couldn't figure out how to turn the dang thing off. He put his foot through it trying to make it shut up." Abigail and I sat in the back laughing. Momma tried to reprimand us for speaking poorly of Mr. Wilkins, but soon her shoulders were bouncing along with us.

I joined Abigail to share the news with her family. Inside, we discovered Nettie resting on the sofa. She said, "Sara came to visit. She offered to let me spend the afternoon with my mother. She's sendin' Ted when he comes in." Surprising, but it made sense.

Abigail started to explain our news. Her father got a sour look on his face. I feared he might say no because he thought it was charity. The disappointment was building in Abigail's voice. Her mother was also unhappy, while her brothers and sisters cheered.

I interrupted, "We're hopin' ya don't mind it's all broken up, but it still works. My grandfather can't sell it and he needs it out of the storeroom, so he said we could work for it. He thought ya might be able to fix it some. It was my idea. Momma didn't agree at first, but she finally said yes."

I finished breathless. Everyone looked at their father. He said, "Your granddad can't sell it?" We nodded. He thought for a minute, and said, "Ya sure?" Abigail nodded and I repeated that it was my idea and yes, I really wanted to work for the television.

Looking at his wife with the sour look still on his face, he gave his permission. Everyone was cheering. We told him about the terms of the agreement and the broken antenna. I told him Daddy could bring it out in his truck. That was the deal breaker. He didn't want my daddy taking time to fetch a television for him. Nettie interrupted, "Ted's goin' to the store for me. We ordered a baby swing for tendin' the garden and such. He can pick up the television when he goes to town. Is that alright?" He thought for a minute before nodding. Ted was family and allowed to help.

After it was settled, I said my goodbyes. In the car, I told Momma about Nettie being there. She looked puzzled, saying, "Nettie's here?" I nodded. Turning the engine off, Momma told me to wait.

Soon, she was helping Nettie down the steps to take her home. Settled in the front seat, Nettie said, "I'm sorry. Sara said she wanted to give me time to visit my momma. I thought she was being nice. Her husband was waitin' in the car to drive me. He was real friendly, nothin' like the stories Ted tells. Grandma Em was restin'. I didn't know what to say. I mean they're family."

Momma said, "You did right. The last thing you need is trouble." Thinking out loud she continued. "We have to find J.P."

At Abigail's, I didn't think of Grandma Em or how Nettie got there. I was consumed with news about the television. I wondered if Momma knew what Aunt Sara and Uncle Roy were up to. She drove fast. As we neared the fork in the road she rolled down the window to listen for Daddy's tractor. We drove until she heard the familiar sound. She stopped beyond our house saying, "Missy, run and get your daddy. Tell him to get to the big house."

I jumped out. Running across the field, I landed in mud up to my ankles. The sound of Daddy's tractor was getting louder. I ran through the grove to find him with Ted. I was yelling and waving my arms, but they couldn't hear me over the roar of the tractor. Ted caught sight of me. He motioned for Daddy to cut the engine. Ted yelled, "Is Nettie O.K.? Is the baby comin'?" I shook my head no.

Daddy bolted off the tractor. They ran toward me. I quickly relayed the story about Aunt Sara. We all took off toward the big house. Ted didn't wait for us, but I almost kept up with Daddy. I could see the house. Aunt Sara's car wasn't there, only Momma's.

I ran up the back steps. Pulling the screen door so hard it slammed against the house, I followed to Grandma Em's room. Ted and Nettie were sitting on the edge of the bed. He held her as she cried. Grandma Em was in her chair by the window, her face red with anger. Momma quietly stood in the corner, while Daddy stormed back and forth saying horrible things about his sister and her husband.

I looked at Momma. She pointed behind me into the hall. I turned to see the parlor empty, except for the frame with the baptism gown. The picture of Grandma Em and Granddaddy Tucker was no longer on the mantel along with the clock. Everything was gone except the pictures of my family.

I moved on to the dining room, again empty. I ran upstairs. The baby's room was intact, Daddy's was untouched, but Aunt Sara's room was empty. I opened the door of my grandmother's room that was now Ted and Nettie's. I gasped loud enough for everyone to hear. Daddy and Ted pounded up the stairs. In the middle of the floor was a pile of clothes, pictures, Nettie's hair brushes, and personal items. The furniture that was once Granddaddy Tucker's was gone. Like downstairs, even the pictures off the walls were missing. Ted pushed by me to pick up the brush and his wedding picture. He said in a low voice, "I don't want Nettie to see this."

Momma came up behind us as I started to speak. "How could Aunt Sara be this mean? Where are ya gonna sleep?" I was shaking my head in disbelief. With Nettie so close to delivering and not well, how could they do this?

Momma said, "Missy, we're gonna need your bedroom furniture. You have the only big bed besides Daddy's and mine, and your furniture is a matching set with two bureaus. You can use a bed and one of the bureaus from the boy's room." As bad as I felt for Nettie, I didn't want to lose my furniture, but I agreed.

She started barking orders. "You men take Missy to the house and get that furniture. Tell Nettie to stay with Grandma. They can sit in Em's room. I'll make sandwiches for supper. Bring the pie on the counter. Now go while I start cleaning up."

She was forgetting about the parlor. I asked about that big empty room. She said, "I have an idea for that too, one room at a time. They need somewhere to sleep tonight."

It was quiet as we ate. The worst part was the look on Grandma Em's face. I didn't know what she was thinking, but we soon found out. That was the last time she spoke to her daughter. The next day she had Nettie call Mr. Farnsworth to make a new will. He arrived with four witnesses from town to make sure there was no doubt of her intent when she cut Aunt Sara out of her life.

We worked all evening getting the room ready for Nettie. Daddy and Ted took a few minutes to check the barns for missing equipment and Grandma Em's car. It appeared they only targeted the house.

After we had a place for them to rest, we settled the women for the night. The men took a flashlight and lantern to bring the tractor in from the field. Momma and I stayed at the house while they were gone.

I was tired, but ran to the car for my books. I worked on Math and English while Momma started cleaning my shoes. After a time, she walked to the trash can throwing them in saying, "I'll take you to town in the morning and buy some new ones."

Overwhelmed by exhaustion, I started to giggle. It was infectious. Momma joined me. We were trying to keep quiet, but couldn't contain ourselves. The men walked in on us. Ted shook his head in disgust. After a minute, he let out an involuntary snort. Daddy looked on in shock, before joining us. Laughter was the only response to a day like that.

The next morning Momma let me sleep in. We left just before the shoe store would open. I picked a new pair of saddle shoes like the cheerleaders wore, but they didn't cheer me up. My mind was with Nettie and Grandma Em. I found it difficult to focus during the day.

Getting off the bus at the big house I found the door locked. Momma came to let me in. I followed her into the parlor to find a flowered sofa, two small red velvet chairs, side tables, and a few pictures on the wall. A large mirror hung above the fireplace. The room looked wonderful. Grandma Em was on a red chair, with Nettie on the sofa smiling. "Isn't it beautiful?" Grandma Em nodded her approval.

The furniture came from Nettie's friend Velma. Her mother died suddenly after Christmas, but the house was still intact. The parlor set was about ten years old, but like new. She was happy to help Nettie. I smiled, remembering Grandma Em's anger when Momma got new furniture. Now Grandma Em's parlor was nicer than ours.

Momma pointed toward the dining room furniture they also bought from Velma. It was similar to Grandma Em's 1930 Depression set complete with a buffet, server, table, six side chairs, and two arm chairs. Returning to the parlor, Nettie motioned for me to join her. Taking my hand, she said, "Thank you for the beautiful bedroom. I love it 'cause it was yours. It's the kindest gift ever." It made sleeping in Ted's single bed almost worth it. Staying until he came in, we left them to enjoy their new rooms.

At home I found a surprise waiting for me. Ted's twin bed had
a four-poster frame, matching white dresser, and nightstand. In
the corner was an upholstered chair covered in white and purple
floral fabric, with coordinating bedspread and curtains. I
immediately ran to tell Momma how much I loved it and her. She
said, "I'm glad you love me, but that's a gift from my parents."

That evening at supper she said, "Sara came by today. She tried
to say she was sorry."

Daddy looked up. "Sorry? Does she understand what she did to
Mother? And Nettie? Did she even think 'bout the baby? She's
always sayin' sorry, but it means nothin'."

"As you can guess it was Roy. Sara told him your mother was
giving Samuel money for college. Roy thought that money should
go to Leroy," Momma said.

Daddy sat back shaking his head. "So he takes Mother's
furniture?"

She nodded. "He took it to Huntsville for Leroy and Jessie. He
wanted your mother to give them money, but she refused and he
was ready for it. He had a truck waiting. Sara tried to excuse it by
saying they just took what was fair for Leroy."

He simply shook his head.

She continued, "Your mother was so angry, she just kept saying
'bad' and 'out.' I was afraid she'd have another stroke. I had to
make Sara leave."

Daddy was silent. He tried to return to eating, but was too
upset. He moved to the front porch. We had an explanation, but it
didn't make it right.

That evening was a warm prelude to summer. Momma and I
joined him after the dishes were finished. On our way through the
parlor, she turned on the radio with some music to ease the
tension. If he was looking to find some peace, that didn't happen.
From my seat I could see a car in the distance. As it came closer I
saw the light on the roof. I pointed it out to Daddy. At the fork it
started to go real slow. It continued that pace past our house.
Sheriff Hosper nodded at Daddy. I could see the flash of his white

teeth as he smiled. Daddy returned his nod, but with a look of disgust. The car continued to crawl toward the big house. I said, "Do ya think he knows 'bout Miss Emily's family?"

Daddy said, "No. This visit's for me. He knows what Roy did and he's tellin' me there's nothin' I can do 'bout it." I hoped he was right, but his words didn't ease my fear. Soon, Hosper made a return trip past us, again moving real slow. An involuntary shudder traveled up my body with a frightening chill.

Ted took the television to Abigail's, helping her father attach the broken antennae to a series of boards strapped to the chimney. It wasn't pretty, but it worked. At school we started talking about programs from the previous evening. Charlotte and Virginia immediately ridiculed Abigail with remarks about watching television at my house. With a puzzled look, I said, "My house? Momma doesn't let me have friends on school nights." Turning to Abigail I continued. "Didn't you watch it on your television?"

Abigail was beaming. Rubbing it in a little more she said, "They got it set up in time for *I Love Lucy*. Wasn't it good last night?" she asked turning specifically to Charlotte. There was shock and disbelief with a few of the town girls embarrassed to know Abigail was one of the special ones. It didn't stop Charlotte and Virginia from tormenting us about other things, but never again for being the country bumpkins who were too poor to have a television.

Grandma Em and Nettie continued to work on the gown each day. The two new chairs were side by side permanently. Nettie was feeling worse each week. Either her mother or mine stayed at the house during the day. As the delivery date approached, I saw that look of fear in Momma's eyes more often. It was different from her everyday expression of concern.

Work and extracurricular activities were limiting my time at the big house. I missed Grandma Em. I also missed Addie. As I looked across the field, I often wondered about life inside those walls. The short visit of her relatives turned into a long stay. More than two months after they arrived, they disappeared during the night. One Saturday morning as I was cleaning I heard a faint knock at the back door. It was Addie. My heart jumped. Momma came out to give her a hug as she did many times. Life experience made me give it a conscious thought.

I was excited to show her the television, assuming she'd never seen one. I was disappointed to find she had been watching television long before me. She told me about daytime shows I hadn't seen. It dawned on me that as I complained about the girls tormenting me at school, she had listened, but never commented. Was it because she didn't want me to feel left out or was she embarrassed that her privilege was a benefit of working for the white women in town. The thoughts stopped me from showing her my new bedroom furniture. I was suddenly aware of my selfishness as well as my good fortune.

I shared news from the big house including the story about Aunt Sara, and our concerns for Nettie and the baby. We talked about school and my job at the store. I didn't tell her about Abigail's television, or how it stopped Charlotte and Virginia. I also didn't share how our television helped me at school. Standing there with Addie it seemed silly and unimportant. Today, I'm ashamed of my insensitivity and my complaints about such insignificant things.

On her way out, Momma popped her head into the parlor. "Take care of yourselves and call me at the big house if you need anything."

Normally I'd be disappointed to not see Grandma Em, but I missed Addie. She usually helped Miss Emily clean houses on Saturday, but that week she was allowed to spend a full day with me. I needed to enjoy our time. Now that she was back, I wasn't able to make other plans for Friday or Saturday evening. I hoped Abigail wouldn't notice.

We ate sandwiches in the parlor as we watched the television. The joyful feeling of that day remains with me. There was a peacefulness being with Addie. We didn't do anything special. Spending time together simply felt good.

Chapter SEVENTEEN

SPRING 1956

Nettie didn't make it to full term, delivering three weeks early. The baby was in an incubator, and Nettie was dangerously weak from loss of blood. Ted wouldn't leave her side the first couple days. Once she began to improve, her mother and sisters took over. Ted returned to work during the day, but traveled to the hospital every evening. He was exhausted from the schedule and the worry. To let Ted rest, Daddy slept in his childhood room to help Grandma Em during the night.

Finally, Nettie and the baby came home. We put a twin bed in the parlor for Nettie as she healed. The birth erased the fear from Momma's eyes. The baby was tiny, but beautiful, with fine light hair. I was glad she wasn't cursed with a dark curly mess like mine.

For the next several weeks, everyone pitched in. Nettie's family spent many days helping, and Momma worked on Nettie's vegetable garden. One day, when the bus arrived at the big house, I noticed James's truck behind the barn. I climbed the porch steps, but the door was locked. Through the window I saw Nettie, the baby, and Grandma Em sleeping in the parlor. Momma was nowhere to be seen.

I walked down the ramp toward the side of the house to find Miss Ada, James, and Momma walking toward me. Miss Ada carried a burlap sack. James followed with a long-handled hoe and small hand shovel. Fortunately, she came several more times. Momma's specialty was flowers, but Nettie needed the vegetables which was Miss Ada's area of expertise.

Everyone knew we came dangerously close to losing Nettie. Many neighbors and towns people dropped off gifts for the baby, with kind words for Nettie's recovery. Even Virginia's mother brought a present to the house. The kindness of our little community was touching, whether they were planting a garden or providing for the baby.

Cal's arrival from college went almost unnoticed. I was glad to have him home. One night he told us about a girl he was dating. He was hoping to visit her over the summer, but Momma warned it wasn't possible anytime soon. He was needed on the farm, and he owed it to Daddy. She suggested he invite her for the Baptism. Nettie's forced recuperation delayed the event, so that visit was more than a month away.

Addie and I didn't see much of each other, only Friday and Saturday evenings. During the day we both tended to our business, me helping at the big house and Addie working with Miss Emily. At the store I frequently saw colored maids shopping for their Misses, but never Miss Emily or Addie. Many of the women were full-time maids, but some were part-time. Miss Emily was very definite about her role. She was a cleaning lady. She never hired on full-time, though many in town asked. I often thought it would be easier to work for one family instead of juggling several. In retrospect, it helped her stay in control. She could say no to a request of working extra, or decide to stop working for a particular individual if they treated her badly. Miss Emily never worked holidays, but spent them with her family. Evidently, she was worth it, even if they hired substitute maids for Christmas and Easter.

The weekend of the baptism I told Addie I couldn't see her. Cal's girl, Jean, was coming and would be staying in my room. I would spend those few days at Ted's.

Abigail didn't join us for church. She and her family set up for the barbeque at the big house. Daddy didn't want Uncle Frank or his family invited, nor was Aunt Sara welcome. Nettie didn't have any grandparents, aunts, or uncles in the area, so it was a small gathering.

When we arrived, the baby was asleep in the bassinet next to Grandma Em's chair. She was wearing the gown. It was beautiful. Grandma Em stroked the lace, smiling.

Once Reverend Howell arrived, we moved outside. Grandma Em took her seat on the swing, joined by Ezekiel. Everyone else sat at the tables in the yard. During the ceremony Reverend Howell asked the question we had all been waiting for, "What name do you give this child?"

They had kept it a secret until that moment. Together they announced, "Emily Rebecca." Everyone looked back to Grandma Em, then to Grandmother Gordon sitting at the table. Grandma Em smiled, but Grandmother Gordon was shocked. I turned to Abigail expecting to see the same look, but she was smiling.

I whispered, "Why aren't ya surprised. I mean, they chose Rebecca, Grandmother Gordon's name."

Abigail leaned over whispering, "Rebecca is my grandmother's name too. Isn't it clever?" Clever was the right word.

As my eyes flitted between my beaming grandmothers, they stopped at Ezekiel. He didn't look well. Ill since January, he had missed the remainder of the school year. I didn't want to dampen her spirits, so I resisted asking Abigail about him. However, I couldn't erase the feeling of unease.

It was a wonderful day, but it tired Nettie. Momma was glad I was staying at the big house. We settled Nettie in the parlor. Ted moved the bassinet to his room, with me next door to help through the night. I drifted off happily thinking, 'Another Emily, another good person.'

The next morning Jean departed early, and Cal returned to work. Momma was glad she left. It had been uncomfortable. She was a town girl, everything Momma ran away from. Momma seemed forlorn. She busied herself as a tear ran down her cheek.

I put my arms around her. "What's wrong?" The panic in my voice got her attention.

She looked at me saying, "Someday Cal will leave. Maybe one or two more summers then he'll be gone. He'll marry a girl like her and they'll live in a city somewhere and never come home. Girls like Jean don't want to live like this. They don't even want to visit. Didn't you see her? The way she looked at us and our home. She didn't want to sit in a chair, afraid it might dirty her dress."

Staying at the big house, I missed those moments. Just like Grandmother Gordon, Jean thought being a farmer's wife was shameful. With her mother, Momma defended her life. However, she couldn't stand up to Jean for fear Cal would support his girlfriend. At first, I was angry with Jean for making Momma feel bad. As she talked, I began to understand it wasn't really Jean, but Cal who hurt Momma. Although it might not be Jean, one day Cal would likely marry a woman who'd look down on us.

One evening Grandfather Gordon called to ask if he could come out to speak with us. He sounded serious. Momma asked if Abigail or I did something wrong. I couldn't imagine what it was, but with Grandmother Gordon it could be anything. I was relieved when he came alone. He would cushion the blow.

Daddy and Cal cleared out on the pretext of work. Momma invited him to sit in her parlor for the first time ever. He appeared more nervous than we were as he took a seat. He began, "You have a lovely home, Melanie. I appreciate you allowing me to come. I want you to know it's been a joy having the girls at the store. They're a big help. They take care of the bottom shelves, unpack the crates, and move things for us. They made it possible to add items we couldn't stock before. We don't know what we'd do without them. We'd like them to continue over the summer. I can provide transportation in the morning if you can pick them up in the middle of the day." He went silent, more scared of Momma than she was of him.

We were expecting criticism or a complaint. It took a moment to gather our thoughts. Momma looked toward me to say, "Would you like that?"

I didn't have to think. "Yes, please. We could pay off Abigail's television and start earning clothes for school. Is that alright?" He nodded. I turned to Momma saying, "Can I call Abigail?"

Her parents gave permission as well. Grandfather Gordon arranged to pick us up a few mornings a week and Momma would collect us at noon. I was excited and relieved.

The following week school came to a close. I needed a break from Charlotte and Virginia. I was looking forward to spending more time at the store. It would allow Abigail to buy clothes for the fall. I wasn't growing, so there were fewer dresses to pass on.

Saturday, I enjoyed the evening with Addie. During that summer the only time Addie had for me was late Saturday with a rare Tuesday or Thursday. She was old enough to fully contribute to the family income, and there was little time for play.

Chapter EIGHTEEN

SUMMER 1956

Grandfather Gordon didn't need our help as much as he said, but it allowed them to see Momma and me on a regular basis. When she arrived the first Wednesday, he invited her to join them for a bite to eat while we minded the store. It became a weekly event.

In early July Grandfather Gordon picked me up for work. When we arrived at Abigail's, she came out to say she was unable to go. Ezekiel was very ill and her parents wanted the family at home. I called Momma from the store to relay the story. Concerned about Nettie's health, Momma debated what to do. She decided it was too important and took Nettie to her parents' home.

A few days later, Ezekiel died. Reverend Howell offered to hold the funeral at church after Sunday services and donated a plot in the children's cemetery. Word traveled around town. The ladies planned a gathering on the church grounds. Momma made a cake and cookies, Grandfather Gordon supplied the cokes and coffee, and everyone else brought the food. Grandmother Gordon put a jar on the counter to help pay for the coffin. She started with a sizable contribution of her own.

I was in awe watching our town come together for Abigail's family. Many people stopped in the store just to make a donation. I marveled at the generosity of our community.

Grandma Em wanted to attend the funeral, but we didn't know how to get her into the church, so Daddy would stay behind. Nettie tried to ease her mind with assurance the family felt her sympathy.

On Sunday Ted and Nettie took the car to help transport her family. Cal was to drive Momma and me, but at the last minute Daddy said he needed him on the farm. Grandfather Gordon agreed to take us. He gathered Momma and me, before returning to collect Grandmother Gordon at the store. Momma moved to the back seat, allowing her mother to sit in the front. As she approached the car I noticed a look of disapproval on her face. I hoped Momma didn't see.

We were dressed appropriately for a funeral. Momma wore her black dress with three-quarter sleeves. It was fitted to the waist, flaring out in an A-line. It had a black cloth belt that accentuated her small waist. She carried her black purse and wore black heels. On her head Momma wore a piece of round black lace. As we drove to the church Grandmother Gordon said, "You should have told us you didn't have a proper hat. We certainly could buy you one if J.P. won't let you."

Momma kept her cool as she replied, "You know I don't wear hats. I never did. It would be inappropriate to wear one today. The attention shouldn't be on me and a silly hat. This is about Ezekiel. It's as it should be, but thank you for the offer."

I caught Grandfather Gordon's face in the rear-view mirror. A small smile creased his lips. It was gone before his wife shot him one of her looks. Her pursed lips made the wrinkles around her mouth more pronounced. A slow red heat was climbing up her neck. I wanted Momma to look at me, but she kept staring out the window. Did her face show fury or a smile?

At church our car was in the dirt lot with Abigail's family truck. I thought about the last time I was there for a funeral. I was very young when Granddaddy Tucker died, but the familiar feelings returned. The sorrowful memory filled my body, but now for Abigail. Ezekiel was too young, having lived a life filled with much difficulty. His death was an unfair tragedy that left behind enormous grief.

We entered, surprised to see Ted, Nettie, and her family sitting in the Tucker pew at the front of the church. We hadn't sat there since Granddaddy died. Uncle Roy and Aunt Sara maintained their claim to the seats, and Daddy never challenged them. That day, Ted took a stand for his wife and her family. My eyes quickly scanned the crowd looking for Sara and Roy. They were sitting at the back of the church. I expected to see him in a rage, but he gave a brief nod and dropped his eyes. I was shocked by his compassion. Samuel smiled briefly with a nod as well.

Uncle Frank and his wife sat to the left at the far edge. He didn't look up as we moved forward. We took a seat in the second row with Abigail and two of her siblings. Grandfather and Grandmother Gordon sat farther back in the church, respectfully allowing the family a place of honor.

I reached for Abigail's hand and held tight as we both began to cry. There was a slight commotion at the back of the church, but hiding our tears, we didn't look up. Ted stood, and stepped away from the pew. Following his eyes, I saw Grandma Em, with Daddy on one side and Cal on the other. They walked her to our row. She sat on the end next to Momma. Nettie reached over to squeeze her hand. Cal and Daddy took seats behind us.

The regular Sunday service was tainted by the aura of sadness. The church was packed, with almost everyone staying for the funeral. We remained in our seats while Reverend Howell went out to greet the few parishioners who left. Everyone quietly waited for what was next. I sandwiched Abigail's hand between mine.

When Reverend Howell returned, he asked the men to bring in the coffin. The brothers, along with Ted, Daddy, Cal, and Samuel were the bearers. The coffin was of nice wood, with brass handles. The towns people had given generously. I was glad

Grandmother Gordon thought of the collection. Occasionally she did have a redeeming moment.

The service was simple. Reverend Howell didn't know Ezekiel. He didn't include personal stories about the wonderful boy who was kind, thoughtful, and loving, but talked briefly of death, and especially of someone so young. After concluding his remarks, he invited others to share their thoughts. The family members, overwhelmed with grief, were unable to speak.

After a few minutes we heard a soft voice from the back. It was Miss Walters. She talked about the quiet student in her country school, bright and sweet, a child who suffered bravely all of his life with no bitterness or anger. She said, "He was often too weak to participate in the fun, but found joy in other things including his love for books and willingness to help the younger children. He was a wonderful young man we were blessed to know. He touched the lives of everyone who knew him. He was grace on earth."

No more was needed. Reverend Howell motioned for the bearers to come forward. He invited everyone to the cemetery for a closing prayer. Abigail and I walked hand in hand. As we moved down the aisle, I recognized many children from school. I was surprised to see Charlotte and Virginia with their families. Their faces weren't taunting or nasty. Instead, they were streaked with tears. It was difficult to believe they were capable of such humanity.

I looked to the other side noticing Uncle Frank's empty seat. I was surprised he left. I expected him to stay for Grandma Em. He hadn't seen her since the stroke. I wondered how someone could walk away from his own sister in their final years.

I noticed Aunt Sara sitting alone. Uncle Roy's absence worried me. My mind went to the farm. No one was there and he knew it. I couldn't tell Daddy or the boys, but Daniel was at the back of the church. He looked at Abigail and me. I mouthed, "Uncle Roy. The farm?"

He nodded, silently saying, "It's fine." I should have known Daddy had it covered.

Momma stayed with Grandma Em. We could hear the movement of the people behind us. It was a quiet procession to honor Ezekiel. As we approached the cemetery, my eyes went to the pile of dirt in the corner. I suddenly couldn't breathe. Abigail squeezed my hand tighter as she reached up to steady herself on my arm. I found the strength to continue because she needed me.

Next to the hole was a table with flowers. A small concrete cross with his name chiseled in the horizontal piece sat nearby. Nettie's parents looked to the people around them, grateful for the kindness. Later I learned Daddy bought the grave marker, but the family never knew.

Abigail's parents wanted to escort their son to his final resting place, but did not want to linger there. They asked Reverend Howell for a simple prayer as the men placed the coffin on the boards across the hole. Everyone bowed their heads. His voice resonated in the quiet as he prayed, "For the soul of Ezekiel, may he be welcomed by our Lord. For the family left behind, may they find peace knowing their son and brother is home with the Father. May his short life have meaning and his goodness not be forgotten. We pray the kindness he demonstrated throughout his life be an example to all. Lord, let his love live on through each person here as we share it with those we meet. Look with kindness on this child we commend to your tender care. Amen."

Reverend Howell picked up three flowers. Giving one to Abigail's mother and one to her father, he placed the third flower on top of the coffin. The family followed his example. I went to the table with Abigail. The flowers eventually ran out, but the people continued to process past Ezekiel. Many reached out to touch the wood as they walked by.

Tables and chairs were set up on the church grounds. There were not nearly enough. The food provided was not adequate for the large crowd, but people didn't care. Gracious as they went through the line, each person took small amounts of a few things. Many sat in clusters on the grass or under the trees. No one left. Even those without food stayed.

Daddy and Cal moved Grandma Em outside to the table with Nettie and her parents. Many people stopped to pay their respects to the family and expressed their joy at seeing Grandma Em. Usually these gatherings didn't last but an hour. That day everyone waited for the family to signal the end. It continued on as Abigail's parents delayed leaving, not wanting to return home without their son.

Nettie made the first move by calling the family together. They climbed in the car and truck with everyone watching. After they pulled away, others began to leave. There was no rush. It was a slow, sorrowful departure. There was a feeling of finality no one wanted.

Cal and Daddy helped Grandma Em into our truck. Momma and I climbed in the back of Grandfather Gordon's car, with Grandmother up front. She asked him to take her home before running us out to our place.

At the store Momma got out, giving her mother a warm hug. Grandmother Gordon did not respond at first, standing with her hands at her side. Momma held her until she returned the hug. Momma said, "I love you," before she let go.

Momma joined her father in the front seat. Grandmother Gordon watched us drive away. I waved to acknowledge her as she stood alone. She waved in return. Reflecting on Reverend Howells words, I hoped it was a new beginning for our family. I prayed Ezekiel's life and death would change our relationship with Grandmother Gordon and bring peace.

Daddy stayed at the big house until Ted and Nettie returned. Unable to sleep, I heard him come in after I was in bed. Thoughts of Abigail consumed my mind. I cried for my friend, for her family, and for their great loss. Mixed with my tears were prayers for them, for Ezekiel, and for Grandmother Gordon. I prayed she wouldn't die with anger in her heart and for the time needed to love one another.

In the morning the telephone rang as I heard Grandfather Gordon's Cadillac pull into the drive. Momma met me in the hall saying, "Abigail's waiting for you." I was glad.

I hoped Grandmother Gordon would greet me with a smile and perhaps a hug, but that was too much to ask. Her lips slightly curved as she said good morning, but the warmth I wanted wasn't there. It would take more than one sermon and a night of prayers to change her. I wasn't going to wait for her to be nice. It had to start with me. If Momma could do it, so could I.

At noon Momma pulled up out front. I went to Grandfather Gordon first. Wrapping my arms around him, I gave him a hug and kiss. Next, I turned to my shocked grandmother and repeated the motions. I smiled with a wave goodbye as I ran out the door. Bouncing down the steps I told Abigail, "The meaning of Ezekiel's life. I'm passin' it on."

Momma ate with her parents Wednesday. When they returned from the apartment, everyone was smiling. I was encouraged. It was the second time I offered my special goodbye. Grandfather Gordon was ready, graciously accepting my hug and squeezing me tight. My grandmother leaned in, returning my kiss on the cheek but without the hug. That would take time. Momma watched with a smile.

We paid off the television. It freed our income for other things. We bought something for the baby and fabric for Abigail's mother. She could make clothes for her children and hopefully something for herself. We bought her father a wood carving tool, and little things for her siblings. Abigail objected to using my share for her family, but I insisted. However, she refused to buy anything for herself.

Toward the end of the summer I told Grandmother Gordon about Charlotte and Virginia. I explained how Momma remade my clothes each year, but now there were fewer to pass on. She listened as I shared my concern about the potential abuse. Nodding, she agreed to give it some thought. I was encouraged.

A week later she came out of the storeroom having a fit. She held up a dress with a piece of lace missing from the collar. Next a skirt, then a blouse, each with something wrong. She said, "Look what they sent us. We can't sell these and they're refusing to take them back. I'm half inclined to never purchase from them again. What a waste."

Grandfather Gordon interrupted, "Will they fit the girls? Melanie could fix them. Maybe the girls will want them for a discount."

I raced over to see, but all three items were Abigail's size. Grandmother Gordon had kindly devised a solution for my problem. She picked three beautiful items others would envy. I encouraged Abigail to buy the clothes. At first, she resisted. Grandfather Gordon explained if she bought them at cost it benefited the store. With all three of us working to convince her, she eventually agreed.

When it came time to leave, I gave my grandmother a long hug and whispered, "Thank you." We ran out to show Momma the clothes. Abigail's mother was a good seamstress, yet we never thought to have her make the repairs.

That summer's end came quickly. I had turned a corner with my grandmother. I looked forward to more time at the store and Christmas. Though she was never a warm cozy person, there was love between us.

It was time for Cal to return to school. We didn't see Jean again. We assumed they were in contact but didn't know for sure. He never spoke of her. I thought he was being considerate of Momma. Later we learned she broke up with Cal after her visit. Though we were relieved, in time there would likely be another Jean. Our fear was the next girl could be worse.

Chapter NINETEEN

FALL 1956

A t the beginning of tenth grade, Charlotte and Virginia spared Abigail, instead making me their target. Their teasing centered on my inability to drive. With the new baby, Ezekiel, and my job, I overlooked an important birthday. In June I had turned fifteen.

I didn't care about driving until they made it important. Abigail didn't have to worry. The youngest person in our class, her fifteenth birthday wasn't until the following May. To ease the abuse, I asked if I could get my permit. Momma took me at the end of September. Abigail joined us for the trip to the county building. We stopped for breakfast at a diner and planned a morning of shopping after my test.

I emerged with permit in hand, expecting to drive. I reminded Momma the boys were allowed. She told me to climb in the back. "They drove the truck around the farm long before they got their permits. You'll be practicing on country roads first."

I began to argue. Abigail caught me off guard by supporting Momma. "You're lucky to learn to drive. Ya should be happy."

I gave her a nasty look, angered by her betrayal. She turned away to look out the window. Momma shook her head as she rolled her eyes in the mirror.

We stopped at one store, but it wasn't fun shopping. I was angry with Abigail, and she with me. She stood off to the side, unwilling to look around. Momma finally said, "Let's go, girls. We're done."

It was a quiet ride home. Abigail thanked Momma but didn't acknowledge me. She slammed the door before walking away.

Momma let me have it. "It's not like you to be so inconsiderate. What got into you? Maybe I won't teach you to drive after all. Perhaps you need to experience a little more of Charlotte and Virginia."

I was in shock. What did I do? I looked at her in the mirror, puzzled, with my mouth open. It made her angrier. She continued, "You don't think you were acting like a spoiled brat? You have the chance to silence those girls, but what's Abigail going to do? How will she stop them? Did you ever think about that?"

I answered, "She'll get her permit and shut them up." I wasn't acting like a brat to Abigail. I was angry at Momma, upset because she wouldn't let me drive.

Momma looked in the mirror saying, "What makes you think Abigail will get a permit? Nettie didn't learn to drive until Ted taught her. Their father still doesn't know. He won't allow it for Abigail either."

I was shocked, saying, "But Nettie drives the truck. I thought she learned when she was younger." Momma shook her head no. I felt terrible. I begged, "Please take me back. I want to explain. I thought she'd get her permit in May." Momma wouldn't turn the car around. I needed to say I was sorry in person. I pleaded, but she said the telephone would have to do.

I called Abigail immediately, hoping she would talk to me. I waited a long time to hear her voice. I said, "I'm sorry. I didn't know ya wouldn't be allowed to drive." She thanked me for the call, but simply said she'd see me in the morning.

That evening I met Addie in the field. I didn't want to make the same mistake. As we laid back to watch the clouds move overhead, I asked, "Are ya learnin' to drive?"

"There's no need, I can't drive round here. Mama said 'fore I go away," she explained.

My ignorance at the difference between her life and mine made me ask why. She was silent a few minutes, before saying, "It's not safe, so there's no reason."

Momma was right. I didn't understand how fortunate I was. I had freedom and privileges I took for granted. I decided not to tell Addie about my permit. This time, I chose to be sensitive to my friend.

We talked about the new school year, the teachers, and for the first time she talked of a special boy. She looked away as she said, "There's a boy in my class who likes me. His name's Henry. He's tall and real skinny, not built strong like Papa. He's the intellectual type."

She said it so proudly, "the intellectual type." I asked, "How come all of a sudden I'm hearin' 'bout Henry? Have ya been hidin' him?"

She smiled. "No. He just moved here. His momma brought him and his sisters to live with family down by the factory. She got a job there cleanin'."

"Where's he from?" I asked.

"Toward Tuscaloosa," she replied.

"Why'd they come back here?" I asked.

She said, "So he could go to school."

I was confused. "Don't they have a school in Tuscaloosa?"

She answered, "He wasn't in Tuscaloosa. They were a ways out. Henry was ridin' a bus every day more than an hour each way. This is better."

I continued, "Does his daddy work at the factory too?"

She contemplated my question. In retrospect I think she was deciding how much to tell me. Addie was always cautious about sharing information about her life and that of the other colored families. That day she decided to give me a glimpse inside. "They came here to get away from him and for Henry. He's a beater. Henry says growin' up his whole life that's what his daddy did. He beat on his momma. He went too far when he started beatin' on Henry. He decided Henry shouldn't be takin' time to go to school 'cause it took so long to get to and from, and studyin' at night. Henry couldn't be workin' for the family. His daddy started beatin' on him every day to teach him. His momma tried to help, but he beat her near to death. That was it. She didn't mind takin' a beatin' but not her children."

I was trying to process the story. It wasn't the first time I heard of a boy being forced to drop out of school to help the family. Thinking of Abigail's older brother, Ted, and even Daddy I said, "That's not unusual in the country. Lots of boys drop out."

"But he's the smartest boy in the class. He's goin' to college. Gonna be somebody," she answered.

Showing my ignorance, I asked, "Couldn't he go to a school closer to home so he could work?"

She said, "There weren't none."

The confused look on my face propelled her on. "Every town don't have a colored high school. Most people gots to go a long ways. The only reason we got one is 'cause of the cannin' factory."

Still puzzled, I said, "Why?"

"Cause of the school, people'll come here to work, and they might even work for less if they can bring their children to get educated."

"So, all the kids in your school, their parents work at the cannin' factory?"

She laughed. "No silly, just some of 'em. The others come from all over. We're the only colored high school for more than fifty miles."

I asked, "Do they all walk to school like you?"

Again, she laughed. "Fifty miles? No, they come in buses."

I shook my head, so confused. "But you don't ride a bus. How come they get one?"

"I'm not talkin' 'bout school buses. Some take the regular bus that runs through here every day. Others take church buses. They stop and pick people up along the way. And some of 'em come in truck buses. People put a cover over the back with benches inside. They charge somethin' to ride each day. There's one that comes through here. He stops and lets us ride for free if there's room. Sometimes we just stand on the bumper."

I thought back to the many times I watched for Addie, but often didn't see her. Was she in one of those buses? There was so much I didn't understand about her life. I assumed every town had a colored school that included grades one through twelve. I was surprised to learn most colored schools ended at the sixth or eighth grade. I took education for granted, but not everyone had the same opportunity.

I was embarrassed. We watched the clouds in silence. After a time, I said, "I'm sorry. I didn't know."

Again, there was quiet in the field. I needed to break the silence condemning me. I asked, "Is he handsome?"

She giggled with embarrassment. "Of course, I wouldn't like him if he wasn't. He's dark, but that's alright 'cause he's real smart. Mama doesn't like him, not yet. She's just seen him. If she talks to him, she'll change her mind 'cause he talks real fine."

I asked, "What's he goin' to college for?"

She smiled. "To be a teacher like me. We got it all planned. We get good grades and he's workin' to save."

"Ya never told me that. Did ya always want to be a teacher?" I said.

She shrugged her shoulders as she replied, "Yeah, but Henry knows how to do it. He's gonna help me."

I listened to Addie's dream of attending college, marveling at her plans. Henry's arrival in our town had a significant impact. His goals and desires inspired many to want the same. As she was talking, I prayed Uncle Roy would never find out. He and his friends would make sure those dreams never came true.

We watched the stars begin to appear one by one. Our time was nearing the end. I hated to leave her, sad to say goodbye. We'd see each other the next week, but it was the realization that someday we'd leave that field for good. Our conversation about the future reminded me the day was coming. Our friendship would end. We would move on to new lives not allowed to exist side by side.

The next day Abigail joined us for church and dinner at the Hotel. She returned home with me, but we didn't go into the field or watch the clouds. I was careful to never take Abigail out back. We sat on the front porch, entering only through that door, watched television in the parlor, or stayed in my room. I didn't want Addie to see her, or know there was someone else in my life. It was silly. She certainly knew I had other friends, but I felt guilty. Abigail was the friend I didn't have to hide.

That day, Abigail talked about her father and his rules. Her family knew Nettie could drive but kept the truth from him. Remembering the times Momma or Ted drove Nettie to see her parents, I assumed it was because they didn't want to be without the truck. I never realized it was so her father wouldn't know.

I didn't press Momma to drive. I occasionally got behind the wheel if it was just us, but never with Abigail or in town where Charlotte or Virginia could see. As a result, the harassment escalated.

In early November Momma picked us up after work. The evil allies were across the street at the gas station. Abigail turned to me saying, "Why don't you drive?" She turned to Momma. "Would it be alright?"

Momma shot a look toward Charlotte and Virginia. Shutting down the engine, she moved to the back seat. "You girls sit up front," she said with a smile.

I wanted to say no, but it would cause a scene. She tried to assure me I'd do fine. I never drove in town, only on country roads with an occasional car passing by. I wasn't convinced it was the best way to put those girls in their place.

My grandparents watched from the window. I waited until there were no cars in sight before pulling away from the curb. I wasn't turning around in front of Charlotte and Virginia. I continued four blocks, making a very wide turn after they were out of view. I took several turns on side streets, returning to Main Street. Thankfully Charlotte and Virginia were gone. I drove Abigail home, and on to our house. From that day, Momma sat in back and I drove.

Thanksgiving came with a new twist. Momma invited her parents to our home. Saturday, she came in the store making small talk before asking the big question. It surprised everyone. I expected a sour look from my grandmother, but instead saw a woman on the verge of tears. Her expression was soft with a slight curve to her lips as she said, "That would be lovely." Momma gave each of her parents a kiss as she left. I gave them an excited hug and kiss as well.

Daddy, Ted, and Daniel took an afternoon to go turkey hunting. They got two, a big one for Ted since Nettie's family was joining them, and a small one for Daniel. Momma kept his to prep for Thanksgiving morning. Grandfather Gordon provided our turkey from the store. Thanksgiving morning Momma and I prepared both turkeys, double potatoes, and stuffing with the extra in baking dishes for Daniel. We sent a jar of Grandma Em's green beans and an apple pie as well.

I helped Daddy deliver the food. The sagging porch and railing of that dilapidated ramble of a house was repaired. The missing shutters were in their places and the junk strewn around the yard was gone. Daddy heard my gasp. Smiling he patted my knee saying, "Daniel's been workin' hard."

The children came out to thank us for the bountiful meal. I gave Daniel the written instructions detailing how to cook everything. He nodded, but the elusive smile didn't appear. He returned to the house that I hoped would someday be mine. He was no longer seeing Ruth. She had graduated the previous June and left for secretarial school, renewing my dreams.

We set up the dining room with Momma's special china from the hutch, a gift from her parents for her eighteenth birthday. I asked when she used them before. She smiled and said, "Never. I was waiting for my parents." She went back to her task, not saying another word.

Momma and I wore dresses, with Daddy in a shirt and tie. Grandmother Gordon entered looking to the right to see our parlor, then to the left to see Momma's china and crystal. She smiled saying, "Melanie, your table is beautiful."

I took their coats while Momma led them into the parlor. Daddy fixed the men a drink in the kitchen, with a glass of wine for the ladies. It was like watching a television show instead of sitting in our own home. The only thing missing was Cal. At the last minute he called to say he was spending the holiday with friends. Momma was heartbroken, but tried to hide her disappointment. It was still a special day, surprising all of us.

With Thanksgiving over, we looked toward Christmas. Cal was coming home and there was a new baby to celebrate. Abigail and I were bartering to buy gifts for our families. She had so many people, but when I offered some of my credit she refused. I talked her into letting me buy the gifts for Ted, Nettie, and the baby from both of us.

I easily found gifts for everyone, but my biggest challenge was the Gordons. Ted bought Nettie a camera to take photos of Baby Emily. Looking at the pictures one day, I realized what I wanted to give them. I borrowed the camera. Sharing my idea with Abigail, she offered to have her father make a frame. It needed four slots, one for Momma and Daddy, one for Ted's family, one for Cal, and one for Abigail and me. She objected, but I assured her they would want her in the picture as well. Nettie gave us a sample picture to show their father. Not buying anything from the store, allowed me to keep it a surprise.

When Cal arrived, Christmas officially began. Momma made Divinity Fudge, we ventured into the woods for our tree, and on Sunday the four of us decorated it with the candles and ornaments. I placed my gifts underneath for everyone to see.

Abigail and I took a break from the store over the vacation. On Christmas Eve we were going to Grandmother Gordon's, but that morning Momma started preparing salted ham and potatoes. The smell from the kitchen woke me. Coming downstairs I was curious why she was cooking so early. She smiled and said, "It's for Daniel. It's his Christmas bonus. I want those children to have something special to eat. He's leaving at noon. I need to get it ready."

I joined her, anxiously waiting for him and Daddy. After we packed the food, Momma brought a box from her room. I opened the top to look inside. Slapping my hand, she said, "Just a couple gifts from Santa."

Upon arriving, Daddy instructed Daniel to carry everything to the truck. Momma followed with a pie. Giving him a hug she said, "You take this to those children and have a Merry Christmas." He was embarrassed, but grateful. I stood behind her waiting to be acknowledged, but he dropped his head as he turned to leave. I was disappointed. I wanted him to know I helped.

Later Momma and I walked across the field to deliver a Christmas cake. I took Addie a book covered in purple fabric with a bouquet of pink roses embroidered on the front. The lined pages could be used as a journal, diary, or for a story. She had a gift for me as well. I opened the wrapping to find a collection of hair pins with fancy ends. I said, "They're beautiful. Thank you."

She said, "They're gonna make ya the envy of Charlotte and Virginia."

I laughed and said, "It'll take all of these and then some."

Momma said, "Hush, your hair is fine. Don't give those girls the time of day."

Miss Emily added, "And I like the new style. It looks real nice."

I had started growing my hair out. Each night we rolled it in Spoolie curlers trying to turn the kinks into waves. It was uncomfortable sleeping, but I was desperate.

We visited for a few more minutes, and wished them Merry Christmas. I thanked Miss Emily for her kind words and Addie for my beautiful gifts. I gave her a hug as I said goodbye, happy she was still my friend.

Momma and I stayed at the big house in the afternoon while Ted and Nettie took Baby Emily to the Gordons. Because of Grandma Em, they couldn't join us for our traditional Christmas Eve.

They were gone longer than expected. I drove home to get ready, returning so Momma could go next. Grandma Em was up from her nap. She didn't look well. The previous week she came down with a cold she couldn't shake. I told her stories about school and the store, but she didn't perk up.

Ted and Nettie finally pulled in the drive. Sending Nettie and the baby in, he waited to take me home. He told me about their surprising visit. "Grandmother Gordon was nice and didn't say one bad thing 'bout bein' a farmer. I almost went outside to check the address. She hugged and kissed the baby the whole time. My little girl turned her into mush. Ya should've seen it." He was laughing as he finished his story. "Sorry we're late. She didn't want us to leave."

I smiled saying, "She's different now. She still doesn't smile much, but at Thanksgiving she was nice to Daddy." I was happy he got to see our new grandmother. Cal would meet her that evening.

Everyone was waiting for me. I gathered my present from under the tree. The ride seemed to take longer than usual. I was anxious to get there. As we walked in, Momma and I gave each a hug and kiss hello. Daddy shook Grandfather Gordon's hand, leaning in to kiss Grandmother Gordon on the cheek. I turned to see the shock on Cal's face. He didn't know what to do. He awkwardly reached out to shake their hands. I released a little burst of giggles. We moved beyond the greeting spot into the living area.

Grandfather Gordon got everyone a drink as we visited with a new air of familiarity and comfort. Cal was shaking his head and gawking in amazement.

Everything was wonderful: the food, the conversation, and the atmosphere. We talked, told stories, and laughed with everyone smiling. When Momma and I started to clear the table, the men pitched in. Grandmother Gordon said, "We're not wasting our time doing dishes. Please everyone." But Momma insisted. She took care of the food, Daddy washed, Cal and I dried, and my grandparents put the dishes away. We continued to visit, but it wasn't the formal atmosphere of the past. It felt like a family.

Once finished, we returned to the living area. It was nicely furnished, though dated. Most were the same pieces from Momma's childhood. The exception was a new television in the corner.

We began handing out the presents. In the past Momma and Daddy gave them one gift from the family. This year they were overwhelmed by the surprises from Cal and me. I held mine back to be last. Momma opened the box on her lap, assuming it was another piece of china or linens. Instead, inside were packs of flower seeds, garden gloves, canvas with different sections containing a garden spade, claw, and mat for her knees. Next, she removed a crystal flower vase carefully wrapped in tissue paper. Grandmother Gordon gave my mother something special, truly for her.

Daddy opened the box on his lap to find a black leather pouch. Unlatching the buckle, he unrolled it to find a series of pockets with various tools, screws, nuts, bolts, and a small roll of heavy wire. We were shocked by the useful gift. Looking up he replaced the surprised look with a smile. "Thank you very much. This will be perfect in the field. Ted will appreciate it. He won't have to walk to the barn if I break down. Albert, Rebecca, I am truly grateful."

I looked at Grandmother Gordon. She was nervous, with a tight smile on her lips and fear in her eyes, afraid the years of cruelty would make it impossible for him to accept the new her. As he spoke I watched the fear wash from her face. The tight smile was replaced with a genuine one.

It was time for them to open the gift from Momma. I was concerned the usual table cloth and napkins were too impersonal, but on top was an envelope. I recognized Momma's note card with small flowers from her garden shellacked on the cover, preserving a little piece of her forever. Reading the words, Grandmother Gordon's eyes began to tear. She passed it to Grandfather Gordon. He smiled, looking up at Momma. "The best present ever. Thank you." Lowering his eyes back to the writing on the card he read, "Wednesday dinner for life." The promise of those special midday visits continuing even after I was gone was the kindest gift she could give them.

Grandmother pulled back the tissue to see the beautiful table wear. She glowed as she said, "I'll use them for Easter when we're all together."

Momma said, "Maybe sooner if you like." Her parents smiled. No doubt, it was the happiest Christmas ever.

Next Cal exchanged gifts with them. They unwrapped a book about the history of Alabama. My grandfather was very pleased. It was a welcome addition to his collection. Cal picked up the large box addressed to him. As he lifted the lid, pulling back the paper he jumped, pumping his fist. He reached in, removing a jacket with his college name across the back. Cal thanked them profusely as he tried it on. They were beaming, pleased with his reaction.

Finally, it was my turn. I opened mine first, keeping their surprise for last. My box was small and light. Tearing off the paper, I saw the wording across the top. I looked up squealing, "Thank you."

It was a camera. Grandmother Gordon took a bag from under the table. Inside were rolls of film. A simple thank you was not enough. I rushed to give each a long warm hug as I whispered, "Thank you. Thank you. Thank you. I love you."

She squeezed me in return. Grandfather Gordon whispered in my ear, "You are a special gift to us. Thank you!"

I knew he was thanking me for giving them a family, though he was responsible as well. He started the process by offering Abigail and me a job, even though he didn't need the help. My role was breaking the ice that surrounded my grandmother. I whispered back, "You're welcome."

The final gift of the night was mine. I carefully retrieved the rectangle. Kneeling in front of my grandparents, I said, "Open it together. I'll hold it. I want you to see it at the same time."

It was a surprise for everyone. As my grandparents tore the paper, I watched their faces. Her hand went to her mouth as she gasped. They removed the paper to expose the frame made of walnut, and oiled to a beautiful shine. Rose buds were carved at each corner connected by a trail of vines. There was a piece of glass in each opening holding the four pictures of my family and Abigail. I was anxious for everyone to see. Grandfather Gordon pulled his wife close. He said, "It is the most precious gift, truly a treasure. Thank you."

I explained, "It's not just from me. It's from Abigail too. Her father made the frame. She's like my sister. You do as much for her as you do for me. We love you."

Grandmother Gordon nodded saying, "It's as it should be, definitely."

She asked Daddy to hang it on the wall where it could be seen from everywhere. I put film in my camera to record that Christmas. I snapped pictures of Momma and Daddy, then of Cal with my grandparents. Cal took a photo of them with me. I cherish the reminders of that evening.

We were happy in the moment, but it was not to last. There was a knock at the door. It was Sheriff Hosper asking to speak to Daddy outside. My first thought was Addie and her family. There was always that fear. My mind raced to Uncle Roy. He knew we were at the Gordons. It was a perfect time to hurt them. How could he on Christmas Eve?

Daddy was gone a few minutes. He returned, leaving the door open while he got his coat. Sheriff Hosper stepped in saying, "Good evenin' folks. Sorry to ruin your celebration." Though the room was full of people, his eyes were focused on me. I felt my whole body tense, in part with fear of why he came, but mostly because of the way he looked at me.

Daddy interrupted my thoughts. "Tom Crandall was drivin' home. He saw lights down over the bank. It's Ben. They called in to Hosper. He saw my car out front, thought I'd want to go with him. Tom thinks he's dead. Doc Batt's headed out to make sure. We'll drive out to talk to Daniel. Cal, get your Momma and Missy home. Albert, Rebecca, I'm real sorry, but I need to go. Daniel's one of my hands and I don't want him to hear 'bout his father from someone else. Melanie, I'll see ya at the house. Roland'll drop me off on his way back to town."

After Daddy closed the door, I felt a cool breeze across my face and an involuntary shiver throughout my body. Our wonderful Christmas was over. Grandfather Gordon asked Cal and me to help him in the store, while the women went to the kitchen. We gathered some canned goods and he wrapped packages of meat from the cooler. As we worked he asked Cal about school. Cal didn't have a steady girl, but talked of his many friends. As the result of a writing class, he wrote several articles for the school paper. Enjoying it so much, he changed his major to journalism. Momma and Daddy didn't know. Daddy insisted Cal major in Accounting. Places always need someone to manage the books, providing Cal solid job opportunities. I was sure Daddy wouldn't approve of the change.

Momma came in carrying our coats. My grandparents walked us to the door at the front of the store. Cal took the box waiting on the counter to the car. Grandfather Gordon said, "Take it to those children. Tell Daniel people in town heard and wanted to do something. Maybe he'll take it. He's awful proud." Momma assured him she'd insist. We all hugged her parents as we left.

Everyone was quiet in the car. About a mile out Cal said, "Who were those people? They weren't my grandparents."

Momma and I laughed out loud. She said, "Well, they are your grandparents, the new and improved version."

Chapter TWENTY

FINAL DAYS OF *1956*

Driving home we passed Mr. Emerson's hearse returning to town. His normal speed told us Ben was dead. We came upon Ruth's father, Buck, with the truck hooked up to his wrecker. Cal slowed. Weeds and brush were stuck to the front. The windshield on the driver's side was smashed, with a hole in the middle. We tried to see where it went over the bank, but the darkness limited our view. We continued on in silence.

At home we waited for Daddy. When he came in, his tired body fell into the chair. Momma asked, "Was he dead?" Though certain of the answer, we wanted confirmation.

He nodded. "Yeah, his head went through the windshield. Pretty sure he was drunk. There was an empty bottle on the floor."

She asked, "What about the truck?"

He frowned. "It'll be fine, but it's not Daniel's. When I took care of the farm, he wouldn't sign over the truck. The thing's still in Ben's name. The boy needs it for the farm, and those drunks in town'll try to take it and everything else."

I asked, "But what can ya do now? He's dead." He shot Momma a telling look. He had a plan, but wouldn't share it in front of Cal and me. Angry, I continued. "Daddy we're not children. We care 'bout Daniel too. If there's somethin' ya can do, we aren't gonna tell."

Momma gave him a slight nod. Turning toward us he said, "When Hosper walked away, I took the registration. I'm gonna see if a friend of mine can fix it. He works at the courthouse. There was also a wad of bills in his shirt pocket. I took that for Daniel, but couldn't give it to him tonight. Hosper said he'd have to hold the wallet 'til everything's cleared up. I don't know if there was more money in there, but Daniel'll never see it. Those leeches in town'll be all over it. I'll take Daniel first thing Wednesday mornin' to get his license, and see if I can take care of that truck. Missy, ya can't tell anybody. Not even Abigail."

I assured him I understood. I was surprised Daniel didn't have a license. He drove Daddy's truck on the farm. I never gave it a thought. Because he couldn't use his father's truck, he never forced the issue.

Momma asked how the children took the news. He sadly said, "Not a sound from any of 'em. Daniel asked what he needed to do, but I told him I'd take care of the body. Emerson said we could make arrangements Wednesday. With tomorrow being Christmas, he didn't want to deal with it 'til then."

Momma started thinking out loud. "I wonder if those children will have anything for Christmas. Do you think he got them anything before he died? What if they wake up to nothing but what I sent?"

Daddy reassured her. "Daniel bought little things when we were in town. Your mother wrapped 'em. They'll have somethin' to open in the mornin'."

I asked, "What 'bout Daniel? He won't have anything."

"I took care of Daniel. He needed a rake for his tractor. I bought one off of old man Harvey. It's used, but in good shape. It'll work well. We'll take it up in the mornin'." It wouldn't be a present under the tree, but he'd appreciate it.

Momma added, "And they'll have food. My father sent groceries. Missy, we can make breakfast if you want to get up early.

Hotcakes, sausage, and scrambled eggs will give them a real surprise." I nodded in agreement. We talked a bit longer before she shooed us to bed.

In the morning, we made their breakfast while Daddy was taking care of the animals. We packed it in a box with towels wrapped around each dish to keep it warm. In light of everything they were going through it seemed like so little.

Ted and Cal were waiting at the barn with the rake hooked up to the tractor. Daddy took our food along with Grandfather Gordon's. Our breakfast was ready when they returned. Daniel was grateful for the rake, and asked Daddy to thank Momma for the food and presents. She said, "It's probably the nicest Christmas since their mother died." The irony of her statement wasn't lost on any of us.

We ate breakfast before opening our gifts. I was grateful to have Momma, Daddy, and Cal gathered for Christmas, but my thoughts continually turned to Daniel and his family. How sad it was for them.

We were going to church at eleven, to the big house to exchange gifts around three, then staying for supper and the evening with Grandma Em. Ted and Nettie were going to have Christmas with her family. Nettie would have a day with someone else doing the cooking. It was easy to forget she had the constant responsibility of caring for Grandma Em, though she never indicated it was a burden.

At church all eyes turned our direction as we entered. There was no time to talk. The music began immediately, followed by the readings, and Reverend Howell's sermon about the season. His words didn't help Daddy's mood.

After the service, people asked about Daniel's family. Ruth and her mother, Jane, came to talk with Momma. She was Momma's best friend in school. Momma told them what little we knew, explaining that Daniel was meeting with Mr. Emerson the next day. She assured them Daddy was helping. Ruth listened, her deep concern for Daniel evident on her face and in her voice. I thought she broke up with him to go to secretarial school, but maybe it wasn't her choice.

Soon Daddy was calling us to leave. He was obviously angry. On the ride home he said, "They come to church pretendin' to be upstandin', but they're a bunch of crooks. I knew they'd be after money from Daniel. I told ya there'd be trouble. Doug Jennings says he won that truck in a bet. He's goin' to Hosper to get it. The rest of 'em started talkin' 'bout how they're gonna get their money takin' that farm. I told 'em everything's in Daniel's name. If that good for nothin' bet that farm or truck they should have checked to see if he owned it. Told 'em if they go after a bunch of orphans, I'd make sure everyone knows. I'll paste their names on a billboard. Like those kids don't have enough problems. Doug had the nerve to say 'it won't matter once the state takes 'em, they won't be takin' nothin' from orphans then.' They're gonna get those kids taken away from Daniel. They've suffered enough. They can't lose each other."

I expected anger, but her voice was calm. "They won't take the children if Daniel has a proper home. They never take children if there's a woman in the house. He needs to get a woman living there."

Daddy was near yelling, "Daniel hasn't got money to hire help. He can barely afford to keep 'em fed and in clothes."

"Oh, for goodness sake, tell Daniel he needs a woman living in that house so the state won't take the kids. He'll solve the problem." She was being cryptic.

We rode along in silence. Momma was shaking her head at his denseness. Suddenly he turned to her asking, "Do ya think Ruth'll still have him?"

Momma nodded. "She's miserable at secretarial school, and begging to come home. He couldn't offer her a future, not with his father alive. He was being a stand-up man when he asked Buck to send her away, but she loves Daniel and now he can give her a life. Tell him to get a woman living in the house and soon."

As I listened to her words my heart began to race. Daniel wanted Ruth to leave because he couldn't marry her. All this time I was foolish enough to think it was over. But it wasn't. He loved her, and her reaction at church showed she loved him.

At home Daddy called his friend. He didn't care if it was Christmas. Explaining the problem with the truck, he asked if the registration could be put in Daniel's name, and dated for some time last year. After Daddy hung up he said, "They leave empty slots in the books for emergencies. I told him Doug Jennings was tryin' to cause trouble for the kids. It was all the reason he needed. He's glad to help if it means stickin' it to Jennings. Melanie, tomorrow while I'm gone ya need to call Bob Fillmore. Tell him 'bout those vultures in town and to get the papers ready. He's a good man. He helped us with the farm. He'll know what to do."

It was time to go to the big house for Christmas. I couldn't erase Momma's suggestion from my mind. Daniel wasn't free. My parents seemed unaware of my pain, so focused on helping the children. I was glad we were going to Ted's because I needed the distraction.

Grandma Em was weak as she struggled to open her presents. I saw the worried look on Momma's face. After a couple hours, Ted and Nettie left with the baby. We guided Grandma Em in to rest. It was quiet in the house. Momma brought a chicken to roast with stuffing and mashed potatoes. We made cherry cobbler with vanilla ice cream for dessert. We set up the dining room while Daddy and Cal finished in the barn. It was lonely without Nettie, like the house was missing something.

When the men came in, Daddy asked, "Where's Mother?"

Momma looked concerned as she said, "Still sleeping. She doesn't look good. That cold was too much for her."

I went in to check on her. She was awake. I sat on the edge of the bed, telling her supper was almost ready. She smiled, indicating it smelled good. Daddy came to help her into the dining room. She seemed a little better that evening, even smiling at times. I was relieved. It was nice being together as a family at the big house.

Ted and Nettie returned late that evening. Baby Emily was tired and cranky, so we hurried to leave. Daddy told Ted he'd be gone much of the next day. Daniel's difficulties had temporarily escaped me as I focused on Grandma Em, but now they returned.

That night I crawled into bed with a mix of emotions. I was heartbroken knowing Daniel would never be mine, combined with sadness for him and his family, worry for Grandma Em, joy for our Christmas with the Gordons, and concern for Abigail's family as they navigated the holiday without Ezekiel. With those thoughts, I drifted off to sleep.

I awoke in the morning to find Daddy and Cal gone. I knew he'd tell Daniel about Momma's idea. I prayed Daniel no longer loved Ruth and would tell Daddy he loved me. I was anxious all day, waiting for him to return.

News from Daddy at supper was that everything went well. Daniel got his license. They checked on the truck. It needed a new windshield, but wouldn't be ready until Friday. Sheriff Hosper stopped to get the registration, but it wasn't in the glove box. He told Buck he'd call the courthouse later in the week to get a copy. By then, it would show Daniel's name to match the title, and both dated for when the farm was signed over.

Daniel wanted a private burial in the family cemetery on his farm. Ben would be laid to rest next to his wife. Daniel didn't want town people there, only the children and our family. He selected a simple casket. Daddy arranged for someone to dig and fill the grave.

As Daddy kept relaying information, he was neglecting to tell us what really mattered. I waited as did Momma. She finally stopped his rambling. "What about the kids and the state? Did you talk to Daniel?"

He burst out laughing, saying, "Ya don't care if the truck runs or the coffin's gold-plated. Just tell me, is there gonna be a weddin'?" He continued, "Well, I don't know for sure, but I wouldn't be surprised. I told Daniel 'bout your thinkin'. At the garage he talked to Buck in the office. They came out smilin'."

Neither of them gave a thought to how I might feel. Daniel needed to do something, but I was heartbroken. My parents continued talking about the children, the things that needed to be done, and Daniel's future. I quietly listened, overwhelmed with sadness and on the verge of tears.

To escape, I went to visit Grandma Em. She seemed better, not as tired. I told her all Daddy accomplished for Daniel and the possible marriage. She detected the sadness in my voice. She placed her good hand over mine as she looked into my eyes. She carefully formed the words, "Not for you."

I couldn't help it. I began to cry. She took my hand saying, "Shhh ...you college."

I looked up to see her nodding with a smile. I had been focused on a life with Daniel, and never considered college. My time with her helped. It temporarily eased my sadness.

Baby Emily stayed with us while Nettie cleaned upstairs. It lightened the mood. The baby loved sitting on Grandma Em's lap and playing with her fingers. They were very close, our two Emilys.

I stayed late. As long as Grandma Em was awake I took advantage of the opportunity. I missed her when she was ill. I was glad she was better.

The next morning Daddy was up early, gone with Daniel. They were back in time for the noon meal with Cal. Momma was giddy the entire time. Daddy rolled his eyes, frowning at her. She did look silly. He said, "You'd think Daniel was proposin' to you instead of Ruth." They both laughed, but I didn't join them.

That afternoon Addie came over. She was working most of the vacation, but James brought her home partway through the day. Momma went to help with Grandma Em. Alone, I told my friend, "I think Daniel's gonna marry Ruth." I didn't try to hold in my emotions. Addie knew about my early dreams, the disappointment, and the return of my hopes. She understood my pain. I continued, "They're makin' plans and nobody cares that I'm losin' him. The only dream I ever had was marryin' him and livin' here with Momma and Daddy."

She put her arm around me saying, "I know it don't feel like it, but it's gonna be alright. Daniel needs a wife now and you can't be that. Ya can't raise those boys. They need someone who can take care of 'em proper."

I knew she was right, but dreams don't die that easily. We listened to the drone of the television, but my mind was elsewhere. After a prolonged silence she said, "Let's make cookies. Sweets are always good when you're hurtin'."

I nodded. "Peanut butter alright?" She smiled in return.

As we prepared the dough, Addie shared stories about the Christmas decorations in the white ladies' homes. Trying to lift my spirits, she described the beauty of some and the ugliness of others. As we were making the crisscross to flatten the balls, I accidently flung a fork of flour that landed on her arm. She responded by deliberately flipping a fork full my way. She immediately began apologizing until I shot one back. We coated each other in white powder until the bowl was empty. We fell to the floor in two heaps of giggles. While the cookies baked we worked together cleaning the mess in the kitchen, but our efforts couldn't hide the evidence in our hair. I wanted to take a picture of us, but knew I couldn't develop it. It would remain a picture in my mind only.

Enjoying the cookies in front of the television, I asked her about college. I didn't share Grandma Em's comment, or that maybe I was considering it for me.

She said, "Mama's savin' as much as we can. Henry and me are studyin' to get scholarship money. It's real hard, but I'm tryin'." I assumed her income was necessary for the family, but Addie was working for her future while my only concern each week was what I'd buy myself.

Time with Addie helped. Her words of wisdom gave me something to think about. I also realized her dream of college could be mine as well.

Later Daniel dropped Daddy at the house, keeping the truck overnight. Cal was taking the car to visit friends. It was Momma, Daddy, and me. We had sandwiches in front of the television so it didn't feel so lonely.

When the telephone rang Momma was out of her chair and half way to the kitchen before I could lift myself off the floor. She came back beaming. "He did it. Ruth and Daniel are getting married Sunday. Jane asked me to make a cake. We have to pull a wedding together in two days. We need to get that house cleaned for Ruth. See what it's like inside. She'll have enough on her hands taking care of them. She needs a fresh start. They'll be out in the morning for the burial. I'll talk to Daniel then, and see if we can start tomorrow. The wedding is going to be family and us. Those children will need clothes. We need suits for the boys and a dress for Amy. Missy, come help me. I saved the boys suits in the trunk and some of your best dresses. Let's see what we've got. They can try them on tomorrow. We're having a wedding!" She went over to sit on Daddy's lap. Giving him a kiss, she said, "Finally, those kids are getting a chance at life. Daniel's getting married!" With that she hopped up and motioned for me to follow.

Momma seemed oblivious to my despair. We gathered the clothes and cleaning supplies. Finally, she said I could go to bed. I welcomed the escape, but slept fitfully. I woke to check the clock regularly. Daniel's marriage was the right thing, but it didn't erase the pain.

We dressed in casual pants with boots for the burial. Reverend Howell wasn't coming; Daniel didn't see the need. He didn't ask Daddy or anyone to speak knowing they likely couldn't say anything nice.

Ruth and her parents were there when we arrived. Jane said, "Daniel asked us to wait here. The children will be out soon."

Ted and Nettie pulled in. Abigail was at the big house with Grandma Em and the baby. We waited another ten minutes before the family joined us. Daniel and his brothers headed for the barn, while Amy walked to Ruth's car. They emerged carrying shovels. Daddy said, "I made arrangements to have the grave filled in."

Daniel said, "We want to do it."

Daddy got two shovels from the back of his truck. Ted grabbed one from his. Buck asked if there was another in the barn. The boys retrieved a spade with a broken handle that was still usable. We started across the field with Daniel and the children leading the way. It was a quiet procession.

His tractor and wagon were by the grave. Leaning the shovels against a tree, the men unloaded the casket, placing it on the boards across the hole. Everyone gathered around as Daniel nodded at Amy. Pulling a piece of paper from her pocket, she slowly unfolded it to read a poem. It was simple, a child's thoughts about death, and the dream of her parents being together. Though none of us were mourning his passing, all were brought to tears by her words. Our grief was not for this particular loss, but for the loss of their childhood and family. After she finished, the children held hands and recited a childhood prayer. We joined them with, "Amen."

The men lowered the casket. Gathering the shovels, they began dropping the dirt. The sound of it hitting wood echoed, causing me to shiver. Amy buried her face in Ruth's coat, covering her ears. It was a reminder that the man we all despised had been a father loved by his children.

Daniel looked at the mound as he said, "May ya now be at peace." Turning to us he continued. "Thank you for bein' here today and for everything you've done." His voice quivered with emotion. Unable to say more, he dropped his gaze. The silence indicated the end of the service.

He offered everyone a ride in the wagon with his brothers sitting on the wheel hubs of the tractor. Amy cuddled in as Ruth's arms wrapped around her. Everyone was quiet.

At the house Momma pulled Daniel aside. She rejoined us saying, "Daniel and the children don't have anything planned right now. I suggested we have supper here tonight. We can gather at six thirty. Jane, will y'all come back then?"

She nodded and offered to bring pies. Ruth looked at Momma. "Here?" she asked.

Momma smiled saying, "Yes Ruth, here. Missy and I'll get this house in shape. You come back later." Nettie offered to help as well. Abigail would take care of things at the big house.

Amy helped us unload the car. The house was generally picked up, but dusty and dirty. From the front door we walked to a room in the middle of the house with a beamed table that had a bench on each side, an old tattered sofa, and an odd side chair. It was where they lived.

We opened a set of pocket doors into the parlor. It was overflowing with furniture covered with sheets or blankets. We found a cabinet and hutch with linens and china. At the edge of the room was a settee with two upholstered chairs, an end table, and a coffee table. Under a blanket against the wall was a dark brown piano. Momma said, "She played at church and for the choir at school. Your momma was very talented." She looked at Amy as she continued, "She played for you children all the time hoping you'd love music like she did."

Amy stared at the piano, silent. Momma said, "Let's uncover the rest of these things and get this house ready for Ruth. She'll have enough on her hands with all of you."

Amy nodded. She was just three years old when her mother died. They didn't have time to build a relationship or make memories. With Ruth, maybe she'd have a little of what I had with Momma.

Nettie was at work in the kitchen cleaning the cupboards and washing every dish. The kitchen was a large shed structure on the side of the house, an obvious addition. At the back of the house was the original cooking room with a large stone fireplace, a bread oven, and old cast iron pot rack. There was a bed against the far wall, a chest of drawers in the corner with a chair next to it, and a door into a bathroom. On the floor were a couple pairs of pants, a flannel shirt, and dirty thermal underwear. They were Ben's clothes. Amy stood in the doorway. Her eyes filled with tears as she turned away. We were moving them along so quickly, we overlooked the fact they had lost their father. He may have seemed useless to us, but not to them.

Momma said, "I'll take care of this room and the bathroom. Just help me with the bed."

We moved it outside. It smelled like urine and vomit. I wondered how many nights their father came home drunk. More importantly, what were those nights like for the children? Momma decided to clean the room, but leave it empty, allowing Ruth and the children to determine its use.

She said, "You start cleaning the dining room. Amy can help you. Move the table and benches to the kitchen, and push that old sofa and chair out on the porch. The boys can haul it away later. After you clean the floors we'll move the dining furniture in and clean the front room for tonight. We'll do upstairs tomorrow. Let's get this house presentable."

I vacuumed the walls, floors, and light fixtures like Momma did during spring cleaning. I could see the difference with each stroke as I removed the dust and cobwebs that had accumulated for years. What looked dirty and old was coming back to life. The walls were a cream-colored paper with a light lace doily pattern on the surface. I was surprised to see something so fancy in that rundown farm house. Just as the remnant of the exterior impressed me, I was in awe of how lovely it must have been inside as well. I had a moment of wistfulness, wishing I was getting the house ready for me, but seeing Amy with Ruth that morning reinforced I wasn't the right person.

We moved the dining furniture into place. Momma smiled at the final effect saying, "This was always such a beautiful room. Amy, choose linens and china to set the table."

I tackled the front room. Amy came in, opening the lid of the piano to run her fingers over the keys. I said, "Ruth plays. Maybe she could teach you." She looked up for a moment with a wistful look in her eyes.

Momma went upstairs to look around. Coming down, she went directly to the kitchen. Nettie called Amy for help with the dishes. Momma walked back through the hall motioning for me to follow. On the second floor there were two bedrooms open, one for Amy and the other for the boys. At the end of the hall was a locked door next to another bathroom with a locked door inside. I said, "They have two bathrooms?"

She nodded. "Ben put this in when she was expecting Amy. She was so sick and weak, and needed a bathroom close by. Whatever was wrong caused problems in that way, so he took one of the bedrooms up here to make this for her."

I asked, "They never knew what was wrong?"

Saddened about the death of her friend, she didn't speak, but simply shook her head no.

She pulled a key ring out of her pocket. "I found these in the dresser downstairs. Let's see if they open the doors."

She tried each key until we heard a click. Inside was a double four-poster bed with a cedar chest against the foot board. The walls were lined with a mirrored bureau, a tall chest of drawers, and a dressing table with a red velvet stool. It was their parents' bedroom. There were two doors to the side. Momma unlocked the first to find the bathroom, and the second was a closet filled with their mother's clothes. Momma looked in the drawers. The tall chest was empty, but the bureau was full of her things. The furniture was not covered with sheets, but preserved as it was the day she left. Momma said, "We'll talk to Daniel first, but this needs to be their room. We can get it ready."

We heard voices downstairs. Momma motioned for me to follow. Daniel and his brothers were in the kitchen. Nettie and Amy had sandwiches waiting. Half the day was gone. The boys approved the new arrangement as they sat down on the benches to eat. Momma asked Daniel if she could speak to him in the front hall. After a minute, I heard their footsteps on the stairs. Soon they rejoined us in the kitchen. Momma nodded at me to indicate that after the boys left we'd tackle that room.

The boys returned to work. Momma asked Amy to help Nettie in the kitchen while we went upstairs. Sorting through her friend's clothes, Momma saved a royal blue sweater, a few skirts, a coat, as well as the brush, mirror, and comb set for Amy. We boxed the remaining items. Together we cleaned the room to get it ready for Ruth.

When we finished, Momma took the jewelry box to the kitchen. She asked Amy to have a seat next to her. Showing her the several pieces of jewelry inside, Momma said, "Daniel wants you to pick something for each of you. He has your Momma's ring for Ruth, but he wants the boys to have something to give their wives. He trusts you to do that."

Amy carefully began organizing the pieces into piles, then reorganizing. Finally, she said, "I want to keep this cross necklace and ring with all the colors. Do ya think the boys'll mind?" Momma shook her head no, so Amy continued. "The red necklace and earrings are for Patrick, and the pearl necklace and watch for Eddie. I want to give the bracelet to Ruth for a weddin' gift. Would that be alright?"

Momma assured her, "I'm sure it'll be fine. Maybe the bracelet can be a gift from the three of you." Amy nodded as Momma continued, "Do you know what that ring means? It's a dearest ring. The diamond is for D, E is the emerald, the purple stone is amethyst, ruby for R, emerald E, sapphire is the S, and the yellow topaz is for T. See, dearest. Your papa bought that when you were born. After three boys they were so happy to have a girl. You should have that ring. Save it for when you're older. You don't want to lose it."

Amy asked, "Can I keep the box? I'll keep it in here."

Momma agreed adding, "You keep everything in there until the boys get married. That cross necklace was a gift from your grandparents on your momma's wedding day. I wouldn't wear it to school. You should save it for special occasions, like the wedding on Sunday." Amy was beaming.

Touching the necklace, she asked, "Did ya know my mother?"

Momma nodded, "Yes, we were all friends: your mother, Jane, and me, but she was closer to Jane. She was a quiet soul, and I was a little too brash. Jane was more like your momma. Like Ruth. When your Papa asked her to marry him, she told Jane first. She was so happy. He was good to her and loved her so much. I wish you could have known the man he was back then. Your momma's death changed him."

Amy carefully watched Momma as she spoke. Amy asked, "Do ya have pictures?"

Momma nodded. "I have one picture of her with Jane and me, and a picture of her and your Papa on their wedding day. I hoped we'd find some here. Maybe it hurt too much to keep them. I'll make sure you have one."

We returned to work. Amy and I helped with the food, while Momma mopped around us. We put the potatoes and carrots in pans of water ready to cook. Amy made a sign for the door that said, "Take off your boots."

Momma told her to wear one of the new dresses, and save the prettiest one for the wedding. She assured her we'd be back in time to start the potatoes. The three of us headed home.

We dropped Nettie, thanking her for the help. At the house we washed up, dressing like we were going to Grandmother Gordon's. As we were leaving, Daddy and Cal came in. Momma informed them clothes were on their beds and to be there by six.

We returned to find the sofa, chair, and bed removed from the porch. Letting ourselves in through the kitchen, we got to work. Amy came to help. She was wearing my pale green dress with pink flowers around the collar and hem. It had a high waist with pink sash waiting to be tied in a bow. We made a fuss over how lovely she looked, pleasing Amy.

Momma reached in her purse removing something wrapped in tissue. Amy carefully pealed back the paper to reveal a frame from

Momma's bureau. The image of she and Daddy was gone. Amy stared at the picture of her parents.

Momma said, "She was beautiful. She looked just like you. The photographer kept telling them to be serious, but they couldn't stop smiling. They were happy and in love. You pick a special place for that picture."

We heard the boys upstairs getting ready with Daniel's raised voice directing them to put the clothes on. I was anxious to see him. Though he was marrying Ruth, thinking about him still made my heart flutter.

Daddy and Cal arrived at the front door. Following the boys into the kitchen, Daddy gave Momma a kiss on the cheek. "I told these boys they better get used to it. There's gonna be a woman in the house from now on tellin' 'em what to wear. So, Momma, do we pass inspection?" Daddy backed up, saluting her. Cal, Daniel, and his brothers joined him, before crumbling with laughter.

She smiled as she said, "Yes, you pass. You look wonderful. Now stop fooling around. J.P., I need the potatoes mashed."

Daddy saluted again. "Yes, ma'am." Turning to the boys, he said, "See, what's comin'?" We all erupted with laughter. She shook her head as Daddy kissed her again.

Soon a knock signaled Ruth and her parents' arrival. I looked at Daniel. There was a nervous, shy smile on his lips, but his eyes revealed the truth. You could see the love, mixed with fear, and relief. He was now officially head of the family, and soon to be married. Overshadowing their new beginning was grief.

Momma started giving orders. "Go greet your company. We'll take care of things here."

Ruth and her parents were in the front room admiring the lovely home as we carried food to the table. They expected the inside to be run down, so it was a pleasant surprise. Ruth was beaming as she said, "This is such a beautiful home. I never imagined." Turning to Daniel, she took his hand saying, "I love it. It will be our home always." He was pleased, smiling at her.

Momma directed everyone to their seats placing Daniel at the head of the table and Ruth to his right. Cal was at the other end with me, the boys, and Amy next to Ruth. The four adults sat on the other side. My eyes caught the picture on the piano. Amy's gaze rested on her parents, content and warmed by their presence. I whispered, "Perfect spot." She smiled.

It was a wonderful evening of conversation and laughter. How long had it been since that house was filled with such happy sounds? Daniel was talking about the farm and his plans when Buck interrupted. "We were savin' it for Ruth after secretary school, but we're gonna give it to her now. I bought Ms. Miller's car. It's in my shed. I was gettin' it ready today. We just need to get it licensed."

Jane sheepishly added, "And you'll need a car to come to church. All of you."

Daniel and Ruth would be a younger version of my parents; a farm boy, a town girl, three children, with a truck and a car. It was meant to be. With each day I was becoming more convinced.

As we progressed to dessert, Ruth admired the china. "It's beautiful. We could use this until Amy gets married, then it can be hers. Would that be alright?"

Jane said, "I always loved this china. I remember when your grandparents gave it to your mother. They'd be happy to know you're enjoying it. Maybe you could invite them to visit after you get settled. They stopped by the gas station yesterday. They were asking about you."

She was nervous as she finished, shyly looking at Daniel to see his reaction. Amy's mouth was agape as were the boys, shocked by her words. Amy asked, "We have grandparents?"

Jane waited for Daniel to answer. He looked at Amy saying, "Mother's parents live in town. I haven't seen 'em in a long time."

Jane was gaining courage, interjecting, "True, but that wasn't their choice. And they've seen you. They're at school every morning to see you get off the bus."

Daniel looked at her. His face was that of a tortured child, willing her to stop, but she was on a mission. She continued, "They lost everything when your mother died. Not just their daughter, but losing all of you was the worst heartbreak. It would mean so much if you'd allow them to come to the wedding. I promised to ask."

Jane was shaking as she finished, fearing Daniel's reaction. Patrick responded, "If they wanted to see us why didn't they? If they never tried, why should we?"

Momma answered, "Your father wouldn't let them."

Still angry, he shot back, "They didn't even bother."

"Yes, they did." It was Daniel, with his head bowed. Looking at them he continued. "They came a couple times after she died. The last time they tried, Dad was drunk. He shot at 'em, and said he'd kill 'em if they came here again."

Momma and Jane were nodding at the incredible story. Buck interjected, "I had to put a new radiator in that car. He put a bullet right through it. They drove straight to my garage that day. They were real shaken up. The radiator was empty and the car overheated. I was surprised there wasn't more damage."

Jane looked at Buck saying, "The car? That's what was important about that day, the car?"

Everyone laughed, but Buck replied, "I was impressed. Imagine, a bullet went through that engine and didn't do more damage than that."

Even Daniel was laughing. Jane looked at Ruth shaking her head saying, "Your father's incredible. Only he could make this story about a car."

It broke the tension. Amy said, "Daniel, if they've been comin' to see us, can we go see them?"

Jane quickly said, "There is nothing they'd like more. They've missed you."

Everyone looked at Daniel. He lowered his head for a moment, before slowly starting to nod. He spoke in a very hushed tone full of emotion. "I'd like to see 'em."

Amy asked, "Can we go tonight?"

Daddy said, "Take our car. Ya can bring it to the farm in the mornin'. You should all go."

Daniel studied Daddy's face, gathering strength from his gaze. His siblings looked to him for a decision. His role was clear. He hadn't been a boy since his mother died. He'd been a man with all the responsibilities of a family.

He said, "Thank you, sir, if you're sure?" Daddy nodded.

Ruth said, "We could invite them to the wedding."

Amy was excited, but the boys were apprehensive. However, they deferred to Daniel.

He turned to Jane, "I uh, I'm not sure where they live."

Ruth gently touched his hand so he'd turn to face her. "I'll show you." The fear on his face dissipated, replaced with a look of relief. He had someone to share his burden.

Jane saw them off. She returned to collapse on the chair next to Buck. He put his arm around her, planting a kiss on her cheek. She looked at Momma. Both were smiling. Daddy laughed saying, "Did that go as ya planned?"

Simultaneously they replied, "Exactly!" Everyone laughed.

We continued to enjoy the conversation, not in a rush to leave. We talked about the wedding and the future. There'd be great challenges, but also much happiness.

We worked together until every dish and pot was clean. Soon we were ready to leave.

Daddy and Cal followed us out, but stayed behind. They didn't want to leave the farm unprotected. Daddy asked Buck to drop Momma and me at home. It was dark at the big house as we drove by. It was a shame Ted and Nettie missed supper, but their responsibility to Grandma Em offered little freedom. My thoughts went to her. I hoped she was better.

Saturday morning Jane called to tell Momma about the reunion. Their grandparents offered to take care of Amy and the boys while Daniel and Ruth went on a honeymoon. It would be their gift. Amy was excited at the prospect, but the boys were not, wary of their grandparents. Momma hoped eventually they'd accept them. Maybe time together would help.

Daddy and Cal came in to eat. Daniel went to town with Ted to pick up his truck. Momma assumed he'd accept his grandparents' offer. She started rambling about where they'd go, how wonderful it would be.

Daddy sat back in his chair, watching her move around the kitchen. The look on his face was not happy. It was shock mixed with anger. "What are ya talkin' 'bout? Daniel can't leave that farm."

She looked at him, with anger matching his. "Those kids deserve a fresh start. His grandparents are willing and he should accept for Ruth."

Daddy rarely used foul language, but he was furious. "What the hell's wrong with you? Stop actin' like a school girl playin' dolls. This is real life. A man died, kids lost their father, bastards in town are tryin' to take everything they have, and all ya can say is 'Ruth deserves a honeymoon.' I spent the mornin' gettin' men to sit at that farm so Daniel can get married. How's he supposed to leave? Even two days is too long. He'll come back and there'll be nothin' left. But, hey, if he can't support 'em that's fine as long as Ruth gets a honeymoon. Melanie!"

Daddy stood up with such force that his chair toppled. Not stopping to pick it up, he stormed out the back door. She was silent, the anger gone, humbled by his words. She simply said, "Oh my. I didn't know."

She looked at Cal and me, embarrassed by her behavior. She followed him to the porch leaving the door open. We could hear them through the screen. She apologized over and over, adding, "I thought maybe they could have something that was normal."

He was exasperated. "We're tryin' to keep things together for those kids. Ya don't understand what's goin' on. Hosper stopped at the garage, and told Buck he needed to watch out for Daniel. Those bastards in town don't care if the property's his, or that truck or those animals. They tried to get Hosper to confiscate everything. Yesterday I met with Fillmore to make sure he has all the legal papers, but that means nothin'. We didn't want to upset you girls, but ya gotta let Daniel be a man, protect what's his, and ya need to help Ruth be his wife."

The emotion in Daddy's voice made me catch my breath. I looked at Cal. He nodded whispering, "It's bad."

"Do ya think they'll hurt Daniel?" I needed to know. I was afraid.

Cal shrugged his shoulders. "Daddy's tryin' to take care of things. The good news is Hosper and Buck are friends. For once he's helpin'. We were up there all mornin' fixin' the gate. Daddy hooked up chains and a couple of locks. I don't know if it'll make a difference. But if it slows 'em down 'til Daddy can get there, that's the idea."

Momma came in, going straight to the telephone. She called Jane, stretching the cord to the hall. She relayed the story. Cal rose from the table, patting me on the back as he left. After hanging up she said, "I was going to let you spend the afternoon with Grandma Em, but I need you. We have to finish cleaning that house today." I assured her I was glad to help. We gathered the pressed suits and shirts to take with us.

Pulling into the drive, Daniel and the boys were working near the house. I caught my breath. Momma turned to see what caused my alarm. There was a shotgun leaning against the fence. We both stared until Amy drew our attention to the porch. We put on a smile before joining her.

Amy was glad to have the company. It only took a couple hours to clean the bedrooms. When we finished, I hated leaving her there alone. Outside, I was relieved to see the boys were nearby. Momma told her she'd be back the next day to do her hair for the wedding. Daniel followed us to the gate, arranging the chains and locking it securely after we left.

Addie came over that evening. We helped Momma decorate the cake, making roses to circle the base while she worked on the intricate design of the top layer. Addie's company took my mind off Daniel. She was the one person who fully understood my pain. Her kindness and compassion eased my heartache.

Abigail joined us for church. I was glad when it was over, anxious to return home. We didn't go to the Hotel, but brought her back to stay with Grandma Em and the baby. We walked to the big house. I was glad to see Grandma Em, even for a short visit.

I struggled getting ready for the wedding. My hair was unmanageable. Momma tried to rush me so she could leave for Daniel's. I started to cry, expecting her to say my hair wasn't worth it, but she didn't. Together, we made it presentable.

She whispered, "It's best for Daniel and those children. It's not meant for you. You're destined for something more out there. I always knew this would be Ted's life, but never for Cal or you. Be happy for them. How gracious is God's plan?"

I thought she was ignorant of my pain, but she knew. Maybe she thought avoiding the subject would make it easier, but it didn't. I wished she had acknowledged it earlier. I needed her.

My mind wandered to the unknown. Rarely had I ever left our little town. Trips to the county seat or the hospital were my limited experience. Momma was thinking beyond those boundaries. Her intent was to help me redirect my envy of Ruth and look ahead to new possibilities. Her words helped a little.

The ceremony was beautiful. Ruth and Daniel were lost in each other. At times Reverend Howell had to repeat his words, causing us to laugh. Amy was beaming beside Ruth. She'd have a woman to fill her mother's empty place, to be a friend, confidante, and companion. Selfishly, in my pining after Daniel, I hadn't thought about the needs of Amy or the boys.

After the ceremony we moved to the basement of the church for cake and coffee. Daddy left the car for Daniel and his family, which now included his beautiful bride. He was my first love and I thought my future. That day I lost Daniel and the life I planned. But amidst the grief my future began.

Chapter TWENTY-ONE
1957

The next morning Nettie called with panic in her voice. Something was wrong with Grandma Em. Doc Batt was on his way. I grabbed my boots as Momma and I ran to the car. When we arrived I had to see Grandma Em. Her eyes turned toward me when I entered. I kissed her, saying, "I love you," before rushing out.

Daddy and the boys were clearing a new field. I drove up the road until I saw smoke from burning brush. Daniel saw me first. Dropping his shovel, he hurried toward me. Ted and Daddy followed, with Cal staying back to manage the fire. I ran toward them yelling, "It's Grandma Em!"

Meeting half way, I shared what little I knew. Daddy told Ted to take care of things as we left. By the time we arrived at the big house, Doc Batt was there along with Mr. Emerson's hearse. Rushing to get to his mother, Daddy forgot to put the car in park. I slid over to shut down the engine.

Mr. Emerson was in the parlor with hat in hand. I ran past him to Grandma Em's room. Thankfully, her eyes were open and moving. Nettie pulled me aside to explain it was another stroke. They were taking her to the hospital. Daddy followed Mr.

Emerson to get the cart as I knelt down beside her. I whispered, "I love you." She closed her eyes in response.

Momma draped a quilt over the cart. Grandma Em's body was limp as we moved her. We carefully wrapped her, and the men secured the straps. Momma and I helped carry her to the hearse. Daddy climbed in the back, directing us to follow in the car. Before we closed the door, he said, "Call Buck. Tell him to take care of Daniel."

We watched them pull away. I couldn't breathe. I knew Grandma Em would never return. As we were leaving, I looked back at Nettie on the porch. The big house was now officially hers.

At the house, we quickly gathered clothes and food. Soon we were on our way. It was a quiet ride. I didn't want to hear, 'She'll be alright.' I didn't want to dream about something that would never be. Momma respected my silence.

We waited for Daddy outside the emergency room. He appeared and fell into Momma's arms. He cried as she held him. After a few moments he pulled away to say, "She won't recover. Maybe days or a week. They're takin' her to a room upstairs. She'll be glad to see ya, Missy. She can't talk, but she'll know you're here."

Thankfully, we were alone in the elevator. After exiting, we walked the long corridor. I glanced in rooms as we passed thinking, 'Whatever it is for you, it's much worse for us. Grandma Em is dying. My Grandmother is dying.' My young mind couldn't fathom anything more tragic. Perhaps one of them was dying as well, but they weren't part of my world and their problems didn't compare.

We waited for her to arrive. She was so still when they wheeled her into the room. I looked for the rising and falling of her chest. It was so faint, barely detectable. Her eyes fluttered open. We gathered around, each kissing her. My tears came heavy with breathless sobs. Momma put one arm around me, holding Grandma Em's hand with the other. In my peripheral vision, I saw

Daddy wiping tears from his face. There were no words, just a quiet sharing of our sadness.

It took me a while to recover. Even then I took deep breaths, each followed by a long slow exhale. It was an automatic response to the stress of the moment, but it stopped the tears. I sat on the bed to look into her eyes. I heard a moan from deep in her throat. She slowly blinked. It gave me the strength to speak. "I love you." She blinked slowly again. I called my parents to see.

Momma said, "Emily, let's try something. I'll ask questions, one blink for yes and two for no. If you understand, blink once." She blinked once. Momma said, "Do you like boiled greens?" Two blinks, Momma laughed. "She hates boiled greens. She ate them so much as a child she'd never make them in her own home." She blinked once. We asked more questions, mostly silly things we knew the answers to. Each time she responded with the appropriate one or two blinks.

Getting serious, Daddy asked, "Would ya like me to call Sara?" She blinked twice. He tried again. "She's your daughter." She blinked twice, turning her eyes to Momma then back to Daddy. In her silence she bestowed the kindest gift. He said, "Melanie's your daughter?" She blinked a very slow yes, allowing her eyes to rest on Momma.

Momma took her hand, kissing it gently saying, "I love you too."

Grandma Em blinked once before closing her eyes. I continued to watch and listen for her shallow breaths. Every time she rested, it worried me. We were waiting for her to die. That thought took me back to the day she stopped speaking to us. We lost so much time for reasons I still didn't understand.

We took turns going to the cafeteria; Momma and I in one shift and Daddy the other. While he was gone we heard Uncle Roy's voice in the hall. I looked at Momma. She said, "Hurry, get your Daddy."

I turned to see Roy filling the doorway. I pushed my way past to rush toward the elevator. I anxiously waited for it to arrive.

When the door opened, Daddy was inside. I told him about Sara and Roy. He took off running as I followed close behind. We could hear Roy yelling at Momma. Daddy didn't wait to find out why or what he was saying. Charging into the room he took Uncle Roy by surprise. Daddy threw him against the wall with such force he crashed to the floor. Daddy was a wild man. Bending down to grab Roy by the shirt he said, "Get out. She doesn't want ya here." Roy tried to get up, but Daddy pushed him down so hard it made Roy catch his breath. The next words out of Daddy's mouth came as a frightening, guttural growl that made Aunt Sara gasp. "Don't ever come near my family again."

Before Roy could get his wits about him, Daddy dragged him out of the room. Closing the door behind him, he turned to Sara. "She doesn't want ya here. Go home and don't come back. Ya made your choice. Ya chose that filth of a husband over her. Now get out."

She turned to Daddy with her nose up in the air saying, "If she doesn't want me here, she can tell me herself."

She was unable to use words, but Grandma Em could tell Sara how she felt. I said, "She blinks. One blink means yes and two is no. Watch I'll show ya. Grandma Em, is this Sara?" One blink. "Do ya like boiled greens?" Two blinks. "Do ya like Mildred Kane?" Two blinks. "Am I Missy?" One blink. "Does she have a boy named Chuck?" Two blinks.

You could see Sara believed. She took Grandma Em's hand saying, "Mother, ya want me here don't ya?" Two blinks. "I'm your daughter." Looking Sara right in the eyes, her gaze not faltering, Grandma Em blinked twice. "But, I love you." Two blinks. "Ya can't mean that." One blink. "Ya want me to leave?" One blink. "It's J.P. He's makin' ya say this." Two blinks. "Mother don't ya love me?" Two blinks. "No, Momma." One slow blink.

Daddy watched, then said, "Sara, go. She doesn't want ya here." Grandma Em blinked her eyes once. Sara took a step back like she'd been hit. She raised her eyes to Daddy. He looked intently into hers saying, "It's time ya were held accountable for your choices. Ya stole the things most precious to her. Ya took 'em from her in her final months. Ya knew what it would mean. Ya knew she wouldn't forgive ya, but did it anyway. Ya decided you didn't want a mother anymore. That was your choice. Now go."

Sara was looking at Daddy, but I was watching Grandma Em. I said, "She blinked once."

Sara looked at me with shock and pain on her face. Daddy's voice came to us, quiet, "Give her peace in her final days. She doesn't deserve your selfishness now."

She looked back to Grandma Em with a final plea, "Mother, please. I want to stay." Grandma Em moved her eyes to Sara's face and blinked twice.

Sara tried to look at Daddy, but he kept his eyes on Grandma Em. As she moved away from the bed, Momma stepped in to take her place. Sara slowly walked to the door. She opened it to leave, never turning back. I expected Uncle Roy to come storming in, but he didn't.

Daddy stayed, but Momma and I went home to sleep. I had a restless night, afraid she would die before we returned. We left early for the quiet drive, each lost in our own thoughts.

Daddy was sitting by the bed when we came in. He looked up giving us a smile. Was she better? I went to her bedside. She looked at me, blinking once. That simple gesture made me happy. I'd have one more day with Grandma Em.

Daddy went home to check on the farm, shower, and change. We settled in. Momma pulled out knitting needles and a skein of pink yarn. "I'm going to teach you to knit. We can make a sweater for Baby Emily. Help me wind this into a ball."

I climbed up on the bed, leaning back next to Grandma Em. Momma looped the skein around my hands, ordering me to keep them taut. I asked Grandma Em, "Did ya ever knit?" She blinked once. I began asking what she knitted and for whom. It became a guessing game both serious and fun. Momma wound the ball while I chatted. "Did ya ever knit Daddy a shirt?" Two blinks. "How 'bout a sweater?" One blink. "Underwear?" A noise emitted from

Grandma Em's throat that I took as a laugh. I watched her eyes blink once. I howled. "Momma she blinked once! Tell me, were they pretty blue underwear? Oh, he must have loved 'em. Did he wear 'em to feed the pigs? No, I know, to drive the tractor. I bet they softened the seat." Momma and I were laughing. Grandma Em's eyes were a constant flutter. She was laughing with us.

It was a wonderful day. We talked and laughed with Grandma Em. She closed her eyes every now and then to rest. During those periods, we focused on knitting to relieve the sadness.

Daddy returned earlier than expected, anxious to see his mother. You could see the relief on his face. She was glad to see him as well.

He said, "Fillmore came to see me. Sara and Roy are causin' trouble. They tried to get us kicked out of the hospital, claimin' Mother arranged for Sara to have all rights in the event somethin' happened. She wanted all property that belongs to Mother and notification to the hospital she was in charge. He told her it was against Mother's wishes, that the proper papers were filed and witnessed by four people. He told 'em Mother designated me to oversee her affairs and 'til the reading of the will that's all he could say. Roy started yellin'. The secretary called Hosper, but that did no good. He won't protect 'em. Fillmore contacted the hospital and sent papers to keep Sara out, but that means nothin'."

Daddy had the boys checking our house during the day. Abigail and her mother were at the big house with Nettie. Her father and other neighbors were also on alert. Jane was spending her days at Daniel's. There was so much to fear with Daddy not there.

That evening there was a knock at Grandma Em's door. I saw Mr. Jefferson through the window. Daddy stepped into the hall. He returned to tell his mother about the visitor, and ask if she wanted to see him. She stared at the ceiling before blinking once. My parents looked at each other. Without a word Daddy guided us into the hall. He held the door as Mr. Jefferson entered. Daddy closed it, but hovered outside as Momma walked me a short distance away.

My mind was focused on Mr. Jefferson and the reason for his visit. I was surprised Grandma Em consented to see him. She was never kind to the coloreds. And what could he possibly want? My thoughts traveled to the porch swing. At the time it was a surprising gift, but I assumed it was because of Momma. This was another piece to the puzzle.

Daddy periodically glanced through the window. When Mr. Jefferson stepped into the hall wiping tears from his eyes, he dipped his head. Daddy nodded in return. Mr. Jefferson proceeded to the elevator without looking back.

We returned to the room. Daddy was sad, not angry. I went to Grandma Em, seeing tracks of dry tears on her face. What brought this odd collection of individuals together and with such emotion? Would Daddy think I had the right to know? Likely not, but I hoped Momma would. She told me about Grandfather Gordon and Mr. Jefferson, so maybe she'd trust me again.

I focused my attention on Grandma Em. I told her stories to keep her engaged, but she was weak. She struggled to keep her eyes open, moving them toward me with great difficulty. I looked to Daddy, but the tortured look on his face said he already knew. He was gently holding her hand, his eyes focused on her face. He said, "Missy, tell her 'bout the weddin' or school. Her eyes might be closed, but she's listenin'."

My sad voice filled the room. The feelings of the first day returned. How quickly we became comfortable with the blinks, confident they'd continue. Every now and then Momma told me to let her rest. I tried, but after a few minutes I started talking again. I couldn't spend my time with her in silence. I pretended she was hearing me, and imagined her response.

I didn't want to leave. I feared the opportunity to be with her might not come again, but Momma said it was time to go. I couldn't make my body move. She gently guided me away from the bed. I turned one last time to say, "I love you."

Daddy told Grandma Em that Cal, Ted, Nettie, and the baby were coming to visit the next day. The meaning was clear, 'Stay alive one more day.' The end was near, and everyone needed to say goodbye.

At home I went straight to my room. I didn't change, or pull back the covers, but fell on the bed into a deep sleep. The next morning I woke to Momma stroking my forehead. She whispered, "Daddy wants us there early. She had a bad night. I have breakfast ready. Nettie's father and brothers are coming to take care of the animals. Cal is getting cleaned up. Get dressed and come down."

What did a bad night mean? It was all bad, days, nights, everything. Would she be able to blink answers today or know I was there? We should have stayed with Daddy. What if that was my last time with Grandma Em? I wasn't ready for her to die.

Cal drove us in the car. Ted, Nettie, and the baby came separate in their truck. Momma and I were spending the day, but the rest would return home for chores. It was our last time together as a family with Grandma Em.

Daddy was somber. You could see the tiredness on his face. I went to Grandma Em. "It's Missy. Open your eyes if ya can hear me." It was a tremendous effort, but she opened them. I said, "That's ok. I'll talk, you listen. Everybody's here. Baby Emily came to see ya, and Nettie, and the boys." She opened her eyes giving a slow blink before closing them again.

I took Baby Emily allowing Nettie to visit. Each person took a turn at the edge of the bed, telling her how much they loved her, and saying goodbye. Occasionally she opened her eyes, but most of the time they were closed. We didn't know if she was listening or sleeping, but each one continued.

After a couple of hours, it was time for them to leave. Ted and Cal needed to tend the farm, and Baby Emily was fussing. Several times they said, "Well, we're gonna go," but stayed. It was a very long and sad goodbye.

After they left, Momma, Daddy, and I sat by her side on a death watch. Each time we engaged her, she opened her eyes to reassure us. I watched for each breath, staring so intently that I didn't realize Momma came up beside me. I said, "Sometimes I don't see her chest risin' at all. She stops breathin', then starts again."

Momma squeezed me as she said, "She's not struggling and she's not in pain. We need to pray that God takes her peacefully." However, I couldn't pray for that, not yet.

We stayed with her while Daddy went for supper and coffee. He returned with the concern and stress more pronounced on his face. He said in a low voice, "I called Sara. I told her to come, but Roy's not welcome. She'll have to choose if she wants to say goodbye."

I was shocked he offered, but Momma wasn't surprised. She rested her head against his chest saying, "I hope she'll come."

Momma and I were like everyone else. We couldn't bring ourselves to leave. About eight the door opened. It was Aunt Sara and Samuel. Daddy looked behind her ready for battle, but they were alone.

We visited a few minutes, but left shortly giving them time with Grandma Em. Before leaving I went to her, saying, "I love you. I'm glad you're my grandma. I'll be back tomorrow. Please be here."

My parents held my hands as we walked down the corridor. I was looking for Uncle Roy. Daddy was too. It appeared she came without him. Daddy left us at the elevator, afraid to leave the floor. Momma hugged him for a long time, kissing him goodbye.

We were too emotional to talk, so it was another quiet ride. At home I looked across the field. Addie's light was on. I missed her over the Christmas vacation. As children, we planned each day, not allowing anything to separate us. That year with her working and the events consuming my life, Addie was not a priority. I had no control over Grandma Em, but losing Addie was a choice. I couldn't let that happen.

Momma urged me inside. I said, "I need to see Addie. Her light's on."

My voice was choked with tears. Momma nodded. It was almost ten, but I needed to make the effort. I pulled on my boots before trudging across the field. I arrived unannounced at her back door. My mind thought of why. With Abigail or anyone else I would have called first. Addie had a telephone, but all communication between our families was in person. With party lines in the country, we could never risk anyone overhearing a conversation. It was one more way we hid the relationship between us.

I knocked on the back door. Miss Emily peered through the curtain before she unlocked the latch. She stepped aside to let me in. I removed my boots on the stoop. My mind flashed to Uncle Roy. What would he think of me going into Addie's house and using the back door? She was forced to use back doors everywhere, but not me. Standing in front of Miss Emily, I paused, looking at the threshold, aware of the significance of entering her house. Did she know my mind was telling me to defy Uncle Roy and the rules of Alabama? The step I took was theatrical, so dramatic in my intent. She watched with curiosity, but didn't question me.

I explained, "Excuse me for comin' so late, but your lights were on. I need to see Addie. I missed her over Christmas. I want her to know." There was so much emotion in my voice.

She nodded, motioning toward the stairs. I walked past, but stopped. Turning back, I said, "Your father came to see Grandma Em. His visit meant a lot to her. Will ya tell him somethin' for me, please?" I held back the tears so I could continue. "Daddy told me not to tell her where the swing came from. He was afraid she wouldn't use it. But she kept askin', so I told her. She wasn't angry at all. She loved that swing. Daddy doesn't know, but Mr. Jefferson should."

She was silent, but I could see how deeply it touched her. I didn't know the connection, but through his actions and Grandma Em's reaction a loving tie was evident. I left her staring after me as I went in search of Addie.

I peeked around the door to her room saying, "Can I come in?"

We rushed toward each other. Clasping hands, we began to spin and spin until we fell on the bed. The laughter was missing, but the comfort of her presence was reassuring. Staring at the ceiling, we talked like we were in the field. I said, "Grandma Em's dyin'."

Speaking those words tore at my heart. I sobbed uncontrollably. She took my hand, and held it tight. I said, "I'm losin' everything. Grandma Em, Daniel…"

She said, "You're not losin' me."

I nodded. "I hope not. We're growin' up and you're movin' on with Henry. And we don't see each other much. Everything's changin'."

She replied, "I'm here now and you're here. Even when everybody says you and me shouldn't be friends, we keep goin'. And we'll keep on 'til we both know it's time. But we'll decide."

I nodded. "Please not now, alright? It's not time. Not for me."

She said, "Me neither."

Our conversation turned to girl things including Henry, Daniel, Ruth, and college. We talked until midnight. Miss Emily popped her head in. "Cal's at the back door. It's time, but ya come whenever ya need. Ada wants to see ya 'fore ya go." I nodded, giving Addie a hug. It was time to say goodnight, but not goodbye.

Downstairs Miss Ada motioned for me to sit next to her on the bed. "Child, we missed ya. You're carryin' a heavy load. I said a prayer askin' God to take special care. Tell your Daddy this family's hurtin' for him. He's a good man."

I wrapped my arms around her, enjoying a warm hug in return. As I moved to leave she said, "Bless ya, child."

James was waiting in the hall. He also sent a message of sympathy to Daddy. I looked at the faces around me and the kindness of each one, grateful to know them.

Cal and I started across the field. He put his arm around me. My escape from reality was over. The weight of my grief and the dread of tomorrow returned.

Grandma Em died on Sunday, January sixth. The last two days she didn't respond, not opening her eyes again. Daddy never left. We brought him a change of clothes each day so he could be with her. The boys made one more trip to the hospital. Aunt Sara came with Samuel every day to keep vigil with us. We talked very little, but it was peaceful. Daddy knew they were the last days with his sister.

I wasn't looking forward to the funeral, but it came anyway the morning of the eighth. Reverend Howell would officiate as he did for Granddaddy Tucker. In the church, Grandma Em was waiting at the front. I grabbed Momma's hand. Her arm wrapped around my shoulder to propel me forward. We sat in the front pew while Daddy talked with Reverend Howell.

People started arriving. Uncle Frank and his wife were across the aisle one pew back with their son Bernie. Abigail and her parents sat a couple rows behind us. Mr. Jefferson came in with Miss Emily, James, and Miss Ada, taking a seat at the back of the church. Daddy saved the other front pew for Aunt Sara and her family. She arrived with Samuel, visibly upset. She motioned for Reverend Howell to begin. Uncle Roy would not attend.

The service was not long with some scripture and a couple of hymns. Reverend Howell talked about Grandma Em growing up in our little town, how hard she worked as a farmer's wife, the friends that filled the church, and the family she left behind. He smiled as he spoke of her good life, the tough woman we often feared, and the kind heart that touched many.

After the service our men with Samuel, Daniel, and Daddy's cousin Bernie carried her to the grave where everyone gathered for a short prayer. Daddy left as soon as the Amen was over. Everyone followed. Aunt Sara moved toward her car, but Daddy placed her hand in the crook of his arm saying, "I'm not lettin' ya go." She began to cry. He put his arm around her, and held tight.

Momma moved toward Miss Ada, James, Mr. Jefferson, and Miss Emily at the back of the parking lot. I joined her to thank them for coming. She couldn't invite them for the dinner, but wouldn't be deterred from gratefully acknowledging their presence. I greeted them, "Miss Ada, Miss Emily it's nice to see you. Hello, Mr. Jefferson," and a nod to James.

A sudden commotion behind me turned my attention to some men gathered with Uncle Frank. He looked directly at me saying, "Miss! Mister! That's right, show who ya are, girl! They shouldn't have been in our church. None of ya should. The likes of you don't have the right."

Daddy was on him, followed by Ted and Cal. Samuel stayed by Aunt Sara, with fear etched on their faces. Daddy grabbed Uncle Frank by the shirt as he pushed him back against a car. The other men cleared out, leaving him to deal with Daddy alone. With his face so close their noses almost touched, Daddy said, "Watch your manners. That's my daughter you're talkin' to. And they're welcome here 'cause I invited 'em."

Uncle Frank spit in Daddy's face and said, "Who are you to tell me anything, boy!

Daddy growled, "We both know what gives me the right." He paused a moment letting his words have their full effect. Then he continued, "This is a day for the family to honor my mother. I expect ya to do that."

"She weren't no family of mine. And neither are you. I don't have to keep your secret anymore. Ya best get over there with your kin!" Uncle Frank had a look of satisfaction on his face.

Momma gasped in fear, but Daddy wasn't shaken. He lowered his voice almost to a whisper, but I heard, "Ya think I don't know? You're wrong. My father made sure I knew everything. That feed store is mine if I want it. All it takes is one call. I have all the facts and the papers too. So, you'll keep your mouth shut. Right now, I'm happy bein' a farmer, but that might change. If anything happens to me, my family, or Jefferson, I'll take it all."

Uncle Frank's face went gray and he began to shake. I wasn't sure if it was fear or rage. It could have been both. I looked at his wife. I definitely saw fear on her face. Daddy let go as he added, "And in case you're wonderin', my boys know too. They know what's rightfully mine and theirs, and they know how to get it. If ya think it ends with me it doesn't. Now we can live in peace or not. It's your choice. With Ted workin' the farm maybe it's time I let my wife move back to town. I always liked your house. Don't forget I'm lettin' ya live there. As long as nothin' happens to my family or anyone else, life goes on as it is."

Daddy took a step back wiping his face with his sleeve, but he never dropped his eyes. Uncle Frank moved away. His wife followed with her head down, ashamed to look up.

Daddy went to Mr. Jefferson. "If ya have any trouble, let me know. Your kindness touched my mother in her final days. The swing was her favorite place to sit and brought her much peace. Thank you."

Mr. Jefferson didn't speak, but nodded at Daddy. James escorted the women to the truck, while Mr. Jefferson climbed in his car. We watched them drive away before turning back toward the church.

The parking lot was clear of everyone but my family and cousin Bernie. As Daddy approached, Bernie reached out to shake his hand. Bernie said, "I'm sorry for the loss of your mother. I apologize for my father. It'll be alright." Daddy nodded and thanked him for coming. Bernie didn't join us but followed his parents home.

Aunt Sara was clearly panicked. Daddy took her hand. In a low voice he said, "I'll take care of this family."

Momma and I were both frightened, but for different reasons. I was scared of what I didn't know, but Momma was afraid of the truth. Did Daddy go too far protecting Mr. Jefferson? Was it my fault? I knew not to use the title Mister or Miss in public. Emotionally preoccupied with saying goodbye to Grandma Em, I wasn't thinking. Would something happen to them or Daddy because of me?

In the basement, people were waiting for the family. Momma told us to start the food line. Samuel and Aunt Sara joined us at a table. He talked about school and New York. It was good to hear he was happy. They took their time eating, delaying the inevitable. It would be the last time we sat together as a family.

As people finished, they stopped to pay their respects. Suddenly Samuel jumped up. We followed his eyes toward the door. Uncle Roy was there. Daddy stood, followed by Ted and Cal. Roy locked eyes with Daddy before averting them to his wife. He said, "Sara, let's go. Ya don't need to be here. Samuel, get your mother."

A look of hatred passed across Samuel's face, but Aunt Sara quietly rose. She gingerly touched Daddy and said, "It's time." He wrapped his arms around her and whispered in her ear as he let her go. She and Samuel followed Uncle Roy without another word.

The intrusion signaled the end of the meal. Daddy couldn't settle again. Together we thanked the ladies in the kitchen. We silently walked to the parking lot, exhausted from the events of the previous week. Daddy was visibly dragging. He tossed the keys to Cal saying, "Me and my girl are sittin' in the back. You kids get us home."

We said goodbye to Ted and Nettie. It was a new beginning for them. The responsibility of Grandma Em was no longer their burden. I could only imagine the mixture of emotions. Was there relief or just sadness? Would the house feel empty and lonely? It would for me.

It was a quiet ride with only music on the radio. At home, Cal immediately went upstairs to change. Daddy collapsed on the sofa and closed his eyes. Hearing Cal pound down the stairs, Daddy called him into the parlor. He put both arms around Cal, giving him a hug and a pat on the back saying, "We gotta get ya back to school tomorrow. Momma'll take ya to the bus."

Cal nodded. Daddy headed toward his room to change. Cal pinched me before draping his arm around me. He said, "Make me a sandwich 'fore I go fight the pigs."

I smiled saying, "Gladly!"

Even though he just had a full meal at the church, he inhaled a sandwich, cookies, and glass of milk. When Daddy came down, he said, "Good thing you're leavin' tomorrow. I can't afford to feed ya."

After they left I went to my room, and threw myself across the bed. I slept fitfully. I should have gone to school, but Momma decided it could wait one more day. We took Cal to the bus station in the next town over. She was grateful for the company and me for the extra time. I wasn't ready to go on with life.

Momma went to sort through Grandma Em's things. She said I didn't have to help, but I wanted to. I cleared out the table next to her bed. Picking up her Bible, I looked inside. My name was written on the front page under Grandma Em's. Momma said, "She wanted you to have it."

Leafing through the pages, I found a picture of Grandma Em holding me. In the drawer were more pictures of her with everyone, including Granddaddy Tucker. Momma divided them into piles for each of us. I chose a rare picture of my grandparents smiling. She placed the few extra in a box for Aunt Sara.

It was difficult, but I felt her presence. I was glad I helped. Later Daddy and Ted moved the bedroom furniture upstairs, leaving Granddaddy Tucker's roll top desk and Grandma Em's chair in its place by the window.

Momma and I delivered the box to Aunt Sara. She came to the door, graciously accepted the pictures, but did not invite us in. We stopped at Abigail's to get the school work I had missed. That evening I attempted to concentrate, but I was not successful. My thoughts were with Grandma Em and how my life would change.

On Thursday I returned to school, depressed to be there. Abigail understood. She was still living with the pain of losing Ezekiel. Remembering his death forced me to think of my grief from a different perspective. Grandma Em lived a long fruitful life, most of it in good health, while he had dealt with constant illness and pain. My thoughts went to his family, especially his mother. My grandmother's death did not compare to their loss.

Chapter TWENTY-TWO
EARLY *1957*

After Grandma Em's death I couldn't speak of her. Daddy was quiet about his loss as well. Momma was a talker. She shared her grief with Jane and her parents. After a couple months I was ready. I wanted to hear stories about my grandmother's life and gain clarity about the events surrounding her death, especially regarding Mr. Jefferson and Uncle Frank. I wrote the story in my mind. It was a love story that explained everything including why Grandma Em was unhappy.

I approached Momma for confirmation of the facts. We were in the kitchen baking a pie for supper at the big house. I asked, "Do you think Grandma loved Granddaddy?"

She was not shocked by my question. She continued rolling the dough as she chose her words, "I think there was a sort of love. They were married over thirty five years. There was a partnership and likely some love."

"But not like you and Daddy? I mean did they hug and kiss?" I continued.

She responded in a very sad tone. "No, they weren't like that."

"Do you think they ever were? I mean, did she want to marry him?" I asked.

Momma pondered my question, battling with a decision. She'd begin to speak, then shake her head and stop. Finally, she said, "This isn't for me to talk about."

I was surprised, but wasn't giving up. "You think I don't know, but I do. I remember Granddaddy Tucker's funeral. She didn't cry. If it's someone you love, you cry when you lose 'em."

Momma remained silent. I continued, "Mr. Jefferson cried at the hospital and so did she." I spoke those words then waited for a response. I could see her body tense, but there was only silence.

I said, "That's the secret, isn't it? That's why Uncle Frank was angry? Mr. Jefferson loved Grandma Em, and she loved him."

Momma's eyes turned toward me with the look of shock I was expecting because I figured it out. She pursed her lips, shook her head, and said, "We're not talking about this."

I expected her to confirm the truth and share the story of their love. I heard Daddy tell Uncle Frank everyone knew. But they didn't trust me. I said, "I'm old enough. Ted and Cal know, and so do I. That's why he made her the swing, and why she loved it even more after I told her."

That got her attention. I nodded as I continued. "She kept askin' me and I told her. She didn't get mad. It made her cry."

"Stop! We're not having this conversation." With that she walked out. The back door slammed. I heard the car pull out of the drive. Maybe she'd tell Daddy I knew. Hopefully she'd return ready to talk.

I finished forming the crust in the pie pan and put it in the hot oven to brown. I put the butter and chocolate squares in the double boiler to melt, and continued adding the ingredients to make the filling. I poured the mixture into the shell, put it in the refrigerator to cool, and began the cleanup. Momma finally returned and without a word began cracking the eggs for the meringue. We finished in silence. Daddy came in, but avoided me as he went directly upstairs.

Returning Momma's silent treatment, I grabbed my coat, and left. The walk to the big house gave me time to get angry. I was almost sixteen, but they treated me like a child.

I thought of Grandma Em. Many things now made sense. I understood why she disliked Miss Emily. She was the daughter that should have been hers. She objected to my friendship with Addie, afraid someone would tell me the truth. Miss Ada and Miss Emily at the big house working in the garden had a reason. Miss Emily did it for her father.

By the time I got to Nettie's, I was furious. They didn't think I could understand, but Grandma Em would. She'd share her story with me. I imagined us on the porch swing as she told me about her forbidden love, her forced marriage to Granddaddy Tucker, and the sadness every time she saw Mr. Jefferson. I'd listen without judging because I felt a kinship to her situation. I hid my love for Daniel and my friendship with Addie. I could have understood what she sacrificed.

Sitting in Grandma Em's seat on the swing, I gently caressed the carvings as she did so many times. The gravel crunching brought me back to the present with my parents' arrival. I didn't want to be alone with them. Moving toward the door I knocked. Not waiting for an answer, I barged in. Nettie was on her way from the kitchen with Baby Emily on her hip. She gave me a hug, saying, "I'm glad you're here. I need another set of hands."

I hurried to the kitchen before Momma and Daddy came in. I played with Baby Emily while Nettie busied herself with the food. Ted appeared shortly, telling her my parents were in the drive. They plated the food while I carried it to the dining room with Baby Emily on my hip. I could see the car as I passed through, but couldn't tell if they were still inside. I listened for the front door as I moved back and forth between the rooms.

Eventually they came in. Ted went to welcome them and I stayed with Nettie. Let someone else be nice. My parents came in the kitchen, so I took Baby Emily to the dining room.

I had been excited about supper at the big house. Abigail's family was not included. I was looking forward to our turn, and now it was ruined.

Positioning myself next to the baby, I was glad to speak to Nettie, even Ted, but not my parents. I busied myself feeding Baby Emily. I am sure no one missed my intentional snubs to the comments Momma or Daddy directed my way.

After the long painful meal, I offered to take Baby Emily upstairs so the adults could enjoy the evening without the bother of children. Nettie looked at my parents, but I avoided Momma's face. I didn't care to see her disapproval. Nettie nodded, so I gladly left the room.

Later, Momma called up to say they were leaving. I went out to the landing. Avoiding eye contact with all but Nettie, I asked, "Can I put the baby to bed? I'll walk home later."

She looked at the others, before nodding. I took the baby back into her room without another word, and closed the door behind us. I heard their muffled conversation in the hall below, and the front door open and close.

Nettie came up. "Your daddy's comin' back to help Ted in the barn. He'll drive ya home when he's finished." I nodded. It was better than being in a car with Momma.

Baby Emily was an effective distraction, but soon it was her bedtime. I came down to find Daddy waiting in the parlor. He said, "Ready to go?"

I nodded. Avoiding eye contact with Daddy, I thanked Ted and said goodbye. We climbed in the truck and he started the engine, but didn't put it in gear. He was quiet, with his hands fidgeting on the steering wheel. I looked straight ahead, pretending I didn't notice. He said, "Ya can't be mad at Momma. It's not her doin'. It's my mother and my decision. Momma isn't mad at ya for askin'. She's mad at me. It's not the right time. Ya have to understand."

"The boys know. I heard ya tell Uncle Frank. It's just me ya don't trust? Did she tell ya I already know?" I asked.

He was shaking his head. "Ya don't understand. It's my job to protect this family. I'm doin' what I have to. Ya don't know what you're askin'."

I interrupted, "But I won't tell anyone. I hide Addie bein' my friend. Nobody knows, not even Abigail. I know more than ya think."

"Ya don't." His voice was shaking.

I reassured him, "I'm not a child. I just want to understand about Grandma Em, and why she was unhappy. Ted knows, Cal knows, Nettie knows, but not me."

"They needed to know to make decisions 'bout their lives. It's not time for you. I don't want ya worryin', not now. That's my job. I need ya to let this go."

He finally looked at me. I couldn't see his eyes in the dark, but I could hear the plea in his voice. As much as I wanted to stop for him, I couldn't. It was about Grandma Em. I needed to feel close to her, to know her. I continued, "No Daddy. Ted and Cal knew things when I was little, things ya wouldn't tell me. They always understood. Everybody in town knows 'bout my family, but not me. I've never given ya any reason not to trust me! I'm makin' decisions 'bout my life too, ya know. Daniel married Ruth. My dreams are gone. Grandma Em died and now what do I have? Uncle Frank said we should be over there with our family and everyone understood but me."

I was sobbing. He tried to interrupt, but I continued. "Ya think I don't know, but I do. Grandma Em didn't love Granddaddy Tucker. She wasn't happy. She was lonely and angry."

There was nothing more to say. I waited for him to put the truck in gear, but he didn't. He remained silent for a long time. The only sound was the sharp intakes of my breath as I cried.

"She didn't love my father, and he didn't love her." Daddy said those words then sat motionless.

"He loved Ada." It wasn't what I was expecting. I waited for more. "Ada's father was a sharecropper. They lived where she is now. To hear my father talk, she was the most beautiful woman he'd ever seen. But it was more than that: she was kind and loving. Ya know Ada."

He paused to collect himself, then, continued. "She helped his mother here at the big house. They saw each other every day. And she loved him. They hid it, but one day his mother caught 'em together. His parents thought another woman would get Ada out of his mind, but it never did. He loved her 'til the day he died."

Daddy stopped the story, deep in thought. Finally, he continued, "My granddaddy and my mother's father came up with a plan. It was a sale agreement more than a marriage proposal. My mother was four years older, with no prospects, so her father promised a cash interest in the store and equipment at cost. My daddy was under pressure 'cause the deal would help the farm. His family struggled year after year. They were always afraid they might lose everything. He felt an obligation to this place. He could never marry Ada, so a business arrangement didn't sound bad. Everybody worked on both of 'em to get the marriage done. His parents moved to our little house, givin' my daddy the big house to keep him away from Ada."

I could hear the sadness in his voice. He sat just shaking his head. It gave me time to think. His father loved Miss Ada and his mother loved Mr. Jefferson. I could understand why the two families conspired to marry them. It solved the problem for both.

He said, "They made it happen right away so he wouldn't change his mind. But it wasn't what he wanted. The night 'fore his weddin', he went to Ada. He felt like he was betrayin' her. He was still torn up when he died."

Again, he stopped the story to find the right words. "He got married the next day. A couple months later he found out Ada was expectin'. He couldn't do anything 'bout it and by then Grandma Em was expectin' me."

In shock, I broke my silence. "James is your brother? Does he know?"

I couldn't see his face, but from his voice I could tell he was surprised by my question. "Of course he knows. We worked the

At home Momma was watching the news. I told her about the wedding and the gift. I described Tucker James's quilt in the bottom of the chest, the carved spool, and the purple velvet lining in that old barn crate. Momma quietly listened with a sadness I shared. Mine in part was for Tucker James, but also the realization I had forgotten Addie's pain. I had been stupidly and selfishly unaware.

The chest haunted me. It was symbolic of the sameness between our families, and the differences. Momma had a nice cedar chest bought from a store, a luxury Miss Ada couldn't afford. Her chest was an old barn crate made beautiful. They each had special items to store, but my mind dwelt on how poverty forced Miss Ada to accommodate that need.

I compared their life to ours. Momma's beautiful dining room was Miss Ada's bedroom in their home. It didn't have fine furniture, china, beautiful glass, or ceramic knickknacks. Instead, there was a mirror above an old chest of drawers with the veneer chipped away on part of the top, and a corner propped up with a piece of wood in place of the leg. There was an upholstered chair in the corner with a piece of fabric draped over the back to cover the holes in the original tapestry, and a pillow on top of the seat cushion to raise the sagging supports. Instead of pretty pictures on the wall, there was a wood stick mounted on two boards to hold Miss Ada's dresses. The coverlet on the bed was worn, frayed at the edges from keeping it clean. Central in my mind was the chest at the end of the bed, fulfilling a purpose like Momma's, but so different.

I took my life and possessions for granted. James was the first-born son, yet Daddy inherited everything. They were brothers, always together as children, but not equal. James could never truly be a son in the way Daddy was. Even the farm and equipment: Daddy got the new tractor, while James got the hand-me-down. Daddy worked the majority of the land, while James was given only enough to survive. James was the son of the woman he loved, therefore cherished. Yet Granddaddy Tucker lived within the societal rules which relegated James and his family to a lower status, and a life that was less in material standards. How could Miss Ada or James continue living behind our house without anger or resentment? Was it a willing acceptance or resignation? I wondered if they or Daddy saw the injustice.

My thoughts moved on to Addie. While I was worried about Charlotte and Virginia, what were her concerns? I simply lived with peer bullying, while she and her family faced the danger of bigotry. I worried about Abigail not being able to drive, but had missed Addie turning fifteen. I fretted about insignificant things and received silence from her in return. Was it her kind tolerance in all things? Or was she conditioned to exercise forced compliance? Though I had a new awareness, I didn't really have understanding.

The truth of our relationship opened my eyes. We were not only friends; we were family. However, we weren't equal, not in rights or possessions. I was filled with shame. I wanted to change who I was and how I behaved. Addie and I had a little over two years of friendship remaining. I hoped to be a better person for the duration. I intended to try.

We were not invited to the wedding. We lived in separate worlds. The only time we connected was at our two matching houses, in the field between them, or for funerals. I didn't see Addie Saturday evening. The wedding was late in the day because the family and guests still had to work. Sunday evening, after taking Abigail home, I asked if I could go to Addie's for a few minutes, anxious to hear about the celebration.

She answered my knock on the back door, happy to see me. James came into the kitchen as I entered. I was uncomfortable explaining my unplanned visit. "I'm sorry. I just wanted to see Addie. I hope ya don't mind…um…I um…"

I continued to stammer through my reasons until he finally put me out of my misery. "It's fine." With that he left the room.

Addie and I grabbed hands like in younger years. We laughed at our immaturity. However, staying in the past allowed us to be

She listened for a short time. She said, "It's your decision. You'll have to work it out if you're going to stay. Another year and we'll have Missy in college as well. That's why your father's adding fields. Not just for Missy, but Ted has a family to provide for. We need you."

Silence again on Momma's end. Her voice wasn't angry, but sad as she continued. "That means your daddy has to pay those workers."

More silence. She continued, "It needs to provide for you over the next year. Without your help, we can't send money. You made a deal. Let me know if you change your mind." She paused. In a soft voice said, "I hope you'll visit. We miss you."

Choking back tears, she said, "I love you. Take care." She hung the receiver on the cradle, and stared at the telephone. She took a long deep breath, and slowly exhaled.

Daddy came into the kitchen and said, "He's not comin'?"

She shook her head. "He got a summer job at a paper. Kind of copy boy, errand boy, but he's hoping they'll let him write."

"How much money?" he asked.

"Not enough to live on, but he found a second job nights washing dishes. He's trying to find a job during the day on weekends. He said he'll take care of it. I told him, it's not just about this summer. I made it clear he'll need to keep one or two of the jobs during the school year to make up what we lose. He understands." She finished with sadness in her voice.

Daddy said, "Where's he livin'?"

She replied, "At the rooming house. He's working for the widow doing odd jobs and mowing. She offered him free room and board this summer in exchange for painting."

"When's he gonna do that with three jobs?" Daddy said shaking his head.

She explained, "He's doing it now. He already started. He's been painting the outside for weeks and is doing a few of the rooms inside over the summer. It was the plan all along."

He nodded. "I suspected that." He paused a minute. "I'm still gonna prep those fields. If he doesn't pull this off, we'll need that money"

She said, "That's it?"

Exasperated, she looked at the ceiling before leaving the room. He hung his head in frustration as he followed her to the parlor. I stayed behind.

He said, "What would ya have me do? Force him to come home? Punish him 'cause he doesn't want to be a farmer? The boy's goin' to college. He's gonna make somethin' of himself. It's my job to help him." His voice softened. "This isn't 'bout Cal workin' for me. It's 'bout bein' part of the family. If we push too much, he might turn away. Isn't it more important to have our son?"

She knew he was right, but when Ted moved out, she still saw him every day, and was involved in his life. Cal was different. She didn't know what he was doing, or the people that were part of his life. She felt that separation deeply.

I'd think about that feeling of loss and Momma's heartache often. Painfully aware soon it would be for me, I made a vow to always keep her part of my life. She deserved that.

She said, "I'm going to bed." She slowly climbed the stairs as we stared after her.

He walked past me to the back porch. Standing at the rail, he looked out over the field. I was focused on Momma's grief, but there was sadness for him as well. I left him to his thoughts, and went to my room.

After a time, he came in. I expected to hear the sound of the television, but instead heard his voice on the telephone. I snuck to the top of the stairs. He was talking to Cal.

He said, "Your Momma misses ya. She was lookin' forward to ya comin' home. It's a mother thing, but I'm proud of ya. My son's gettin' a college degree. Do what ya can to help with expenses, but I'm here if ya need me."

There was silence, Cal was speaking. Every now and then Daddy interjected with, "I know, son," or "I understand."

Eventually, Daddy said, "Make a plan with your mother. Set time aside, pick a day, call her, and ask her to come. She needs it. She and Missy can drive up to spend the afternoon. If ya can't come here, let her come there."

He relayed a few more parting words. I heard the screen door again. He was on the porch. I was exhausted and wanted to be rid of the sad thoughts. Sleep, as usual, was my escape.

Cal called the next day. He asked Momma to come Friday. He said he missed her and wanted to see her. She never knew it was Daddy's idea. It was better that way. She needed to believe her son cared.

It was a nice visit. We ate with Cal at his favorite diner. He took us on a tour of the newspaper office and his favorite places. He told Momma about his friends and girls he'd dated. It gave her what she needed.

As we were leaving, she arranged to call him every Monday morning at seven. It helped to know they'd talk. If only for a few minutes each week, she was part of his life.

I turned sixteen in June. Momma made an appointment to get my license. She planned a girl's day for Abigail and me. It was more like a vacation than a morning at the county courthouse. Focusing on our plans, I didn't have time to be nervous. I passed the test easily. I was afraid it might sadden Abigail, but she seemed genuinely excited.

After our afternoon of shopping, I dropped Momma at home before proceeding to the big house to share my good news. Driving without Momma was exciting. Abigail seemed happy as well. She put my mind at ease with her words. "Maybe we can drive to work on Saturdays."

I said, "We don't have to. I don't care. This can be just for us."

She smiled saying, "Charlotte and Virginia will pick on us anyway. Even if I could get my license, they'd find somethin' else."

"Yeah, but they'll pick on you. If I don't drive, then it's both of us," I said.

She turned toward me, "I want one of us to stand up to them. We only have the truck. I wouldn't have anything to drive. Daddy bein' old fashioned is better than us bein' too poor." I hadn't given thought to one reason being better than another. For her, being poor was more embarrassing. Often it made her the brunt of their cruelty, but this time it wasn't the reason.

Momma let me drive to work much of the time. Grandfather Gordon ordered new shelving to redo part of the store. He was expanding his stock of kitchen equipment and electronics. Because of the remodel, we got more hours. In the past we made lists from Grandfather Gordon's catalogues, but that summer was different. Abigail was saving almost every cent. She negotiated with Grandfather Gordon to receive some of her pay in cash, and keep the rest on account. He agreed for both of us.

In July she opened a savings account. I decided to go with her. I watched my friend make a down payment on her future. Feeling guilty, I opened an account as well. As I was filling out the paperwork, I thought how silly, but that account received more money than I intended. Each week, she deposited every penny, and I did the same out of shame.

Chapter TWENTY-FOUR

LATE SUMMER 1957

The first week of August, a young couple stopped in the store to stock their new home. The young man said, "My wife and I are hoping to settle here. I'll be working with my grandfather at the feed and seed." I caught my breath. It was Uncle Frank's grandson. Should I introduce myself or stay quiet? There was bad blood between Daddy and Uncle Frank. Would his grandson reject me as a result?

Before I could decide, Grandfather Gordon said, "Well my goodness. Missy, come meet your cousin."

I waited for his reaction. The young man smiled as he moved toward me. He said, "It can't be little curly haired Missy. You're all grown up. I'm Mark, Markus your cousin. This is my wife Liz. It's good to see you." I greeted both of them. He continued, "How's your family? I heard about Aunt Em. I'm real sorry, such a loss for all of you."

We talked for a while. As a child he loved visiting and couldn't think of a better place to live. He recently graduated from college with a degree in business and accounting. He wanted to eventually take over the feed and seed, but Uncle Frank was not in agreement. Mark hoped his grandfather would soften with time. Mark intended to do some accounting on the side to supplement his meager income.

Liz interjected, "We're renting a small house a couple blocks over. It's been vacant a few years, so we're paying almost nothing. In exchange, we're going to fix it up." She was excited, but Mark rolled his eyes. They were so kind that I relaxed and enjoyed the conversation.

I was anxious to tell Momma, but decided to wait until we were gathered for supper. She made dried beef gravy on toast. I loved the thick buttery mixture. We coated the warm toast with butter, adding to the rich flavor.

Daddy came in from the field and washed up, ready to eat. He smiled as he inhaled the delicious aroma. He liked it as much as I did. It was comfort food.

Momma told us about her day, and he shared news from the farm. I waited until they were finished so there would be no distractions when I shared my surprise. Finally, they were quiet. I told them about the strangers buying supplies. After providing general details, I said, "Guess who?"

I was happy to see a surprised look on each face. She said, "We know them?"

"Yup!" I replied. "Guess!"

Daddy didn't like games. He said, "How would we know? I couldn't even try."

Momma said, "Give us clues. Did they live here before? How old are they?"

She was always good about playing. I answered, "They never lived here, but we know him. He visited when he was young. He's the same age as Ted."

Momma was thinking. She said, "How about an initial?"

"M for his first name." I giggled with delight over her willingness to humor me.

"Hmm, M." After another minute she said, "Another clue."

"Ok," I continued. "He's named after his great-grandfather."

They shook their heads. I gave more clues. "Ya know his father and grandfather real well. His father moved away, but his grandfather still lives here."

Had I given it away? They were both thinking. Momma scrunched up her face and Daddy shook his head perturbed as he said, "Just tell us."

Momma said, "One more clue for me," as she shot him a nasty look.

"He wants to join his grandfather's business, hopin' to take it over some day, but his grandfather didn't want him to come. That's why he's rentin'." I paused for a moment to see if that clue gave it away. They still looked puzzled. I continued, "We're related to him."

Daddy's eyes narrowed as he said, "Related? Did ya say M? Do ya mean Markus?"

I nodded, so excited he guessed, but he was not pleased. "Yeah, Cousin Bernie's son, but he goes by Mark. It's him and his new wife. He's real nice. I wasn't sure how he'd be 'cause of Uncle Frank, but he's fine."

He pounded his fist on the table as he stood up. Pacing around the kitchen, he said, "What's Frank tryin' to pull now? I told him I'd take it all! Leave him with nothin' if he took one step out of line."

I tried to allay his fears. "It's not like that. It wasn't Uncle Frank's idea. Mark liked comin' here. It took him a long time to convince his father, and Uncle Frank told him no, but he came anyway."

Momma spoke, "J.P., are you listening? Calm down. You don't know anything yet. Get the facts before you fly off the handle. If you go to town angry, there's no telling what Frank will do. If you threaten his grandson, it might push him too far." He stopped pacing to look at Momma. He forced his hands deep into his pockets to hide the balled-up fists. Their words, as usual, confused me.

He mulled it over and asked, "Markus said his grandfather doesn't want him here?"

I nodded. "Uncle Frank told him not to buy a house or get too settled 'cause he won't be stayin'. But Mark is determined to show his grandfather he can help. He has to take work on the side 'cause Uncle Frank won't pay him much."

He paced for a moment. Turning to Momma, he said, "Maybe it isn't all bad. It could be good to give Frank a vested interest in the future of that store. Problem is, I don't know how much that boy knows. This could be bad. It's one thing to keep Frank in line, but it might be hard to keep a whole bunch of 'em quiet."

She said, "Bernie would know. He's always been good to us. He hated the way his father behaved. And he came when your mother died. Call him. Find out the facts."

I added, "Mark heard 'bout Grandma Em and was real sorry. His father told him stories 'bout comin' out to the farm, growin' up with you, and that Grandma Em was always nice."

Momma got up from the table. "I'll get the number."

He slowly nodded. He said, "Missy, go watch television." I opened my mouth to protest, but she held up her hand to silence me. I felt dejected and angry, but knew not to push.

I turned the television volume low. I positioned myself on the floor close to the hall. He always talked loud on the telephone to yell across the miles. Soon I heard him say, "Hello, is Bernie there?" Then a minute later, "Bernie, it's J.P."

There was a long pause as Daddy listened to the voice on the other end. Then he said, "Yeah, Missy saw him at the store today. Seems he's settin' up house. Bernie, things with your dad and I aren't good. Ya know how it's been over the years, but since my mother died, it's bad. I'm tryin' to figure out how your boy fits into the picture, and well.... how much does he know?"

After a pause he said, "Nothin'? Really?" Another pause as he listened. "Well, I appreciate that. Ya always did good by me. I'm grateful." He was silent again before continuing. "Well, that's how I see it too. We give your dad a vested interest in the future of that store. I'm a little worried 'bout what happens if he wants out or worse, when he dies. This might be the ticket to keepin' him quiet. How do ya know he won't tell your son?"

After a time, Daddy said, "Ya think your dad will keep that promise?" Again, a pause. He continued. "He doesn't respond well to threats. They tend to make him meaner. Can't see how ya threatenin' to cut him off is gonna end it. He only has to keep the deal 'till he knows he's dyin'. This is a temporary fix and puts all the risk on you. What if I sweeten the pot? I agree to turn the store over to your son if Frank goes to his grave with the secret. He never tells your boy or anyone else or the deal's off. Ya think we can get him with an offer like that? No one has to know the store was mine all along. Does he care enough 'bout your boy?"

There was a prolonged pause. He said, "Alright. Make sure he understands if he tells anyone, the store reverts back to me. I'll draw up the papers and get ya a copy if he agrees." After a time, he said, "I'll stay clear and let ya handle it. Thanks, Bernie. Missy said your boy's real nice. I'll have him out soon."

After a few final remarks, Daddy hung up. He and Momma started whispering. I couldn't hear what they were saying. I moved to the sofa. I was trying to fit the pieces together. Thinking back to that little boy outside the feed and seed, I was sure Uncle Frank was like Uncle Roy regarding the coloreds. But how could he hold a lifelong grudge against Grandma Em for loving Mr. Jefferson. She gave him up. Shouldn't Uncle Frank have forgiven her?

Over the next couple of days Daddy was jumpy. He spent more time at the house, but by the third night he returned to his regular schedule. The call finally came, but he wasn't home. Momma said she'd give him the message. I didn't ask about the conversation because I knew she wouldn't tell me.

When he came in she said, "Bernie called. He'll be in town this weekend. He decided to talk with his father in person."

Daddy pursed his lips and shook his head. He said, "I'm not sure what that man cares 'bout more, family or Jim Crow. Bernie might not be able to convince him. This could backfire."

Momma reminded him I was at the table. Daddy nodded at me as he walked out onto the porch. Her eyes met mine for a minute before following him. Angry, I went to my room.

The next few days Daddy was on edge. His comments were, "This is bad Melanie," or "Frank likes to hate more than he loves." He was not optimistic. It was a long time until the weekend.

Saturday during supper the telephone rang. He jumped to answer it. I heard him say, "Alright, good. See ya at eight."

I had invited Addie for the evening. Momma sent me across the field to explain our plans were cancelled. She wanted me to see Bernie, and Addie couldn't be at our house.

We were in the parlor with the television volume turned low when we heard his tires on the gravel. Daddy stepped onto the front porch. Momma and I followed. Bernie greeted Daddy with a smile as they shook hands warmly. He gave Momma and me a kiss on the cheek, as we exchanged pleasantries. Momma invited the men to sit and offered to bring cold lemonade. She motioned for me to follow. I helped make four glasses. I expected to join them, but was told to wait on the back porch while she delivered their refreshments.

She returned, leaving the men to their business. She didn't make small talk and neither did I. We sat in silence waiting for the meeting to be over. It was a nice night, but we weren't feeling the peacefulness of the beautiful summer evening.

It was more than an hour before we heard the engine of Bernie's car. Within a few minutes Daddy joined us. He leaned against the rail looking at Momma as he nodded. He wasn't smiling, but seemed satisfied. "He convinced his father to make a deal." Daddy looked across the field and whispered, "I hope he can trust him."

The next week Momma visited Liz to invite them for a cookout Friday evening at the big house. During the week Liz stopped in the store frequently. One day she joined us on the porch as we ate. She was lonely with Mark working long hours, and seldom home. We invited her to come any time. She became a regular for the company more than the merchandise.

The feed and seed closed at six on Fridays, so Mark was free for the evening. Liz was excited. She was anxious to meet Nettie, and have an acquaintance her own age. I could imagine the two becoming good friends.

Friday was a beautiful day. The sun was shining with clusters of clouds. It was hot, but there was a nice breeze. After work, I helped set up. Momma and Nettie seemed nervous. Daddy and Ted quit work early to start the fire pit. The picnic table was covered with a red checked cloth, matching napkins, and Momma's white dishes. It looked like a party.

They arrived a few minutes early. Liz brought a vanilla cake with a layer of chocolate cream sandwiched in the middle, topped with whipped cream and drizzled with chocolate sauce. The men gathered around the pit with cold beers, while the women sat at the table with iced tea. The air was filled with the women's laughter. Nettie and Liz connected immediately. Momma studied their interactions, nodding her approval.

The men talked as the chicken cooked. Daddy said, "Knowin' your customers will mean success. Missy, get a pencil and paper from the house."

As Daddy talked, Mark took notes of likes, dislikes, wives, kids, specifics about the farms, and their crops. I was torn between the conversation at the women's table and the men, but Daddy's stories were more interesting. At one point he got serious. "The Klan's powerful here and a lot of 'em are on that list. Ya be careful what ya say, and don't sell to the coloreds. That's a sure way to get in trouble."

Mark nodded in reply. "My dad told me. He drilled the dos and the don'ts 'til my head was spinning. And I know nothing's gonna change as long as my grandfather's alive, but someday maybe."

Daddy looked at him. He wisely responded, "Not sure what ya mean."

Mark said, "A business man can't limit his clientele. A sale is a sale, and the colored farmers need supplies too. Someday I hope to run this as a real business."

Ted interjected, "Be careful. Don't say that to anyone. Ya need to toe the line if you're gonna stay."

"I'm talking down the road, when the business is mine and there's a new breed of farmers." He was worried by Daddy's expression. He followed up with, "My dad said you aren't part of the Klan and if I needed something, I could come to you. I didn't mean to talk out of turn."

Daddy's next words were a warning. "Mark, this is Alabama. Ya don't know what a man really thinks or believes or who he's loyal to. And family ties don't always mean you're of one mind. Men here think for 'emselves. Ya never give an answer that could be used against ya or your family. Just nod and smile. Never say either way. It's true, people here know where I stand, but I'm one of 'em and I've got friends. You don't. Don't ever think ya do. Ya ever need anything, I'm here. I told your father I'd look out for ya, but ya gotta do your part. That means check your words and be careful. Don't trust anyone. Protect your family, and your family is that wife of yours."

Mark listened to Daddy, as did everyone. Mark's next words were spoken with serious conviction. "I know who my enemies are and who my family is. My dad left to get away from the poison, to raise his children free of the hatred that was forced on him. He didn't want me to come. I fought for this. I know who my grandfather is. But I want to live here, and if that means I have to smile at the devil for a few years, I can manage that. There's a difference between smiling at the devil and joining him. I can smile real nice. And family? I'm sharing a meal with them tonight."

The silence that surrounded us was so unnerving that even the birds seemed to hold their breath. It was Daddy's move next. He studied Mark for a minute before extending his hand saying, "Man to man."

she's plannin' somethin', and it's for me. I have Tommy. Who does she have? Who will she ever have? So what if she tries to embarrass me. I feel sorry for her. Stop worryin' 'cause I'm not. Now breathe. Ya can't faint on the sidewalk again."

I gave a weak smile. She eased some of my anxiety. I took several deep breaths and tried to relax. She was right. Passing out in front of everyone would be worse than anything Charlotte had planned.

We stayed in our seat while everyone exited the bus. Abigail turned to me saying, "Feel sorry for her." We entered the school with a new motto regarding Charlotte: no fear, just pity.

Charlotte was dressed in a bright pink skirt with flowers appliqued on the front, a matching pink ribbon in her hair, a light pink blouse, and bright pink shoes. She was pink. She flounced in expecting the girls to envy her, but the reaction was shock. She twirled so the hem of her skirt hit us. With a sweet smile, Abigail said, "Charlotte, that's lovely, just lovely."

I nodded in agreement hoping my face did not give away the true sentiments behind the compliment. Our kindness unnerved her, and proved to be an effective strategy.

Beginning that fall I ate with the other girls while Abigail sat with Tommy. It was lonely. Some of them were kind, but none were really my friends. Abigail was with me in class, but with him during free time.

The first few weeks were uneventful. Abigail continued to shower flowery compliments on both Charlotte and Virginia. It interfered with their agenda to hurt, but eventually Charlotte's mean streak emerged. One day she walked past Tommy and Abigail in the cafeteria and said, "Smell the pigs? Tommy, how can you come to school like that?" Then walking up close, actually sniffing around them, she announced, "Oh, I'm sorry, I assumed it was you. Abigail, you smell like a pig farmer's wife already."

I sat a few tables away watching the show. Abigail looked up at Charlotte briefly. She reached across the table to take Tommy's hand, and continued to talk. Charlotte smiled, satisfied as she began walking down the aisle. One of the boys jumped up saying, "Whew, smell that? She's spendin' too much time at the whore house. Hey, Charlotte, don't they tell ya to wash that stuff off when you're done workin'?"

They erupted into whoops and hollers. Jimmy Frank jumped up and grabbed Charlotte's arm as she tried to rush by. He whispered something in her ear. She blushed from embarrassment, but the look on her face also showed fear. She ran from the boys as they continued to call out insults. She motioned for Virginia to follow as she escaped the cafeteria. I expected Abigail and Tommy to be laughing along with everyone else, but they weren't. She looked sad. I remembered the bus and her words, "Feel sorry for her."

I often wondered what Jimmy said. His words or what the boys did caused her to step back the attacks on Abigail. I became Charlotte's sole target.

It was a new and different pattern with Tommy part of Abigail's life. I felt even more isolated. I was grateful to have Liz as another friend. They continued to make strides with Mark's grandparents, though progress was slow. His grandfather moved to being civil to Mark and cordial to Liz, while his grandmother grew in warmth. She occasionally dined with Liz mid-day, or stopped by the house with a little gift or flowers from her garden. Liz began making plans to settle in town and was looking for a home.

Thanksgiving approached. Liz and Mark invited his parents and grandparents to join them. Busy with preparations, her time at the store was limited. Nettie invited her family to the big house. Ruth was hosting her first Thanksgiving as Daniel's wife which would include her parents, grandparents, and Daniel's.

Momma missed Cal, and hoped he'd come home. I was certain he wouldn't, so I developed a plan. When Momma arrived at the store I ran out to the car. Opening the passenger door, I hopped in blurting out the details. "Momma, I want to make Thanksgiving dinner for Grandfather and Grandmother Gordon, but I want to do it like a town girl. Something she'd be proud of. I want to thank them for everything. You know a fancy party with everyone dressed up special, with Daddy in his suit and city dresses for you and me."

She was silent. I continued, "Please. This can show my appreciation."

She reached over to take my hand. "It's a lovely idea. You couldn't think of a better way to thank my mother."

I was pleased. It started as a way to take the pain away from Momma, but became a special gift for my grandparents as well. I explained, "Don't say anything," she agreed.

We went into the store smiling. Grandfather Gordon's eyes took on an inquisitive look, but he'd have to wait one more day. Giving each a tight hug, I said, "I love you."

On the way home, we talked about what to prepare. We would start with soup, then salad, followed by the turkey, stuffing, and mashed potatoes. We decided to add vegetables and breads that would create elegance. The real test would be the dessert. Daddy expected pumpkin pie, but she said, "It's all in the presentation. That's what my mother will be looking for, but the men will care about the food. We simply need to dress it up."

Momma used fancy printing to write an invitation. She drove me in the morning to drop it through the mail slot before they opened. I wanted to see their faces, but she said, "Mother would never deliver an invitation in person. She always believed the receiver should be pleasantly surprised."

At school I had difficulty focusing, anxious to get to the store. When the bell rang I tried rushing Abigail, but Tommy was in no hurry. I waved goodbye and left her behind.

My grandparents were waiting for me. She came out from behind the counter to take my hands. She said, "We found the most beautiful surprise this morning, a lovely invitation. Thank you. We kindly accept."

I wrapped my arms around her as I whispered, "We're excited to have you come." She patted my back, but I wasn't letting go until she gave me a real hug. Finally, her arms encircled me to squeeze tight. I heard her sigh with a catch in her breath. I said, "I love you."

She replied, "I love you."

I kissed her cheek. Stepping back, I turned to see Grandfather Gordon watching us with a warm smile. I leaned across the counter to put my arms around his neck giving him a kiss on each cheek saying, "I love you too. I'm glad you're my grandfather."

He said, "You're a special and wonderful blessing, my dear." I looked back to see my grandmother standing stoic and firm. She was a hard woman. The bell rang to announce Abigail's arrival. We looked toward her, the three of us beaming.

I laughed saying, "So Tommy finally said goodbye?" She blushed, as she dropped her eyes. It took the focus off us.

A giddy excitement was pervasive throughout the afternoon. Liz came by, and joined in the happy conversation. The customers were affected by the good humor in the air, leaving with smiles on their faces.

In preparation, I searched cookbooks for soups, vegetable recipes, and desserts to try over the next several days. Daddy would be our guinea pig. Each night I made a shopping list for the next experiment. It took three tries to find a soup, and even more for a dessert to complement the pumpkin pie. The vegetable dish proved impossible. Everything we tried resulted in the same response from him, "Well, I guess that's one way to ruin peas or beans." We eventually decided to make Grandmother Gordon's recipe for scalloped corn, one of his favorites. It would go well with the turkey and stuffing.

Daddy, Ted, and Daniel again hunted for turkeys. Nettie's father got one for the big house. Our men got a small one for us, and a larger one for Daniel.

Momma took her time telling Daddy he needed to wear a suit. Wednesday she made open-faced roast beef sandwiches with mashed potatoes, gravy, and apple crisp for dessert. He came in to find his favorite meal. We talked and laughed through supper. I shared my plans for the next day. After he finished eating,

I retrieved the boxes, handing one to Momma. Grandmother Gordon nodded permission. We carefully unwrapped the gifts to reveal matching jewelry boxes. Inside were identical heart lockets containing matching pictures of Momma and Daddy on their wedding day. It was special for me, but Momma was staring at the picture through tears. Smiling at her parents she said, "Thank you. This is the most precious gift ever."

I waited for my grandmother to put into words the meaning of the gift, but that was beyond her capabilities. The picture was her apology for not accepting Daddy. Grandfather Gordon brought the evening to a close. "Missy, we'll see you at the store. It was the most enjoyable Thanksgiving. Thank you."

I closed the door after them. Daddy put his arm around Momma, and said, "Well, it only took twenty-five years and one daughter to thaw the iceberg. Missy, you're a miracle worker."

He helped Momma with her locket. I removed mine from its box, and hooked it behind my neck. We spent the remainder of the evening working together. He washed dishes, Momma dried, and I put away. Several times I caught Momma fondling the locket with a smile on her face. It was the happiest of times for our little family of three. The absence of Ted and Cal was not hanging over us like a cloud, but instead our home was filled with joy.

At the store everyone shared stories about their Thanksgiving celebration. Liz was excited because their time with Uncle Frank went well. It was actually a turning point.

School resumed Monday, continuing on peacefully through to Christmas. Even Charlotte and Virginia seemed to be living in the spirit of the season. Experimenting with recipes for Thanksgiving inspired me to try more.

One Saturday evening Miss Ada taught us how to make Sweet Potato pie. We listened to music as we worked. Miss Emily joined us for a fun evening with the girls. *Rip it Up* came on the radio. Miss Emily grabbed Addie's hand spinning her around as they did the swing. I watched in awe, wishing I knew the steps. James came to watch with a rare smile on his face. We applauded as they finished. The next song on the radio was Elvis singing *Heartbreak Hotel*. Miss Emily looked to James. He pushed the table off to the side, while Addie and I moved the chairs. He took Emily's hand leading her into The Stroll. We watched their beautiful movements, two moving as one. Addie took my hand, and guided me through the steps. Slowly, my awkwardness began to evolve into a resemblance of the dance. We continued to dance as each song played on the radio. I reveled in our special time together.

Momma was trying hard to be excited for Christmas, intent on maintaining some of the traditions, though it was difficult. She missed her boys. One day Abigail and I arrived at the store, but Grandmother Gordon wasn't there. Momma had taken her for a ladies' day of shopping. Later, they returned smiling and happy. At first, I was hurt, but realized soon I'd be gone and they needed a relationship that didn't include me.

In early December, Ted stopped at the house to visit. Momma was pleased, but even more when he suggested we all get our Christmas trees on Sunday, followed by dinner at the big house. Baby Emily was ready for her first tree trip. It was a year of transitions.

Christmas came and went. Cal was home for three days. Baby Emily loved tearing the pretty paper off, even more than she liked the presents. We made our annual visit to the Gordons with our entire family. It was a happy and uneventful holiday season.

She gave a chuckle. "When you were born. My parents showed up at the hospital with a big box wrapped in pink, full of baby clothes. They came in and we looked at each other. There was silence for about ten minutes. Thank God your Daddy wasn't there. A nurse came in carrying you. It broke the tension. We had something to talk about. We had you." She smiled at me. "From the moment you were born, you were the healer. That year was the first time they invited us for Christmas Eve."

Through the years and important events, they didn't speak, including her wedding, or the birth of her first and second child. She was a new young mother alone. My mind went to Nettie and Baby Emily. How often she looked to Momma and her own mother for help. I asked, "Did you have anyone to help you with Ted?"

She nodded. "Grandma Em was wonderful to me. The Tucker's were the only family I had until you were born. Even then it wasn't friendly with my parents. My mother was mean to your Daddy. It hurt him and me too. That takes a long time to get over and it needed something special to help it along. I'll always be glad you started working at the store and that you could love them like you do. You taught me how to be their daughter. Next year when you go to college, I'll have them and they'll have me."

She was finished. That was the story and we were living the continuation.

The previous summer at the store was fun with Liz coming in almost every day, my relationship evolving with my grandparents, and spending time with Abigail. I was expecting more of the same, but it was different. Liz was busy nesting in her new home and bonding with Mark's grandmother. Abigail was with Tommy and his family much of the time. Most days it was Momma and me or just me if I had the car. Addie was working every day to save money for college. I felt very alone.

What made it worse was Sheriff Hosper. Whether I was with Momma, Abigail, or alone, I would see his car in the rear-view mirror. Sometimes he passed by, but often he trailed me all the way home. I stopped driving on days I knew Abigail was going to Tommy's, and asked Momma to pick me up instead.

I went to the big house on my days off to help Nettie with Baby Emily, the garden, or canning vegetables. We also painted the parlor and dining room that summer. She was always welcoming, but that town held very little for me anymore.

My grandparents invited me to join them at the diner one evening. It became a weekly date. It was nice spending relaxing time together. They enjoyed telling me about Momma and the accomplishments of her youth. I could see the pride and love they felt for her. I wondered if they still believed she had made a mistake with Daddy.

I learned about their lives as children. My grandfather grew up with one sibling. His father was a small-town doctor in northern Alabama and helped him get established in our little community. I thought my grandmother was a rich town girl. However, she grew up in extreme poverty as a sharecropper's daughter. That was why she feared Daddy and the life he could give Momma. She had worked hard to build a new identity and a different future. Daddy and his prospects were reminiscent of her unhappy childhood. The fine china, fancy dinners, and high manners were an escape from the past, and her attempt to prove she was better than her beginnings. Even the title 'Grandmother' spoke to her desire to rise above her upbringing. In her youth she wasn't a Charlotte, but was more likely an Abigail, suffering abuse at the hands of others. That explained many things, not only her cold nature and stand-offish ways, but also why she didn't want Momma to be a farmer's wife. Was that the reason Momma didn't try to be, and Daddy wouldn't let her?

I learned Momma had aunts and uncles throughout the South. They kept in touch with letters, but each went their own way. I couldn't imagine never seeing Cal or Ted. I felt certain we'd always be part of one another's lives. Even Cal's absence didn't wake me to what would be.

The loneliness of the summer confirmed that I needed to move on. I didn't have a future there. In reality, I didn't have a present. I tried to evaluate my likes and dislikes. My list of favorite things contained two: Choir and Newspaper. Professional singer was out, but I had a talent for researching and writing stories. To fill the emptiness of the summer I read the newspaper, and replicated the articles using people and events I knew. I wrote a collection to share with Mrs. Larsen. I thought she could evaluate if it was a viable career for me.

A week before school started, my grandparents invited us out for supper. Daddy drove Momma's car with Grandfather Gordon in the passenger seat. We three ladies were packed into the back. I couldn't imagine Grandmother Gordon was pleased with the arrangement, but she surprised me. She was happy to share the cramped space with us. Everyone was in a good mood, even Daddy. We had a wonderful time. I enjoyed the closeness of my family. I prayed the four of them would have peace when I was gone. They needed a new way of life that didn't include me. I hoped they'd find it in each other.

Chapter TWENTY-SEVEN
FALL 1958

Returning to school, I gave my writing samples to Mrs. Larsen. We arranged to discuss them Friday after school. When I arrived, she was waiting with my stories in front of her. She said "Before we look at these, tell me about you. Why did you choose journalism?"

I explained, "I like Newspaper club, so I thought maybe it could be a good job."

She asked, "How did you feel writing these stories?"

I replied, "It wasn't difficult. It was easy to copy the format, and write about people from town."

She smiled saying, "Is that it?"

I said, "Yeah."

She said, "I was hoping to hear that it was fun and exciting. I wanted to hear you loved writing. I didn't hear that."

I shook my head, whispering, "No."

She continued, "You shouldn't have to force yourself to write. I fear you've chosen journalism not because it inspires you, but because you can't think of anything else."

I listed the other careers I had evaluated and eliminated. She smiled, nodding her head. "Your thinking is too limited. You don't the road. It was a woman. As we drew near I realized it was Addie. Abigail's presence made me question how to react. I needed time to think. I slowed and looked in the rear-view mirror, checking for cars. Specifically, I searched the road for Sheriff Hosper. The right thing to do was to stop. But I was afraid someone might see me, and I was worried about what Abigail would think. I wanted to speed past, but Addie would know it was me.

I continued to reduce my speed. Addie began walking faster. I pulled alongside. She didn't look, but took off running across the field. I yelled, "Addie, it's me, Missy," but she didn't hear me. I drove forward trying to keep pace.

I yelled louder. Abigail called out the window, "Addie, stop. It's Missy drivin' the car."

Addie turned to see if it was really me. She stopped. I pulled off the road and got out without thinking. Realizing, fear shot through me. What had I done? Now I had no choice. I'd made my decision. I looked first at Abigail, then both ways for other cars. Suddenly afraid, I couldn't hesitate any longer. I ran into the field. Addie didn't move. As I came near, our eyes locked. I said, "I didn't mean to scare ya. I was slowin' to give ya a ride." It was a lie. Until she started to run, I'm not sure I if intended to stop.

She stood motionless except for the heaving of her chest. Many things were running through my mind. My biggest worry was what Abigail would think or that someone might see me. My concern was for me, with no regard for Addie. She was faced with the danger and fear of a slowing car. Would I have reason to be afraid? I was sure I wouldn't.

Aware we were exposed in the open field, I said, "Come with me," but she didn't move. I extended my hands toward her. It reminded me of running to each other, but in slow motion. She stumbled toward me as tears began streaming down her face. I felt her full weight as she collapsed against me.

I scanned the road as I prayed no one was coming. I began moving her toward the car, trying to hurry. As we approached, Abigail leaned over the seat to open the door. I helped Addie in.

Her sobs had subsided, but the tear-streaked face told Abigail everything.

I rushed to get behind the wheel. I looked in the rear-view mirror to check on her and for approaching cars. Glancing at Abigail, she gave me a slight smile. I found the courage to let her in on my secret. "Abigail, this is Addie, my friend. Addie, this is Abigail."

Abigail turned to face Addie. She extended her hand across the seat saying, "It's nice to meet ya." Addie sat for a moment, not sure what to do. She slowly brought her hand up to Abigail's. She nodded, but didn't speak.

I put the car in gear to proceed to Abigail's. I pulled in the drive looking back at Addie. She sank down into the seat, trying to be invisible. Abigail turned saying, "Goodbye Addie. I hope to see ya again." Then to me, "I'll see ya tomorrow. Have a good-night."

Pulling away from Abigail's, I looked toward town. Panic set it. Sheriff Hosper was approaching. I looked at Addie, grateful she was still hiding in the back seat. I waited for him to drive by. As always, he nodded with a smile that made my stomach turn. What could I do? I looked in the mirror. Abigail was standing on the porch. Should I ask her to come with me? But then I would be putting both of us in danger. All I could do was continue home. I said, "Stay down. Sheriff Hosper just passed. He'll be headin' back."

She said, "Don't drive to my house. Go to yours."

I pulled onto the road heading home, terrified, thinking, 'What if he stops me?' It wasn't long before I saw his car returning. I prayed out loud. "Please God, let him drive by."

From the floor in the back seat I heard, "Amen."

As always, he slowed almost to a stop as I came near. With a nod and smile, he touched the brim of his hat. I tried to act normal by nodding in return. I continued on, but my eyes were focused on the mirror to make sure he didn't return. Once he was out of sight I increased my speed faster than I'd ever driven before.

Grandmother said, "He'll come around. This lets him have his pride. She'll be in an upright home, with good morals and values. He wouldn't feel people are speaking badly of him or his daughter."

Momma and Daddy looked at each other. He said, "Nothin' has to be decided tonight."

As they got up to leave, Grandmother Gordon said, "The girls shouldn't drive themselves right now. We can bring Missy home if you need to be with Nettie and the baby."

"J.P.'s driving the girls to school. We can get them home," Momma replied.

Grandfather Gordon said, "I'll pick them up at school and bring them to the store." Momma nodded.

In the morning my parents were in the kitchen. There was oatmeal with brown sugar and milk waiting for me. Momma said, "As much as I don't want my parents involved, we think their suggestion is best. We talked about Abigail staying here, but help would be nearby in town. We decided that's probably better. With Daddy in the fields, we'd be alone. Her father won't hurt her, but he might try to take her. Nettie agrees. She's afraid he'll send her away. Ted and Daddy will take you girls to school. They'll talk with her father after that. So, hurry and eat."

He said, "Nettie and your Momma are takin' the baby to see Anna Lee. For today we need to be careful. Once we get it settled, things'll be fine."

"What 'bout you and Ted. Ya shouldn't go there. What 'bout Tommy?" I asked.

She said, "I called his mother. We thought he should stay home, but if he doesn't see Abigail he'll find another way. They decided school is the safest place. His father is taking him and picking him up until things calm down."

Abigail and I crowded in with Ted and Daddy. As we approached her house you could feel the tension. We looked for anything amiss, but all was peaceful.

The trip to town was uneventful. Tommy was waiting inside. Abigail was strong and stoic until she saw him. She fell into his arms. He picked her up. I could hear her soft sobs as she buried her head on his shoulder. I wanted to follow, but felt like an intruder. They disappeared into Mr. Beaker's office. She didn't need me. She only needed Tommy.

Throughout the day everyone was somber, respectful, and a little on edge. In the cafeteria it was like always, the girls' table, the boys' table, and Tommy with Abigail. The room was quiet with all eyes on them.

He left school early with his father and brother. When the bell rang, we let the other students leave as we slowly gathered our belongings. At the front entrance we saw Mr. Beaker at the end of the sidewalk. After the buses left, he came back toward us. As he opened the door he said, "Missy, your grandfather's pullin' up."

Abigail asked, "Is my father here?"

"No. We don't expect any problems, but I'll walk ya girls out," he answered.

Grandfather Gordon smiled as we climbed into the back seat. We looked for her father on the side streets, at Buck's garage, waiting for us at the store, but he was nowhere in sight. My grandmother guided us to Momma's bedroom. A suitcase from Nettie's and some new clothes from the store were on the bed. She told us to settle Abigail. We quietly unpacked the few belongings. Sitting on the bed, she began to cry. I put my arm around her. There were no words to comfort her.

We worked in the backroom unpacking and pricing new items in silence. Grandmother Gordon frequently popped her head in to give us a weak smile, and make sure we were fine. When the bell rang on the front door we listened to the voices. Customers were coming and going, but never Abigail's father.

At closing time Momma and Nettie arrived with the baby. We heard them talking with my grandparents. We joined them to hear about Daddy's visit with Abigail's father. He was angry, and put up a strong front, but consented to Abigail staying with my grandparents if she didn't see Tommy. Abigail began to react, but Momma said, "You'll see him at school and talk on the telephone. Right now, we have to show your father some respect."

I said, "But then what?"

She continued, "That's not worked out yet, but it will be. He won't want you living here long. They tried to get him to sign so you could marry, but he wasn't ready. Once he's calmed down, Nettie and Ted will talk to him again. Don't worry."

As I was leaving, I said, "I'll see ya on the bus."

Abigail looked at me, but didn't respond. Suddenly, I realized we wouldn't ride the bus together anymore. I was overcome with sadness. One more piece of my life was changing.

Over the next week the mood remained tense. Grandfather Gordon continued to pick us up after school. One morning Nettie received a call from her mother. Her father was in the far field, out of view of the house. Abigail's clothes were in feed bags by the mail-box. Momma went immediately, quickly loading them in the car to deliver to the store.

After school Abigail took her books to Momma's room. Grandmother Gordon sent me to check on her. She was sitting on the bed holding a piece of paper, tears on her cheeks. She softly whispered, "Mother can't come, but she wants me to have a beautiful weddin'."

I said, "Things could change or maybe she'll come anyway."

She shook her head. "He won't allow it and she won't go against him. A weddin' is supposed to be happy, not like this. How do ya plan, knowin' your family won't be there?"

I said, "Ya should talk to Momma. My grandparents weren't at hers. Grandmother Gordon didn't want her to marry Daddy. She thought if she was mean enough, Momma wouldn't go through with it, but it didn't work. It's different for you. Your mother wants ya to marry Tommy. Find happiness knowin' that."

She looked at me. "Who says there'll even be a weddin'? If my father won't sign, I can't get married."

I said, "He'll sign. Your mother said so in the letter."

She said, "Ya think? Is that what it means?"

I nodded saying, "Yeah, I do. He'll be ashamed to have ya livin' off the kindness of my grandparents. He expects his daughters to find husbands. He'll sign."

She said, "I can't be a silly girl plannin' a foolish weddin'. Make everyone understand."

"I will. It'll be a special day for you and Tommy," I said.

"Exactly," came her soft reply.

She couldn't talk about it any longer. We joined my grandparents in the store for a quiet afternoon. Grandmother Gordon invited me to supper and a sleepover on Friday evening. I wasn't sure how Abigail would see it. It sounded like a school girl thing to do. She wasn't feeling young or carefree, so I was surprised she said yes.

Friday after work grandmother told me to get a Chef Boy-ar-dee pizza mix and round tray off the store shelf. It was sweet how much she was trying to help Abigail feel comfortable. Making pizza was a good idea. It helped Abigail relax. We laughed when the dough sprang back as we pressed it to the edge. Grandmother Gordon set up the dining room table which made me chuckle, her good china for pizza. Grandfather Gordon brought four cherry cokes and a bag of Golden Flake Potato Chips in from the store. Taking a bite of the pizza, we laughed at my grandmother as she pursed her lips. I'm sure Chef Boy-ar-dee never graced their table again.

They watched television while we cleaned the kitchen. Abigail said, "I don't wanna get married before graduation. I can't go to school as a married lady. Does that sound ridiculous?" I told her no, I understood. She continued, "Your grandparents agreed to take me in, but not for that long."

I replied. "They love havin' ya here. If Grandmother Gordon had her way the weddin' would be next year. Stayin' a little longer won't be a problem. They'll be honored you're not in a hurry."

We joined my grandparents for the end of *Your Hit Parade*. During the commercial, I turned down the volume. I explained

Abigail's feelings. They nodded their heads. My grandfather said, "We were talking, but felt it wasn't our place to tell you what to do. We agree. Getting married before you finish school is wrong. My dear, we want you to take as much time as you need."

Abigail said, "It was gonna be the last Saturday of June. If it's alright I'd like to keep that date."

Grandmother Gordon said, "That's fine, my dear, whatever you decide."

Abigail gave each of them a hug, satisfied this concern was behind her. We went upstairs to Momma's room. She said, "I don't want the long dress I picked out with Anna Lee. Do ya think she started it yet?"

In support of Abigail's father, Chuck ordered Anna Lee to send the fabric home, but Abigail didn't know. I said, "No. Nettie said she hasn't started. Ya can still change it. But ya have to make a decision. Wait here. I'll be right back."

I ran to the store, returning with the McCall's and Simplicity books. We selected a short dress with a simple tulle veil. Abigail said, "I want your dress to be like mine, but in yellow. It's nice with your black hair." Noticing my surprise, she continued. "I want you with me, just you." I smiled at my friend.

Into the night we talked about what was to be for Abigail and the changes eventually for me. We discussed specific details about the wedding. She wanted to scale it down from the original plans. It would be just close friends and family, a quiet gathering. I had a lot to report. Nettie would be pleased.

In the morning we woke to the smell of pancakes and sausage. My grandmother was humming as she worked around the kitchen. I caught my grandfather watching her, a smile on his face. She was happy. It had taken almost eighteen years and Abigail's family feud for me to spend a night at my grandparents.

On the ride home Saturday afternoon, I asked Momma, "Why's her father so angry? It's just drivin'. Everyone drives."

She took a deep breath with a long slow exhale as she debated what was appropriate to say. I waited as she chose her words. "It's hard to be a man. Your role is to lead and provide. Abigail's father has suffered a lot of failures. Their poverty has brought him shame much of the time. People look down on him, so he finds other ways to hold his head up. Being a strong leader for the family accomplishes that. He can be a man by making rules and requiring everyone follow them. He demands their respect in that way because he fears he doesn't deserve it for anything else. Driving isn't the issue. He wants his family to look up to him for something."

I reflected on her words saying, "Abigail once said her father not allowing her to drive was better than being too poor to drive."

She said, "Exactly. It saves him the embarrassment of people thinking he can't provide for them. Tommy teaching her to drive went against the one thing he has: authority over his children and their respect. That's why he'll never show acceptance. He has to stand his ground to keep what little pride he has." I was sad for Abigail and all of them. The shame of being poor outweighed the love of being family.

Momma and Nettie started making the arrangements for the wedding. Abigail didn't seem to mind. Her dream had lost the excitement. Momma would make both dresses. We decided not to tell Abigail until later. It was too much for her at the time.

Addie came over that night. We were eating a piece of Momma's cake in front of the television. She said, "Is your friend alright?"

I was afraid to speak, unsure what she knew. She continued, "I was at Miss Evelyn's. I saw her out the window."

I said, "That day with her father?"

She nodded. "He ran her up on the grass. It was a good thing that other man showed up. I was afraid her papa might kill that boy."

"Was it bad?" I asked.

Again, she nodded. "As bad as I ever seen. He was dangerous like. The boy went at him tryin' to protect your friend, but her papa threw him off. I was hopin' she's alright."

sign to avoid the embarrassment of cancelling the wedding and forcing Abigail to remain with my grandparents.

Over the next few weeks each of us focused on our own issues. Abigail was concerned with helping Tommy provide for them. Addie, along with finishing school, handled all of Miss Emily's clients. The hope was with time her mother would heal, and eventually return to work. I took care of the applications for the schools in Texas and California.

Cal graduated from college. My grandparents closed the store for the day to join my family at the ceremony. My parents were very proud. He got a job writing for the *Pittsburgh Post-Gazette*. He left from Auburn without returning home, and rarely had time for visits over the years. Momma kept in touch with calls, but missed seeing him.

My graduation came quickly. The ceremony was on a Sunday afternoon. I had my parents, grandparents, and Ted. Nettie was the only family there for Abigail. My grandparents gave each of us a silver bracelet with two charms, a graduation cap and a heart with Abigail engraved on one side and Missy on the other. My parents gave me a set of luggage and Abigail an account at the store to buy what she needed to start married life. We all celebrated at the Hotel.

Tommy was working non-stop fixing up the tenant house on his family's farm. He refinished the wood floors throughout, painted every room, and added new trim. He built new pine cabinets, with Formica counters in the kitchen. His parents bought a refrigerator and his grandparents a stove. Tommy worked late every night to get their new home ready.

Family and friends came together to paint the outside. Momma and I dug up some of her flowers, splitting the bundles. A couple of evenings we traveled out to plant them along the front of the house, around the trees, and at the edge of the back yard for Abigail to see from her kitchen window. Tommy was there, and gave us a tour. He was excited to show off his hard work. It was a very nice home for his bride.

It was time for Nettie to tell Abigail about Anna Lee. She explained Chuck wouldn't allow Anna Lee to make the dress or attend the wedding. Though she was disappointed, Abigail was able to accept the truth.

The time came for Ted and Nettie to speak to her father. At first, he resisted, standing his ground. She told him Abigail would not abandon Tommy nor return home. They emphasized it was unreasonable to expect my grandparents to house her for another year. He finally agreed to sign the paper.

I turned eighteen a few days before Abigail's wedding. Momma planned supper at the Hotel with my family and Abigail to celebrate. She had a cake waiting along with gifts from everyone. It was reminiscent of Abigail's special day several years earlier. I was enjoying the evening when Sheriff Hosper came in. He took a table alone in the corner. Throughout dinner I tried to not to look his way, intent that he would not ruin my special day. As my family was singing Happy Birthday, my eyes caught him watching with a smile on his face. He nodded, with a look in his eyes that made me shiver.

We enjoyed Momma's cake and moved on to the gifts. I wouldn't give him the satisfaction of looking his way again. I kept my eyes focused on those around the table, but I knew he was staring at me the entire time. I could feel the force of his eyes.

As I was extending a thank you to each person, he got up, and walked to our table. Stopping behind Daddy, he faced directly toward me saying, "This looks like a special occasion. Melissa, are ya turnin' eighteen?"

I nodded, unable to speak. He continued, "Well then, Happy Birthday. Not a little girl anymore." The tone in his voice caught everyone off guard. They all turned to see him smile with his eyes focused on me. My family was shocked by his behavior. He said, "I'll let ya finish your party. Melissa, I look forward to see ya soon." Reaching his hand out to Daddy, he said, "Good to see ya, J.P."

smiling with tears running down her face. Over and over she said, "I can go. I can go."

After we collapsed to the ground, I said, "Is your momma better?"

She shook her head, "No. But John James and Sissy are moving out here. She's expectin' again. Granmama'll take care of the baby so Sissy can keep workin'. Mina's movin' back with family and they're gonna rent both apartments at the store for extra money. I have to work, but I'll take care of myself. Sissy's aunt got me a job at a boardin' house with a bed in the attic if I go now. I'm takin' the bus tomorrow. I wanted to say goodbye."

My heart wrenched; I felt sick. I too started to cry. That moment was the end of Addie and me. I didn't say, 'I'll write' because that couldn't be. Our friendship existed in those two little houses and the field between them. It could never go beyond. I said, "I'll see ya at Christmas."

She said, "If I can come." But I knew Addie wouldn't be allowed a vacation or time off to visit family. She would have obligations at the boarding house. Keeping that job would be a priority.

I took her hands, pulling her up. We started spinning, slowly at first, then faster, and faster. The faster we went, the harder we cried. We fell to the ground, hidden in the tall grass. I hugged my friend and she hugged me. We held tight in a goodbye that we both knew was forever. We were going out into a world where our friendship was forbidden, and we'd conform.

There was nothing more to say. She stood up; I slowly joined her. We held hands for a moment. She squeezed mine and I squeezed hers. Without another word we let go. We each walked back toward the homes of our childhood, and the dreams of our future. I didn't look back until I climbed the steps of our porch. She was standing on the stoop at her back door. I reached my hand up, and waved. She did the same. I whispered, "Goodbye, Addie." Then we flashed our porch lights for the last time.

Momma was waiting in the kitchen. She wrapped me in her arms as I cried. It may seem like I had built a life without Addie, or at times had forgotten her, but she was always there, my first best friend, a true friend. It was a loss that I compare to that of Grandma Em. It was deep and painful.

Two weeks later it was time to leave for St Louis. Momma and Daddy were driving me. Daniel's brother was helping on the farm which allowed my parents time to visit with her family.

We were departing Saturday for the long drive. Grandmother Gordon invited the family, along with Tommy and Abigail, for supper on Wednesday evening. Though there was an undercurrent of sadness, especially noticeable with my grandparents, the evening was full of laughter, so different from the tense Christmas Eves of the past.

Thursday was my last day at the store. My grandparents were teary eyed. Liz and the baby came for a final picnic on the porch. Many things signaled life was changing forever: Abigail's wedding, Addie's departure, and now my own new adventure. For so long, everything was the same, with the same people and activities filling my life. My heart ached for the past.

Daddy picked me up at the end of the day. I wasn't ready to say goodbye to my childhood. Grandfather Gordon moved toward his wife. He pulled her close to ease his pain as much as hers. Abigail put her arms around me. My dear friend and I held each other. First, we cried, then we laughed as she said, "It's just till Christmas."

I moved on to embrace each of my grandparents and they hugged me in return. She whispered, "You taught me how to love. Thank you." He kissed the top of my head, but spoke no words.

I stepped back and said, "Christmas! I'll be back to work over Christmas." Turning to Daddy, I nodded, ready to go. They followed us out on the porch. From the front seat of his truck I had a family to support. He was runnin' the store and they lived with his parents in the house. His father thought he was passin' the responsibility of the family on to his son. He didn't know Frank was part of the Klan. Frank threatened to tell the whole town. He scared my grandparents, so they set it up for everything to be my mother's as far as ownership. Frank got to live in the house and run the business as long as he never told."

Daddy's words at Grandma Em's funeral now had meaning. I asked, "So when Grandma Em died, it all came to you?"

He nodded. "All of it. I own it, but I promised to give it to Mark and Liz if Frank goes to his grave with the secret. If he does that, it'll be over."

I said, "That's why you were worried 'bout them comin' to town. Ya didn't know what they knew or if they were the kind who'd tell."

He nodded. I finally understood the fears, the anger at times, and the battles between my parents. My head was spinning, overwhelmed by the implications. It meant Daddy was colored and in Alabama, so was I. I found myself wishing I didn't know any of it. I sat motionless as he looked out the window. It was beginning to get dark.

He was waiting for me to speak. My mind went to Mr. Jefferson. "Why did Mr. Jefferson move here, and why were ya afraid of Miss Emily?" I asked.

He said, "Jefferson had a store for coloreds in Montgomery, but when his father died the protection was gone. It wasn't safe for him there. Grandma Em was the only real family he had. He sold it all and moved here to be close to her. He tried to reach out, real secret like, but she was afraid. She wouldn't acknowledge him. That made Emily mad. She started goin' after James, not 'cause she liked him, but to get back at Mother. My daddy tried to warn James, but he was taken with her. She was good lookin', had fine manners, and was a merchant's daughter. He ignored my daddy. She was usin' him to get close to the family, but James didn't understand 'til after he married her. Then he knew she didn't love him, but it was too late."

I asked, "Why'd James stay with her. Why didn't he just tell her to leave?"

He couldn't answer right away. He tried to speak, but his voice was choked with emotion. He finally said, "To protect us." Again, he took time to collect himself, then said, "My daddy feared Emily 'cause there was no incentive to keep the secret, at least not 'til she had children."

I asked, "Why'd that make a difference?"

He looked at me sideways. "Married to James and us bein' white was protection for all of 'em, even her father. We also meant more money. If James took his crops to market on his own, he got half the price or less than Daddy or me sellin' it."

He gave me a minute before explaining, "And Jefferson was a good man. Knowin' our secret gave him power, but he never used it against us. With him gone, your mother and I are a little worried. With Emily's state of mind, well, I'm not sure what she or the boys might do. We could be in trouble. But if they listen to James, I think we'll be ok."

"Her boys know?" I asked. He nodded yes. "But why would they hurt us? We're nice to 'em."

He said, "Nice? Hmmmm. They might not see it that way."

My mind went to Addie, to the privileges of my childhood, our home, but most important not living in fear. My chest felt heavy, and I couldn't breathe. Guilt and panic were weighing me down. I understood many things now. Daddy stood up for James because he was his brother, but also James held our fate. Momma's behavior over the years began to make sense. I understood why she was afraid.

I whispered, "Does Addie know?"

He nodded, saying, "I expect so, though I'm not sure. Nothin' was ever said."

My mind was working through all the connections that could hurt my family. I thought of Uncle Frank at the funeral. I asked, "Does Uncle Frank know who Mr. Jefferson was?"

"I don't really know. I think probably, and maybe that's why the Klan left him alone. I always figured Frank made sure nothin' happened, afraid of what I might do," he replied.

I fully understood the dangers of Uncle Frank. At any time, he could destroy our lives. I couldn't talk anymore. I was exhausted. He waited a bit, but I remained quiet. He started the engine. We rode home in silence.

At home, Momma was waiting at the kitchen table with sandwiches, but I moved toward the stairs. I wanted to be alone. I threw myself on the bed, and buried my head under the pillow to shut out the world. My mind raced as I thought back through the moments of my life with Addie, Momma and Daddy, Miss Ada, Miss Emily, and Grandma Em. All of them had a true understanding of life among us, even Ted and Cal. I was sure Nettie knew; everyone knew but me. My mind finally stopped and I drifted off to sleep.

The next morning, I slept late. I didn't want to wake up or think about anything, but there was much to do. My mind wasn't on packing. I was consumed with questions, and overwhelmed with guilt that needed to be released. Momma was in the kitchen when I came down. She put two eggs in a pan of boiling water and popped two pieces of bread down to toast. She made poached eggs on toast whenever we were sick with a fever or the flu. It was an appropriate breakfast for the way I was feeling.

I sat down. She placed one plate in front of me and one in front of her seat. Taking her place, she said, "Questions?"

My first question was more of a confirmation. "Nettie knows?"

She nodded. "Ted wouldn't marry her unless she knew. She deserved the truth."

"Did you know before you married Daddy?" I asked.

She said, "He told me for the same reason."

"Do the Gordons know?" I asked.

She said, "Yes, just after I married him. I got in an argument with my mother; she was criticizing my life and your Daddy, so I told her. I was trying to make the point that I loved him no matter what. It wasn't the right thing to do, because then she really hated him for putting me in danger."

"Does anyone else know?" I asked.

She said, "We're not sure. Uncle Frank and Bernie definitely know, and James and his family."

I asked, "Mark and Liz?"

She said, "Bernie said no when they moved here. We don't know for sure now."

Uncle Frank's rejection of Grandma Em, his behavior at the funeral, as well as his treatment of Mark and Liz suddenly had a reason. The issue was not that he didn't want his grandson living here nor was it about the business. Their desire to settle in town interfered with his plan to hurt us. Mark's presence forced him to take the secret to his grave.

She continued, "And Aunt Sara. She knows of course. That's it we think."

I said, "Uncle Roy?"

She heard the fear in my voice and began shaking her head no. "Don't worry, he doesn't know. If he ever found out, he'd kill Sara for embarrassing him. Sometimes she doesn't seem to remember. She's spent most of her life living and believing like Roy. She wants to forget and pretend she's someone else. The family in Montgomery, some of them know. That's why we never see them. It's better if they forget we exist."

"Montgomery?" I asked, "The family that comes to Addie's?"

She nodded, "Different family, but yes. They're Mr. Jefferson's colored family. But I meant the Coopers. A couple of the older girls know, but they've always protected us." I thought back to Momma's anger over the relatives from Montgomery staying with James. I now understood her fear.

I said, "When Nettie was expectin', that's why you were afraid. It wasn't that somethin' might be wrong with the baby, but that it

Chapter THIRTY

2012

M any years have now passed. Miss Emily died less than two years after Addie and I left for college. She never recovered after her father's death. Nettie had a second child, a boy, when Baby Emily was six. They gratefully raised their two children, and James the third works the family farm today. Cal and his family have lived in several places around the country due to his career as a journalist. Though we see him infrequently, we are always in touch. Abigail, fifty-three years later, is happily married to Tommy with five children, thirteen grandchildren, and three great-grandchildren. Daniel and Ruth were finally blessed with three children, but only after they finished raising his siblings. God's timing is perfect in all things. Jessie returned to Leroy, and came home two more times before leaving him for good.

All through college, I returned each summer to work at the store with Abigail. She was a great help and comfort to my grandparents. They didn't live long enough to see me married or to meet my children, but I was grateful to have known them, to have loved them, and to have their love in return.

I completed my studies and took a position as an Occupational Therapist in Nashville. It was closer to Momma and Daddy which allowed for frequent visits. I really enjoyed the work and was glad to have a profession. Eight years later I met my husband. He was a patient, who was rehabilitating from injuries suffered in Vietnam. It took four years before he was ready to marry me. We moved to Louisville, Kentucky where we have lived ever since. We have two children, and five grandchildren. We have led a simple, but happy life.

Jefferson James was killed in action in Vietnam in 1968. It proved to be too much for James and he began to fail. He died four years later. His death was difficult on Daddy. I returned home for the funeral. I watched my father grieve for the brother of his childhood and for the relationship lost. Over the years I couldn't erase the guilt I felt regarding Addie. I saw those same feelings in Daddy.

Her Papa's funeral was the first time Addie and I were both home since that day in the field. She never returned for holidays or summers for fear of losing her housing and job. She received her teacher's certificate and left the South for a new life, moving first to Cincinnati and later to Chicago with Henry. That first meeting was difficult. I wanted our friendship to be like before, but we had changed and there was a distance between us. She was cordial, and thanked me for coming to pay her father respect, but not friendly.

I saw her again when Miss Ada died in 1977. I wanted our meeting to be more, to show that our friendship had been and was still important, but I failed. It wasn't societal rules holding me back. Eighteen years had passed, a lot had changed, but our behaviors were still controlled by the belief system of our childhood. There could be no new beginning.

Ada's death signaled the end. As long as she was alive, I knew where Addie was and about her life. The thin thread that connected us was forever severed. After Miss Ada's death, John James, Sissy, and their family left the farm for good, cutting all ties.

I take this moment to say, "Addie, my best friend. I miss you. I thank you for tolerating my ignorance, both when it was real and for the times it was not. I recognize your bravery and kindness. You lived in fear each day: both in the community and from me. There could never be complete trust. You could not show your true feelings, be it anger or resentment, just acceptance. I will never understand our childhood through your eyes. All of this I acknowledge as I extend my deep and sincere gratitude for the protection you and your family gifted to us.

Most important I want you to know my shame. Because we looked white, we were allowed freedom, rights, and security. We prospered, while you were given only enough to survive. It was not just the rules of society that determined your life, but also the decisions of my family. I ask your forgiveness. I am truly sorry."

I began writing our story almost twenty years ago. Each time I returned to telling this truth, courage failed me. Momma and Daddy along with Ted and his family were still on the farm in Alabama. Though time has passed and progress made, is society ready to accept the reality of our heritage as not important? The labels and rules about who you are or how you identify yourself have not changed. In Alabama, my family and I were colored.

I could not finish this story while my parents were living. Afraid the world would discover we were not white dominated their thoughts and actions. The fear was so deeply ingrained. It is with Cal, Ted, Nettie, and our children that I finally share who we are. We offer this as our apology for allowing fear to control our actions and for standing by while injustice reigned. We speak now to honor our entire family, black and white. Our hope is that the color of our skin will no longer divide us, and that we may celebrate the blood that forever binds us, our *Silent Ties*.

Chapter THIRTY-ONE

S he finished supper, and washed the pan she used to prepare poached chicken with hot apple preserves and her table service for one. Henry had died several years earlier, leaving her alone. There was comfort in their home of almost forty years, though at times the quiet was lonely. Retired from teaching, she filled her days with tutoring, babysitting her great-grandchildren, and reading.

She put away the dishes, and hung the towel to dry. Her eye caught the book waiting on the table. She had been reading it for several days, and should have finished it by now, but overwhelming emotions forced her to set it aside so many times.

She took a seat at the table, and opened to the ribbon marking a place near the end. Sadly, she began to read, slowly turning each page. Staring at the final words, her mind was no longer in the present. Her thoughts went back to the sharecropper's cottage she called home for her first eighteen years, and to the forbidden friendship she had fought to maintain. But overshadowing those memories were the painful feelings of life as it was.

Closing the book, she clasped her hands over the image on the cover. She lowered her head and closed her eyes as her body leaned forward like a woman in prayer. Shaking her head back and forth in small movements, almost undetectable, a tear rolled down her cheek. She didn't wipe it away, allowing it to fall freely. After a time, she opened her eyes. Nodding her head, confirming her decision, she placed her hands on the table. Pushing her tired body up, she looked toward the wall next to the back door. She picked up the book, brought it to her chest, and held it tight. She walked toward the telephone hanging between the frame and the cabinet. She forced herself to move forward, shuffling her slippers across the linoleum. When she reached the wall, she closed her eyes, and bowed her head again.

She opened her eyes to see the trash can resting against the wall below the telephone. Stepping forward, she pressed her toe on the lever. As the lid came up, she saw the foam tray and scraps from her supper. Dropping her hands forward, the book tumbled until it landed face down in the pile of debris. A slow steady exhale took every ounce of breath from her body as she studied the sight. She removed her foot and took a couple steps backward with her eyes focused on the can.

After a moment, she turned to begin a slow walk to the living room. Lowering her body into the recliner, she picked up the remote. She pushed the power button, immediately depressing a number to change the channel. *Jeopardy* was in the final round. She settled back in her chair ready to call out the answers, always confident of her response.

The End

Final WORD
SO YOU DON'T LIKE THE END . . .

During the writing process I asked several individuals to read and critique the story of Missy's life and her friendship with Addie. All but one previewer wanted the ending to be changed. They wanted a renewal of the friendship. Is that what you were hoping for?...

Please visit www.dawndayquinn.com to understand why this was Addie's happy ending; for more about the development of *Silent Ties*; and to learn about "Not Your Typical Book Club."

Thank you for reading. Blessings to all.

Dawn

AUTHOR

Dawn Day-Quinn discovered the magic of books as a child reading for hours, writing, working in the local public library through high school, and moving on to glean more through academic endeavors. She has an entrepreneurial spirit which guided her to create a major program leading to a Bachelor's degree, an interdisciplinary Master's degree, running her own successful design firm, followed by several positions as a college professor as she moved around the country advancing her husband's career. She finally settled in Western Pennsylvania with her husband and four boys.

With a thirst for learning always present, she continued to study at the doctoral level in human learning, theology, and psychology. A course in multi-cultural psychology led to a study of inter-racial relationships in the Jim Crow South. Voracious research and reading formulated her first novel *Silent Ties*.